──────────── ★ ────────────

Roper heard Malkins's stomach heave as they stood together in the scullery doorway.

"Bloody hell," muttered Malkins, briefly looking away and closing his eyes, then forcing himself to look again. "Bloody, bloody Nora."

"My sentiments exactly," agreed Roper. "Poor sod."

The police doctor, Evans, with his feet carefully astride to avoid the puddles of congealed blood on the quarry tiles, had a fingertip placed below Oates's right ear and his stethoscope pressed between Oates's shoulder blades.

"Yes," he said. "He's very dead, Superintendent." Doctor or not, even Evans was appalled. "There must be three or four pints of blood splashed about. My God."

──────────── ★ ────────────

ROY HART

A FOX IN THE NIGHT

WORLDWIDE.

TORONTO • NEW YORK • LONDON
AMSTERDAM • PARIS • SYDNEY • HAMBURG
STOCKHOLM • ATHENS • TOKYO • MILAN
MADRID • WARSAW • BUDAPEST • AUCKLAND

A FOX IN THE NIGHT

A Worldwide Mystery/July 1998

First published by St. Martin's Press, Incorporated.

ISBN 0-373-26280-9

A FOX IN THE NIGHT

ONE

At six o'clock in the morning a fine autumnal mist hung about the King's Minster street-lamps like breath on a mirror. It would be two hours yet before Hannah Blezard's body would be found. In the mean time, here and there, the little market-town was slowly coming to life.

In the yard behind Sylvester's dairy the last of the electric milk-floats was being crated up. Further along the High Street a mechanical road-sweeper was already at work. It was presently passing King's Minster police station where the lights burned for twenty-four hours a day. Not that King's Minster figured dramatically on the county's crime statistics. A few D and Ds on Saturday nights; the occasional car-theft; a break-in, on average, twice a week; some petty thievery; some vandalism; a few domestic incidents—these, more or less, were the sum total of villainy in King's Minster. The last murder in these parts was in 1958—until the day before yesterday, that is.

In Challow Street, the smart new housing development near the infirmary, Terence Clark, Detective Sergeant and one-third of the establishment of King's Minster CID, was plying his electric shaver in his kitchen while he waited for the kettle to boil. Upstairs, Julie, Clark's wife of twenty years through thick and thin, and his two children were still asleep. From the transistor radio on the refrigerator came the news and the weather forecast from Radio Solent. The day was to be yet another clear dry one with perhaps a little rain later this afternoon, at last. The south-western counties had seen no rain in the last three weeks.

In Chaucer's bakery, near the town gate, Arthur Chaucer, a member of the King's Minster Rural District Council, and a leading light in the local Rotary Club, was supervising the first of today's bread and cakes from his ovens. The bakehouse backed on to the river, where Arthur Chaucer's smart little cabin cruiser was tied up at his private mooring, along with several other vessels which were owned by King's Minster's more well-to-do.

The adjacent property was Hawkesley's boatyard. Nothing much would happen in the boatyard until Sam and Charlotte Hawkesley arrived to take off the padlocks at a few minutes before eight o'clock.

A quarter of a mile to the east, where the river opened on to the sea, in a row of cramped mean cottages that fronted directly on to the street—cottages built in King's Minster's nineteenth-century heyday as a wool town—Norman Oates was just surfacing from an unquiet sleep. It had been the second uneasy night in a row for Norman Oates.

North-east of the town by a mile or so, in a secluded fake-Georgian house luxurious enough to be equipped with its own covered swimming-pool, were all the signs of occupation. Lights burned downstairs. Monday's newspapers—the *Financial Times* was one of them—lay in an untidy ziggurat on the glass-topped coffee-table in the well-appointed lounge. The hi-fi equipment in the corner was switched on, although the tape in the tape-deck had run itself out some thirty-six hours ago. The amplifier was switched to feed the two extension loud-speakers by the glass-covered pool at the rear of the house. They were, of course, now silent.

More ominously, yesterday's newspapers still lay on the recessed coconut mat behind the front door; while, outside, the two pints of milk on the doorstep under the pillared porch were also yesterday's.

And a few hundred yards along the same lane, in a thatched cottage with diamond-paned leaded windows, and with a deep front garden that in the summer was a riot of bright colours, Florian Westlake, known to very few by his real name of Ernest George Hawkins, stirred his great Hanoverian bulk in his great Hanoverian four-poster and dreamed. As he would dream until eight o'clock, when Roland Hollister, his companion and very dear friend of twenty years, would carry up his breakfast on a silver tray and clink a silver apostle spoon against a Spode china teacup to wake him.

On the other side of the house with the milk-bottles still on the doorstep, by perhaps some five hundred yards, Ailsa Crispin was mucking out her stable of hacks herself this morning, because yet another half-witted girl had left her to seek wider and more lucrative pastures elsewhere; although Ailsa Crispin was hardy enough to do the work of two girls—or two men for that matter. On her way across to her stables after breakfast she had noticed, through the trees, that several of Mrs Blezard's downstairs lights were on, and so they were in that glorified conservatory that looked as if it had been pupped at Kew. So perhaps Mrs Blezard was entertaining yet *another* man. But surely not in her pool at a quarter past six in the morning. Ailsa Crispin did not quite approve of Mrs Blezard. Too much money, that was Mrs Blezard's trouble. Too much money and not enough to do with it.

At a quarter to seven, Detective Sergeant Clark took up a cup of tea to his wife and gently shook her awake. She stirred irritably.

'What time is it?'

'Quarter to seven.'

'God,' she murmured sleepily, shuffling up from the covers. 'You're getting earlier and earlier.' She took the cup and saucer from him. Some of the tea slopped over into the saucer. He had kept her awake half the night, tossing and turning and talking in his sleep. He had been that way for weeks.

'You've got to see Dr Marchant,' she said. 'You look terrible.'

'I keep telling you,' he retorted spikily, 'I'm all right.'

She knew better than to argue. Just lately he flew off the handle at the slightest provocation. He never used to. He said it was overwork, stress, that Butcher was pushing him. The trouble was that it was beginning to affect her, too. Being a copper's wife was never a bed of roses. A woman had to put up with the same stinking hours, and all the same mental callouses that her husband had collected during the day.

'Try and be early tonight, eh?' she said.

'I'll try,' he said, but she knew he wouldn't. Last night she had persuaded him to go out for a Chinese—just the two of them, without the kids. He had promised to be home by half-past six. He had finally appeared at half-past nine. There had been no Chinese. He had fallen asleep in one of the armchairs before he had even drunk the cup of coffee she had made him. It had been his birthday, too. His fortieth. In two years he would have done his twenty in the force. He could retire. The pension wouldn't be a fortune, but a lot of people lived on less.

'I'd better be off,' he said. He stooped over the bed. She budded her mouth. He gave it a hasty peck. Couldn't wait to be away. If he carried on like this, he wouldn't *live* to see his retirement. He would burn himself out.

'See you,' he said.
'Take care.'
And then he was gone.

CLARK DROVE through the silent and near-empty streets.
They would be busier later. Today was Wednesday, market-day.

At seven o'clock he was signing the duty-book and
climbing the wooden staircase to the office that he shared
with his two DCs. It overlooked the High Street and the
town's memorial to Queen Victoria. The High Street was
wider here, almost a plaza.

He hung his raincoat on the coat-stand beside the door
and draped the jacket of his smart grey suit over the back
of his chair. Then he lit his first cigarette of the day and
drew himself a plastic cup of coffee from the machine
along the landing. His two assistants, DC Wilkie and
WDC Anderson, would arrive at eight o'clock. Clark always arrived early to make a start on his paperwork.
Butcher ran a very tight ship when it came to paperwork.
Clark did not believe in paperwork. Clark's desk was a
muddle. Clark was a street man. This was Clark's manor,
known to Clark like the face he shaved in the morning.
In King's Minster, Terence Clark knew every street,
every alley, every dossing-place where a villain was
likely to hide himself, every drain-cover and every rat-
run; as Clark also knew every villain, miscreant, pervert
and tart in it by face and by name. There were not many,
but there were still too many. In his six years in King's
Minster, Detective Sergeant Clark had fingered more than
his fair share of collars, and seen a fair few owners of
them put away as well; and knew that there were still a
few more walking the streets, despite his strenuous ef-
forts, who had no right to be.

Norman Oates, for instance. One of the Occurrence Reports in Clark's filing-tray this morning concerned a box of blank video-tapes stolen from a van on the Dorchester Road yesterday afternoon while its driver took a break in Ossie Lang's café. Only a small job, not worth a light to a self-respecting villain. Three or four hundred pounds' worth at most. Norman wouldn't have done the thieving himself, because he lacked the nous. But if anyone around these parts needed the services of a fence to slip stolen goods back into the market, then they would make their first enquiries of Norman Oates.

At the bottom of the docket was the red imprint of Butcher's rubber stamp and, on the dotted line the stamp provided, the word ACTION in Butcher's neat block hand. Well, Clark would give Butcher action. He wanted an excuse for a few words with Norman Oates anyway. Especially after what young Susan had told him on Monday evening when she had come home from school. That was likely to be down to Oates, too.

At five to eight—Butcher usually arrived at eight on the dot—Clark shrugged back into his jacket and raincoat and went downstairs again. From the information room, behind the duty desk, news of a traffic accident on the road to Swanage was coming over the radio.

Clark signed himself out in the book. Name. Time—he glanced at his watch. In the column headed DESTINATION, he wrote, suitably vaguely, Harbour End, the name by which the grubbier end of the town dignified itself.

'Off out, then?' enquired Sergeant Harper, prowling out from the information room. Harper ought to have signed off with the night-shift at six o'clock, but had probably stayed on to show Butcher what a conscientious copper he was.

'Sorting out those video-tapes,' said Clark. And that, too, sounded suitably vague. 'I've got an idea or two.'

'Butcher'll be here in a minute,' said Harper. Harper never even combed what little hair he had without asking Butcher's permission first. Two years off his pension was Harper, and still frightened of losing it.

'I know,' said Clark, dropping the ballpoint pen on its length of string back in the crease of the book. He tried to think of something pithy and biting, but it was too early in the morning. And the uniformed Harper really wasn't worth the trouble. 'I'll be a couple of hours, tell him.'

And Harper could be relied upon to tell him. Like lap-dog and master Harper and Butcher were.

At two minutes to eight Clark slipped from the station by its side-door and climbed into his car. At the traffic lights by the old town gate he glimpsed Butcher in his Volvo in the opposite lane, the two of them waiting for the green.

Clark pretended he hadn't seen him.

SAM AND Charlotte Hawkesley arrived together at their boatyard at a few minutes before eight o'clock. Hawkesley took off the padlocks and opened the double gates to the street and hooked them back on their stays, while his wife unlocked the ship's chandlery to the right of the gates and put on the kettle. Their staff of two would arrive at eight o'clock.

It promised to be a fine morning. Business was good, and the twenty-thousand mortgage from the bank would soon be settled.

Hawkesley unlocked the workshop and checked the state of the twin glass-fibre hulls of the catamaran that Chas and Ivor were working on. They stretched almost from end to end of the workshop, thirty-six feet, the biggest job that Hawkesley's had ever undertaken; and next week, God willing, the pair of them would be rolled down the wooden slipway at the back and taken on the river and put under sail as far as the sandbar and back. Hawkesley had a cool eight thousand of his own invested in that catamaran.

In the chandlery, his wife was tipping the daily cash-float into the till. In the summer season the chandlery made more than the yard—passing trade mostly, tourists who came to look at the minster. They bought barometers, reproduction brass riding-lights, and even the occasional ship's wheel to hang on their front-room walls.

She brewed the tea and poured milk into four mugs in her curtained-off cubby-hole at the end of the counter. The teapot was on the go all day in Hawkesley's boatyard, and today looked little different from all the others that had preceded it. It was five past eight.

She heard her husband coming back in from the yard as she was spooning sugar into the mugs.

'Tea up,' she called, as she always called.

But, unusually, there was no cheery response.

'Sam?'

The telephone beside the till tinkled. She drew the curtain aside. He was dialling, the receiver in his white-knuckled hand, his body trembling and his face the grey of wood-ash.

'Sam?'

'Don't go out to the jetty,' he said. 'For Christ's sake, don't go out to the ramp.' She watched him press the receiver closer to his ear. 'Hello? I want the police, please....' His arm shot out and made a barrier to stop her going out through the counter-flap.

'Don't, Charlie,' he said. 'You won't like it. There's a body out there. I think it's Mrs Blezard.'

TWO

ROPER AND PRICE showed their identity-cards to the constable guarding the entrance to Hawkesley's boatyard. The inevitable small crowd had already gathered: a few children on their way to school, a few women with shopping-trolleys, an elderly man walking his dog.

The constable pointed into the yard.

'That way, sir. Turn right at the end of the shed. Mr Butcher's waiting for you.'

A light breeze from the river flapped their raincoats about their knees as they rounded the corner of Hawkesley's boatshed. The early-morning mist was long gone. An autumn sun shone palely now and made the river sparkle like shards of broken glass. On the opposite bank, the clock on the minster chimed the quarter to nine o'clock.

The tableau was assembled at the toe of the wooden slipway that led down from the double doors at the back of the boatshed. At the centre of the group lay the black-clad body of a woman, a foot or so above where the river lapped the boards.

Phil Butcher, in uniform, levered himself upright as Roper and Price strode down the ramp. He proffered his hand. It was cold and moist, and the cuff of his tunic was black and glistening where it had been in the water. His greying hair had been blown into spikes here and there by the breeze.

'How long?' asked Roper, as Butcher's damp clammy hand fell away.

'Twenty-four hours at least,' said Butcher. 'Not that I'm an expert.'

Roper dropped to his heels beside the body. She'd had a good figure, tall, broad-shouldered, well proportioned. Black hair, water still running from it and darkening the oak planks beside her. Black sweater and black slacks. Barefoot. About thirty-five, perhaps, going by the figure. Several rings, two of them sporting diamonds. No wedding-band. A small frond of seaweed trapped between two of her fingers. Roper lifted her right hand. The skin was wrinkled and icy cold. The fingers were stiff, the wrist and elbow still in rigor, so Butcher's guess of twenty-four hours probably wasn't so wide of the mark—except that cold water both delayed the onset of rigor and prolonged it, so it was a long way from a certainty.

And Butcher's other guess, that foul play was concerned, was also not so wide of the mark.

Her right cheekbone was definitely depressed, probably fractured, and the skin over it deeply grazed. The blue lips were swollen and puffy, the lower one split a half-inch or so left of centre. Two of her upper front teeth were broken off at the gums, both to the right of centre. From one stump protruded a stainless-steel pin that had once retained a dental cap. One diagonally struck blow by the looks of it, which had just missed the right-hand side of her nose. Something solid, something blunt. Or maybe it hadn't been a weapon at all. From the undamaged left-hand side of her face she had clearly been a good-looking woman—once. Her eyes stared upwards in the vacuity of death, the scudding clouds overhead reflected in them, beads of river moisture still on the lashes.

'And there's this,' said Butcher, crouched by the body's head.

Roper shuffled sideways as Butcher parted a couple of

switches of the wet black hair. There were several bare patches on the scalp, and not only had the hair been forcibly torn out but in some places several outer layers of skin as well. One patch was about the size of a fingernail. At a guess it would have taken a pretty hefty pull to tug out that much hair at once.

'What do you think?' asked Butcher.

'Could be,' said Roper. Roper had known Butcher on and off for twenty years. He was a good copper, and if Butcher's gut was thinking murder, then he was more than likely right.

The face was a translucent white, as if it had been bleached, its only spot of colour the blueness about the gaping swollen mouth. Two gold molars at the back. Expensive, like her rings.

'Do we know who she is?'

'Blezard,' said Butcher. 'Hannah Blezard. Local woman.'

Roper rose. By some accident of history, the minster seemed to have been built on the wrong side of the river, or perhaps the town had grown up on this north bank in defiance of it. About fifty yards to Roper's right, as he faced the water, was a stone road-bridge, busy with traffic at this time of the morning. To the left, as the river widened, was the older part of the town: some drab-looking cottages fenced off from the river, a few derelict warehouses, a stone jetty with a few cars parked on it. On the opposite bank, the town petered out altogether past the minster and gave way to banks of reeds and grass and trees. Close by, on this bank, a colourful flotilla of small boats was tied up.

'We'd better make a tentative start, Dave,' he said to Price. 'Radio in for Mr Wilson—tell him we've got a suspected foul play. And a photographer. And a couple of frogmen—see if they can find anything in the water. Anybody got a blanket?'

One of Butcher's men was standing by with one. He draped it carefully along the body.

'Do you want any of the lads down here?' asked Price.

Roper wasn't sure yet. She just might have fallen from a boat, or fallen off that bridge. She might be a suicide. And murder inquiries were expensive.

'Perhaps later. We'll see how it goes.'

'Right.' Price turned away and started back up the slipway to the narrow stone jetty.

'Was the tide coming in or going out?' Roper asked Butcher.

'Coming in,' said Butcher. 'It'll be on the turn in about half an hour.'

'How far from the sea are we?'

'About half a mile.'

'And how about currents, undertows—that sort of thing?'

'Sorry,' said Butcher. 'I'm a landlubber. You'll have to ask Sam Hawkesley, the bloke who found the body.'

SAM HAWKESLEY spread an Admiralty chart across the polished mahogany top of his counter and weighted down its curling edges with a couple of glass ashtrays.

'We're here,' he said, bending a stubby forefinger against the chart, about half a mile from where the river bell-mouthed into the bay. 'Poole is over here.' Hawkesley's forefinger moved just off the chart to the right.

'And what's this?' Roper's forefinger zig-zagged over an island of contour lines, all of them close together, about a quarter of a mile out from where the river entered the sea.

'The sandbar,' said Hawkesley. He was about forty,

Roper guessed, bearded and balding, with a good pair of hands that looked as if they earned their living the hard way. The business looked moderately prosperous.

'How deep?'

'A couple of fathoms—twelve feet. In the summer. At this time of the year it's nearer a fathom. It shifts as well. You take out anything with a keelboard, and you avoid it like the plague.'

Roper traced the direction of a set of arrows. 'How about these?'

'Predominant currents,' explained Hawkesley. 'North-east to south-west.'

'So, if she had fallen into the sea, it ought to have been north of the river mouth? Up here somewhere.' Roper's forefinger circled an area of shoreline and sea north-west of the sandbar.

Hawkesley was an intelligent man, and interested enough to be looking for implications.

'Yes,' he agreed. 'That's possible.'

Roper's fingertip traced back along the centre-line of the river. It had occurred to him that if the body had been floating in the river for as long as it looked as if it had, then somebody surely would have seen it. Unless it had floated out to sea and then floated back again this morning.

'If she had fallen into the river, could she have been washed out to sea? And then been washed back in again?'

'It's possible,' agreed Hawkesley. 'The river current's slow at the moment because of the drought. And there's a pretty fierce undertow, up here, by the old jetty.' Hawkesley's finger circled the northern shore of the bell-mouth at the eastern end of the town. 'Between high and low tide there's a sort of whirlpool action. A competently handled dinghy could ride it out easily.'

'But not a floating body?'

'I doubt it,' said Hawkesley. 'It could turn it round and bring it back up here.'

Roper's finger moved westwards, to the landward side of the stone bridge he had just observed outside.

'If she'd drowned in the river west of this bridge? Here, say. What then?'

'It's shallow past the bridge in that direction. Barely a foot deep. Silted up. Has been for years. You'd have a job to drown there. Unless you were drunk—or very determined.'

'So in your opinion, Mr Hawkesley, if she was drowned in the river, then it had to be between the bridge and the sea? Or she was drowned in the sea. Right?'

'Yes,' said Hawkesley, 'I'd go along with that.'

'And it's a strange time of year for a swim, eh, Mr Hawkesley?' said Roper thoughtfully.

'She wouldn't have needed the sea *or* the river for that,' said Hawkesley. 'She had her own pool.'

'You knew her socially?'

'Not exactly,' said Hawkesley. 'But she was pretty well known around here. Blezard's Electronics, on the industrial estate. I think she owns it. Since her husband died.'

'I see,' said Roper. So Mrs Blezard had probably been wealthy; which widened the investigative horizon somewhat. Panic, passion, prejudice—or greed. The motive was always one—or a combination—of those. An old inspector had told Roper that, years ago, and Roper had adopted the dictum as a lifetime creed.

'Did you touch the body, Mr Hawkesley?'

'Only to bring it in,' said Hawkesley. 'Just one of the hands. I hauled her up high enough on the ramp to stop her floating away again. Then I rang your people.'

'You didn't attempt resuscitation?'

'Hell, no,' said Hawkesley. 'I was fifteen years in the Navy. When a drowned body looks like that you know it's been in the water for a bloody long time.'

'How was she floating?'

'Face down,' said Hawkesley. 'All I saw at first was her hair. The rest of her was submerged.'

'But you didn't pull her out of the water by her hair?'

'No,' said Hawkesley. 'Her hand was nearer. So I grabbed that.'

Mrs Hawkesley came from her curtained-off cubbyhole with a couple of mugs of tea which she set down on the counter beside the chart.

'And you saw nothing, Mrs Hawkesley?'

'No,' she said. 'Thank God.'

'And neither of you noticed anything unusual going on during the last couple of days? A strange face in town, perhaps? Anyone in your yard who didn't ought to have been? Anything of that sort?'

They shook their heads. They seemed genuine enough.

ROPER WENT BACK down the ramp to where, at its toe, the recently arrived pathologist, the Coroner's Officer, Price and Chief Inspector Butcher were crouched around the body. The red blanket, folded now, had been put to one side and the sodden black sweater rolled up to the body's armpits. A few feet out, a constable manoeuvred a rubber dinghy; while another, heroically stripped to the waist, hung over the side and was feeling about in the mud on the off-chance of finding a shoe—or, even less likely, a pair.

'How about the frogmen?' asked Roper.

'On their way,' said Price. 'Should be here by lunchtime.'

Wilson, the pathologist, glanced up briefly over his paper mask.

'Morning, Superintendent.'

'Morning, Mr Wilson.' Roper dropped to his heels beside him, as Wilson returned to the job of draining a fluid sample from the body's water-distended lungs with a syringe.

'Death by drowning?' asked Roper.

'No doubt about it,' said Wilson. 'The poor woman's almost waterlogged.' He withdrew his syringe and squirted its disagreeable-looking contents into a sterilised bottle on the planks beside him. 'And that's not all of it. I expect her other lung's the same. Give me a hand to turn her over, will you—and carefully. Here....' He handed out three pairs of polythene gloves. 'Gently please.'

As painstakingly as if it were still alive, Hannah Blezard's body was rolled onto its face. The dark hair was drying rapidly in the breeze that was still coming across the river. On the opposite bank, on the minster landing-stage, a couple of constables were herding away a knot of would-be ghouls who were drawn to occasions like this like iron nails to a magnet.

Where Wilson softly prodded, the puckered flesh stayed indented, like soft dough. One of Butcher's young constables looked in imminent danger of being sick. He went closer to the river. His shoulders heaved helplessly, and he gagged a couple of times and mopped at his mouth with a handkerchief.

A pair of surgical scissors sliced down the seam of the black slacks and the briefs beneath, and Wilson inserted a rectal thermometer.

Roper watched him continue about his business, the Coroner's Officer making the occasional note on his pad at Wilson's instruction, the scene-of-crime photographer taking the occasional photograph. The constable had come back. He still looked green about the gills as he tucked his handkerchief away.

'Sorry,' he said sheepishly.

'Don't worry about it,' said Roper. It took a lifetime to get used to this job. Even after thirty-odd years Roper still had bad moments himself.

Wilson sat back on his heels and checked the rectal thermometer against another that was recording the ambient temperature. The body was as cold now as the river.

'How about formal identification?' he said. 'She got a husband?'

'She's a widow,' said Butcher. 'But I can go along to the factory and find out about her next of kin. If she's got any.'

'Those hands never worked in a factory,' said Wilson. 'Not on your life.'

'She owns it.'

'Ah,' said Wilson. 'That's more like it. Post-mortem examination at two o'clock if the coroner sees fit. Suit you?'

'Suits me,' said Roper. 'But how long do you reckon she's been dead? A day? Two?'

Wilson had begun to put the instruments of his trade back in their black case. He puffed out his cheeks contemplatively. He was a cautious man, and guessing was not his strong point.

'If we can find out when she ate her last meal, her stomach will tell us to within an hour or so. But otherwise....' His gaze raked slowly down the body and back again. 'Of course it *is* only a guess...but I'd say about thirty hours. Give or take, say, four or five...or perhaps six.'

Roper pushed back his layers of cuffs and deducted thirty hours from his wristwatch.

Quarter past nine now—the minster clock chimed again to confirm it; less thirty made it some time plus or minus Monday midnight.

'And how about those broken teeth?'

Wilson was peeling off his mask. It went into a polythene bag and then into his case. He closed its lid and snapped its catches with an air of finality. He liked his little moment of drama, did Mr Wilson. An electronic flash plopped softly nearby, the scene-of-crime photographer taking his shots of the jetty and the slipway.

Wilson stood up with his black case in his hand.

Behind him, the undertaker's men were lifting the mortal remains of Hannah Blezard into a temporary coffin.

'Your guess is as good as mine, Mr Roper,' said Wilson. 'But I'd say the poor woman was knocked half-unconscious. And perhaps was held under water by her hair until her lungs were clogged. Of course, I could be wrong.'

SERGEANT CLARK focused the powerful night-glasses tighter on the yellow front door across the narrow street. The doorknocker was a cast-iron lion's head with a ring through its nose, painted black. One of the door-panels had a hair-line split in it.

'Good pair of binoculars, these, Oatesie,' he said. 'What do you use 'em for? Birdwatching? Eh?'

'That's my business,' grumbled Norman Oates from the bedroom doorway. Sergeant Clark had practically turned the place over. A whole hour. No warrant. A courtesy-call Clark had called it.

'Got a bill for 'em, have we, Norman?'

'I bought 'em off a bloke in a pub.'

'Yes,' sneered Clark. 'I'll bet you did, you bloody little pervert.'

'A proper copper'd be out looking for criminals.'

'I am, Oatesie. I am....' Clark broke off as the yellow door opposite was opened and a baby in a folding pram was wheeled down the single stone step to the pavement. It was followed by a robust but shapely young woman in a leather jacket, jeans and high-heeled boots. She paused to lock her front door behind her and to tuck the blanket tighter around the child in the pram. She was a redhead. About twenty. The jeans fitted her like a second skin.

Clark panned the binoculars up from the yellow front door to the bedroom window above it. Through a gap in the net curtains, he could just make out the shadowy corner of a padded bed-head and the mirror of a dressing-table.

'You really *are* a bloody Tom, aren't you, Norman? A right little peeper, eh? Aren't you, my son, eh?'

'Don't know what you mean,' mumbled Oates.

'Don't you?' Clark slowly laid the binoculars back on the chest of drawers beside the window, whence he had picked them up, and turned to rivet Oates to the spot with the malevolent beams of his dark eyes. Clark levelled a finger at the unmade bed and the large yellow Kodak envelope and the black-and-white eight-by-ten photographs that Clark had, a few minutes ago, spilled from it to the rumpled bedcovers.

Then the finger was aimed at Oates, and crooked.

'Come here, Norman,' said Clark softly. 'I want you.'

And, for all that his mind willed otherwise, Norman Oates found himself hooked up and drawn forward to where Clark stood beside the bed and the heap of photographs.

'Take these yourself, did you, Oatesie?'

'There's no law against it,' protested Oates. 'Anybody can take pictures in the street.'

'And you printed 'em yourself, too, eh?'

'Well…yeah,' agreed Oates. 'But that's not against the law, either, is it?'

'Proper little brief, aren't you, Norman?' sneered Clark.

'Now, look,' threatened Oates. 'You got no right.…'

But Clark's rage broke at last, black and uncontrolled. 'No,' he hissed. '*You* look!'

And Oates flinched and shrank even smaller than he was as Clark's left hand flew out and clamped hard on Oates's neck and rammed his face down over the bed.

Clark's other hand snatched up one of the black-and-white glossy prints and brandished it an inch from Oates's face. His grip fastened tighter on Oates's neck.

'That's *my* little girl, Oatesie.'

'I didn't know,' gasped Oates. 'I didn't *know,* Mr Clark. Honest.'

'Well, you know now, don't you, Oatesie?' said Clark, as he loosened his grip on Oates's neck. And Oates watched him, still rooted to the spot by Clark's implacable eyes, as Clark tugged his black leather gloves tighter and menacingly flexed his fingers in them. 'What else have you got stowed away in this grubby little drum of yours, eh, Oatesie? More Mary-Jane—like last time? Eh? Eh?'

'Nothing,' whined Oates. 'Nothing. Honest. And I didn't know, Mr Clark. Honest, I *didn't* know.'

'But you know *now,* don't you, Oatesie?'

Oates drew back, and his hands rose futilely to protect himself as Clark's tightly balled left fist thumped menacingly into the open palm of Clark's right hand.

'I'll report you,' he whimpered. 'You ain't got a warrant. You got no right even to be in here. I'll see your guv'nor. I will.'

'You, you snivelling little oick,' hissed Clark. 'By the time I've finished with you, you bloody pervert, *you* won't be in a state to talk to anybody. Believe it.'

ROPER DREW Butcher's cut-glass ashtray closer. It was ten to ten. A rumble of traffic rose from the High Street.

'…and a room for the Inspector and me,' said Roper.

'They can use the one at the end of the passage,' said Butcher.

The WPC made a note on her pad.

'How are you off for jacks?' asked Roper.

'Three,' said Butcher. 'A sergeant, and two DCs.'

'The sergeant a local man, is he?'

'The best,' said Butcher, which would have caused Sergeant Clark some surprise had he overhead. 'Got a nose like a gun-dog.'

'Can we have him?'

'Sure,' said Butcher, then, to the WPC: 'Do we know where Terry Clark is, Jan?'

'Yes, sir. Up at Harbour End. He's looking into those missing video-tapes.'

A tic of irritability fleeted across Butcher's pinched narrow face.

'Get him on the radio. Tell him I want him back here. Sharpish. It's important, tell 'im.'

'Yes, sir. Is there anything else, sir?' This last was to Roper. The WPC was a plump pretty girl, her fair hair tied at the nape of her neck with a black ribbon; and Roper wondered, and not for the first time, what brought bright young women like that into a thankless job like coppering. She looked scarcely out of school.

'You got a teapot on the inventory in this place? A good china one?'

'Yes, sir.'

Roper smiled at her. 'Three cups, then. We'll pour it ourselves. And *that* is it. Thank you.'

She went out and closed the door quietly behind her.

'Use your phone, Phil?'

Butcher slid his red telephone across the desk. Roper held out his hand for Price's notebook and Mrs Blezard's telephone number. He dialled the number, waited.

The phone at the other end rang six times. There was a click. Then a long pause. For a few moments it sounded as if the line had gone dead.

Then a voice, a woman's. Curt and crisp and incisive.

'This is Hannah Blezard. I'm sorry, but I'm out. If it's important, leave a message. And if you're trying to sell me something—forget it. Please speak after the pips.' Then three pips.

And that was it. It wasn't the kind of voice that would encourage anybody to leave anything.

'Roper,' said Roper, to put a marker on the tape at the other end. 'One—two—three.' And glanced at his watch. Nine fifty-three. Exactly.

He laid the receiver back on its rest. 'Answering machine,' he said. 'Could mean there's no one in the house. So we'll need a warrant. And you'd better get a man up there. Don't want anybody turning the place over in the mean time.' He slid the phone back to Butcher.

Within a few minutes a car was on its way to the late Mrs Blezard's house in Witling Lane. The warrant would take longer. The due and proper processes of the law were never quick. Only those at the rump end of it, like Roper and Price and Butcher, were expected to act with speed.

The WPC returned with the teapot and three respectable china cups on a plastic tray.

'Sergeant Clark's back, sir,' she said. 'I've just seen him pulling into the yard. And we've just had a call in from a farmer in Witling Lane. There's a plum-coloured Daimler Sovereign parked in the gateway of one of his fields. He can't get his tractor in. He says can we move it.'

'Great God,' muttered Butcher. 'As if we aren't busy enough already. Send someone up there with the master-keys and get him to shift it. And we'll have the bugger for obstruction as well, tell 'im.'

'It's Mrs Blezard's car, sir,' said the WPC. 'Sergeant Harvey's already been in touch with Swansea.'

Which put an entirely different slant on a simple matter of mindless obstruction.

'Sure about that, are we?' asked Roper, looking up at her.

'Yes, sir.'

'Could you find your way to this farm?'

'Yes, sir.'

'Take her with you, Dave,' Roper said to Price. 'And contact Regional Forensic. Tell 'em to truck it away and give it the once-over. And tell 'em to give it priority. And some answers by tonight, please. And *plenty* of photographs.'

Price poured himself a hasty half-cup of tea and gulped it down, then put on his raincoat and picked up his notebook from Butcher's desk.

'Where'll you be?' he said.

'Mrs Blezard's place,' said Roper. 'I'll see you there.'

As Price and the WPC hurried out, a raincoated figure just coming in stepped aside for them in the passage.

It was clear by the truculent way that he strolled in

and closed the door behind him that he had no fear of Butcher, and did not know who Roper was.

'I got the call,' he said. 'Heard downstairs we might have a murder on the patch.'

'Damn right we have, Terry,' said Butcher tartly. 'Where the *hell* have you been?'

'I thought I'd got a lead on those tapes. Thought I ought to check it out.'

'And?' said Butcher.

'No luck,' said Clark. 'The lead was duff.'

'You went out on your own again,' said Butcher, still tart. 'I saw you.'

'There was no one else here, was there?' retorted Clark.

'You should have waited,' said Butcher. 'Taken one of the jacks with you. You only had to wait five minutes, for Christ's sake.'

Clark didn't answer, and Butcher didn't pursue it. He nodded towards Roper.

'This is Superintendent Roper from County, Terry,' he said. 'You're working with him. Sergeant Clark, Douglas.'

Clark's dark eyes met Roper's. He gave a nod.

'Morning, sir.'

'Morning, Sergeant,' said Roper. 'Take a seat.'

Clark sat down in the chair that was still warm from Price. Roper took further stock of him as Butcher poured two cups of tea. The smart raincoat, the well-cut grey suit, the pale blue and white striped shirt, the slightly askew blue and black striped tie, the shrewd knowing face with the copper's eyes, tired and red-rimmed, Roper observed, above a neatly trimmed Mexican bandit's moustache. Roper put him around forty. Which meant that, if he was as good a jack as Butcher had said he

was, then he ought to have been an inspector by now.
One of the black gloves on Clark's lap was split at the
knuckle, a lozenge of white linty fabric showing through.
It looked recently done.

'Do you know a Mrs Blezard, Sergeant?'

'Widow,' said Clark with commendable promptness.
'Number eight, Witling Lane.'

'More,' said Roper over his teacup. 'All you know.'

Clark turned out to be a walking compendium. Mrs
Blezard was moneyed, was in her middle thirties, fond
of fast cars, had a large share in Blezard's Electronics
left her by her late husband—who had been about to
divorce her, or so another rumour had it, when he'd
dropped dead in his factory. Her house was grace and
favour, so the gossip said—owned by Blezard's Electronics, but hers to live in until she died or moved out.
She ran a plum-coloured Daimler Sovereign, a Double
Six, with current registration-plates. Her clothes were certainly not purchased in King's Minster, and her hair-
dresser—at least, her local one—was Monsieur André, a
few doors along from Sylvester's dairy in the High Street.
Two speeding offences this year, otherwise a clean sheet.
And, of course, with a wealthy good-looking widow like
that, rumours about her possible love-life abounded in the
rock-pool community of King's Minster.

And there, thought Roper, were probably enough motives to write a book about. And Butcher had been right.
DS Clark certainly knew his patch.

THREE

CLARK CANTED HIS Cavalier half on to the grass verge in front of Mrs Blezard's tall bank of privet hedge and ratcheted on the handbrake. In front of the gate a white Metro with the County police insignia on its doors was already parked.

Roper climbed out and flexed his legs. It was half-past eleven. The investigative machinery was primed. Price had just radioed in: the Forensic crew were presently giving Mrs Blezard's car the once-over further along this same lane. When they were done, the car was being winched off to the regional laboratory for a more thorough examination. Four divers and their equipment, on loan from their base along the coast of Sussex, would be trawling the river in an hour or two. And Blezard's company secretary would be meeting Roper at the mortuary at half-past one to make the formal identification. Mrs Blezard, it seemed after all, had no known next of kin.

Car doors slammed, and Butcher came across the grass to flank Roper on one side, with Sergeant Clark on the other. In Butcher's black-gloved hand was the buff envelope containing the search-warrant. The magistrate had not been keen to sign it at this early stage. But, then, he had not seen Mrs Blezard's bleached white face and broken teeth. Clark carried a jemmy to force a door if that was necessary.

He opened the black-painted wrought-iron gate and stood aside for Roper and Butcher to precede him up the front path. A few yards further along the same strip of tall hedge an identical pair of gates let on to a tarmac-adamed driveway that went off to the right of the house to a garage. The yellow up-and-over door was open, and the garage was empty.

The red-brick house was neo-Georgian; built, Roper guessed, within the last ten years or so. Sash window-frames painted white, a tiled porch supported on two elegant white pillars over flagged front steps. Considering the season, the front lawn was very orderly, as if it had been recently raked of all the dead leaves. The brace of tall box hedges on the lawn were also lately trimmed by the looks of them.

The bell-handle beside the freshly varnished oak front door was a reproduction of the Victorian sort: a forged iron bar with a looped handle at the bottom. Butcher gave it a tug. The double chime that sounded on the other side of the door was clearly of the late twentieth century. Roper glanced back down the path. The house was well secluded behind its hedges. It would be more so after dark. There were two bottles of milk on the step.

Butcher had tugged on the bell-handle again, but there was still no response.

A footfall on gravel came from the right-hand side of the house. It was the constable who had driven here in the white Metro. He threw up the kind of salute a man can only learn on a military parade-ground.

'There's no one in, sir,' he said to Butcher. 'But there's a conservatory at the back. I tried the door. It's unlocked.'

'We'll try that,' said Roper. 'Anyone been?' he asked the constable as the four of them started up the gravel path between the house and the garage.

'Yes, sir,' said the constable. 'Milkman, the postman and charlady. I told the milkman not to bother and collected three envelopes off the postman.' He reached inside his tunic and brought out three envelopes that he handed to Roper. Two of them were buff. One looked like a bill for the rates, another a bill from British Telecom. The third envelope was blue, the address on it typewritten. It had been postmarked in King's Minster yesterday lunch-time.

'The milkman left no milk?'

'No, sir.'

'So the bottles on the step were yesterday's delivery?'

'Yes, sir.'

'And there were no empties to take away?'

'No, sir.'

So the milk on the step was yesterday's. Not much to go on, but useful all the same.

'How about the charlady? Get her address?'

'Yes, sir. Told her to stay available. Said we'd want a statement.'

'Good,' said Roper.

They had reached the rear corner of the house, and rounded it. Stretching out from the back was an elegant glass conservatory built on the lines of the older hothouses at Kew. Its lower windows were banked on the inside with shrubbery and ferns that made an almost impenetrable screen against anyone trying to look in. Condensation misted the glass on the inside where the shrubbery touched it. Three expensive electric chandeliers, high up in the apex of the semi-circular roof, glowed with mournful indifference to the daylight outside.

'Here, sir,' said the constable. They had reached a point roughly halfway along the conservatory. With his gloved little finger he depressed the aluminium doorlever. The door opened outwards under his touch on welloiled hinges.

Roper kept well to one side of the single tiled step

down to the inside. The conservatory was built over a green-tiled swimming-pool. A strong smell of chlorine caught at his nostrils. The same green tiles made a path around the water. A couple of adjustable lounging-chairs were set out on the opposite side from the door, a towel draped over one of them.

'Go back and keep an eye on the front,' he told the constable. 'If anyone calls, I'd like a word with 'em. And you, Sergeant'—this to Clark—'you can take a look around the outside.'

Butcher followed Roper down the step.

Roper unbuttoned his raincoat. It was close in here. The steamy heat of the jungle. A centigrade thermometer on the door-frame showed close to twenty-two degrees; outside it was down nearer ten. Roper dropped to one knee and stretched a finger into the pool. That was warm, too. So Mrs Blezard had obviously set a great deal of store by her creature comforts.

Roper and Butcher kept close to the outside of the tiles. Near the door that let into the house an ultraviolet sun-bed, like an oversized trouser-press, stood in the corner. Above it was a loudspeaker strapped to the wall and set at an angle downwards. Its partner was strapped up in the opposite corner. Both were silent.

Roper stopped and looked back. The pool was about thirty feet long, eight deep at this end and about four at the other. In front of the two lounging-chairs a railed chromium-plated ladder with rubber-cased treads gave access to the water.

'Super?' Clark's voice echoed hollowly over the tiles. He was standing in the doorway. 'I've just found something. Somebody's polished up a patch of glass on the outside. About that much.' He made a circle with extended thumbs and forefingers. 'It's about the only spot where you can see straight in. Could have been a peeper.'

And that was likely. A place like this with a woman in it would definitely be an attraction for the dedicated voyeur.

'Make a note of it,' said Roper, 'and when the finger-print lads arrive point it out and have 'em take a picture.'

Clark went away again.

The glass-panelled door into the house was unlocked. It opened inwards to a luxurious barn of a sitting-room. All the wall-lights were switched on.

'I smell money,' said Roper.

'They're all the same along Witling Lane,' said Butcher. 'It's the scampi belt around these parts.'

To walk on the carpet with street-shoes was tanta-mount to spraying graffiti in a church porch. It was ivory white and lushly piled; and in the light from the three windows at the far end of the room it showed a mass of impressed footprints in the pile, several of which termi-nated by the doorway in which Roper and Butcher were presently standing.

'Watch it,' said Roper, and carefully skirted them as he took off his gloves and replaced them with a pair of white cotton ones from a polythene envelope he took from inside his raincoat. The central heating seemed to be going at full bore. Drier in here than it had been in the pool, but certainly as hot.

Two lights glowed in a rack of expensive hi-fi equip-ment in the corner beside the reconstituted York-stone fireplace. An amplifier and a tape-deck, both switched on. Roper pressed the EJECT button on the tape-deck and took out the tape. A digitised update of old Glenn Miller clas-sics. The sort of music to smooch by in the small hours. Perhaps an indication that Mrs Blezard had been entertaining someone at some time on Monday. Perhaps late. And perhaps a man friend. Roper dropped the tape back into the deck and prodded shut the plastic cover. The speaker switch on the amplifier was switched to EXT.1. Probably the pool—or, if one had that kind of mind, the bedroom. The ornaments on the stone mantelshelf were quality: a couple of Chelsea plates on wire stands—the one way to ruin a good plate; a Crown Derby piece, shepherd and shepherdess, *circa* 1750. The mark on the base showed it to be the genuine article. The last time he had seen one like that had been up at Sotheby's. It had fetched the best part of six and a half thousand pounds. He replaced it as carefully as he had picked it up, and wondered—and again it had nothing to do with the job—into what lucky hands the artefact would fall. The two plates were equally genuine. A clear two hundred apiece, or Roper was a Dutchman.

The massive brass-framed carriage-clock was quartz-controlled, and very expensive. The Matisse on the wall above it was a print, although he had to look closely at it to be sure. A glass-fronted corner-cabinet near the window was filled with a dozen varieties of early Victorian teapots.

The two settees and four armchairs ranged about the fireplace were as blatantly self-indulgent as the carpet. Upholstered in white kid. The newspapers on the chrome and glass-topped coffee-table were Monday's. The pink one on top was the *Financial Times;* opened at the stocks page. Two coffee-cups, both used, lipstick on one of them. So there had *definitely* been a visitor.

The wall opposite the fireplace was panelled with mirrors—an obvious device to give width and proportion to the narrow room which looked as if it had once been two. The wall-lamps were pink-shaded in translucent oys-ter-shells with gilded edges. A touch too chi-chi.

The double chime sounded in the hall. Butcher went to answer it, treading the carpet as if he were crossing a river on stepping-stones. Roper heard the rustle of news-papers. The Welsh-lilted voice that spoke to Butcher was Price's.

He stopped at the doorway, Butcher behind him.

'How did it go?' asked Roper.

'Running with condensation on the inside,' said Price, 'and the back seat was wet. And the steering-wheel and the door on the driving side had been wiped of prints. One of the Forensic lads found a white fibre caught up in the doorhandle.'

'Did you talk to the farmer?'

'Yes.'

'And was the car there yesterday?'

Price shrugged. 'He didn't know. Said it could have been.'

'Pity,' said Roper. It would have been useful to know when the car had first arrived at the farmer's gateway, because it sounded as if a wet dead body just might have been transported in it.

Price leaned forward and swept an appreciative glance around the sitting-room.

'Very chic,' he observed. 'You found anything?'

'Two used cups on the coffee-table here. That's all, so far.'

'So she had a visitor.'

'I'd say so,' said Roper.

The doorbell rang again. It was Clark this time, who had completed his circuit of the outside of the house, and the two men from the fingerprint section of Regional Fo-

rensic with their black cases. Roper went out to the hall
to join them, treading carefully in Butcher's shoe-prints.

'You'd better start in the sitting-room,' he said. 'There
are two cups in there that might be worth looking at.
Then the pool at the back. DS Clark's noticed a recently
cleaned window out there. Might be a print or two around
that. And watch the carpet in there.' He jerked a thumb
over his right shoulder. 'You might find a male shoe-
print or two. It'd be useful to know the size.'

'Could be some footprints around the pool, too,' said
the senior of the two, a square, bearded man in steel-
framed spectacles. 'Any signs of a forced entry?'

Roper glanced at Clark, who shook his head.

'Perhaps not,' said Roper. 'But look for one just the
same.'

From their cases, the two of them took out some polythene bags that they slipped over their shoes and fastened
in place with elastic bands around their ankles.

Price was nosing around by the front door where the
telephone sat on an upholstered telephone-seat. There
was a grey-cased answering machine beside the telephone. A yellow light blinked demandingly beneath the
MESSAGE legend.

'Anyone know how to work these things?' asked
Roper.

Clark did. He took a ballpoint pen from inside his
jacket, and with its cap end depressed a key labelled RE-
WIND/REVIEW. A muted whirr came from inside the case;
then a soft thud as the tape jolted to its beginning. With
the pen-cap, Clark pressed the PLAY key.

Three pips. A pause. A male voice. Soft. Mellifluous.

'Hannah—it's Rollie Hollister…,' the voice began.
'Florian would like to know if you can spare him a few
minutes this evening. About nine o'clock. Some research.

About clothes. Ten minutes, he promises, that's all. He'll wait for you to ring back.' This was followed by three pips followed by a silence. Then again.

'Stop it,' said Roper. Clark quickly depressed another key. 'Do we know who Rollie Hollister is? And this Florian whoever?'

'Neighbours,' said Clark. 'About a hundred yards, that way. Florian Westlake and Roland Hollister. Mr Westlake earns the pennies, and Mr Hollister does the shopping.'

'Like *that* is it?' enquired Roper drily.

'Nobody knows,' said Clark. 'But it's likely. They're both a bit precious.'

'Nobody's ever called Florian Westlake,' said Price. 'Or are they?'

'It's what's on the back of his books,' said Clark. 'He writes novels—romances—the heaving-bosom sort. Could be just his pen-name.'

That sounded likelier.

'And Hollister?' asked Roper. 'What about him?'

'Ex-actor,' said Clark. 'Back in the forties and fifties. The movies. B-pictures mostly.'

'Faded or retired?'

'Probably faded,' said Clark. 'He wasn't exactly a star.'

'Make a note, Dave,' Roper said to Price. 'We'll pay the gentlemen a call. Find out what time Hollister rang here.'

'See if there are any more,' said Roper to Clark. Clark depressed the PLAY key again.

Three pips.

'Hannie....' Another male voice. Out of breath. 'I know you're in... I saw you upstairs.... Please let me in... We've *got* to talk. Please.... I love you.... Please.'

Then the click of the phone quickly dropped, as though the caller had burned his fingers on it.

'Hold it,' said Roper, because there had been a great deal more in that voice than strangled speech.

'Hold it,' he said again, because Clark hadn't held it and the tape had run on to the next three pips.

Belatedly, Clark stabbed the STOP key.

'Know that voice, do we?'

Clark shook his head.

'Play it back.'

Clark pressed the FAST FORWARD key by mistake, quickly pressed STOP, then REWIND, then STOP again. The tail end of Hollister's voice once more; then the breathless voice. It sounded to Roper like a young voice, although he couldn't be sure.

'I love you.... Please.'

Unrequited love, thought Roper, which was not the least motive for murder.

'Do you know it, Phil?'

Butcher, too, shook his head.

'No,' he said. 'Could be anybody.'

'Try the next one.'

The voice came at once. Yet another man.

'It's Marshall, Mrs Blezard.' Authoritative and businesslike. 'The board has agreed Thursday. Ten a.m. Ring if you can't make it, will you? Preferably tomorrow morning. Thank you.'

'I know that one,' said Butcher. 'Ben Marshall. He's the company secretary over at Blezard's factory. The one you're meeting later. I've played a few rounds of golf with him.'

Clark had let the tape run on again. The three pips had occurred several times, but no voice had followed any of them.

'Run that back,' said Roper. 'Start again where Marshall finished.'

Three pips. A short passage of silence. Three pips. Another brief silence. And again—but this time with a hint of a human breath in the silence. Clark found the volume control at the side of the machine and turned it to maximum and played the section through again. It was *definitely* an intake of breath, perhaps a forerunner to speech. But the caller had obviously changed his or her mind on the same instant and cut off. The same caller each time? Someone with something important to say, something that could not be left on an answering machine? Or simply three different callers who, like many other people, preferred not to talk into a box of tricks?

'Let it run,' said Roper.

'It's Ailsa Crispin, Mrs Blezard,' barked out, before Clark turned the volume control down again. 'Saw your lights on. Phoned to see if everything was all right. Got your bloody machine instead. 'Scuse me for not minding my own bloody business, won't you? But if you're under the weather I'm taking the motor into town this morning to do a bit of shopping. So if you want anything give us a tinkle. Er—goodbye. Goodbye.'

Then came Roper's marker after the next three pips.

'Roper. One—two—three.'

'Stop,' he said. 'Who was the woman?'

'Ailsa Crispin,' said Butcher. 'Next-door neighbour. Runs the riding school. A couple of hundred yards down the lane.'

'We'll see her, too,' said Roper. 'Put her top of the list.' It would be interesting to find out when Ms Crispin had first noticed Mrs Blezard's lights burning. And what morning had been 'this morning'? In any event, all the

calls they had listened to so far had, for a certainty, been
made before nine fifty-three *this* morning.

'Run it,' said Roper.

Three more pips. Silence for perhaps a second, or perhaps even less. Then a click. Definitely another caller
who had changed his—or her—mind. Then came simply
a long silence broken from time to time by the occasional
magnetic splutter of the tape passing the head. That *last*
abortive call had been made some time between nine
fifty-three and now—which was a minute to twelve. It
might have been made by one of the callers who had
earlier rung off. Or even that breathless male voice that
had proclaimed its owner's love, lust, or whatever, for
the late Mrs Blezard. Had Mrs Blezard returned that love,
lust, or whatever? Had it been the owner of that voice
who had joined Mrs Blezard over coffee in the sitting-
room on Monday evening? Or one of the others? Florian
Westlake, or the breather? Or none of them?

'See if you can get the tape out of that machine, Sergeant,' said Roper to Clark. 'Bag it up and we'll run it
over again later.'

THE DINING-ROOM was across the hall from the sitting-
room. At its centre a rectangular glass-topped table on a
chromium-plated steel frame and legs. The chrome and
white leather chairs about it were equally trendy and
equally ugly. Another corner-cabinet like the one in the
lounge, this one full of cut-glass drinking-glasses. Bottles
of alcohol in the cupboard beneath. The carpet was identical with the one in the sitting-room. The room felt as
if it had not been used for some time.

The kitchen was a purely functional clinic: a built-in
split-level cooker; plenty of fitted cupboards; a washing-
up machine—empty; a fridge-freezer—West German—

with little in it. No crockery in the sink. Nothing left to dry on the draining-board. Light switched on, but the venetian blinds over the door and window were down and shut. So the kitchen had most likely last been used on Monday evening. There were no signs of a struggle—or of much else, for that matter.

THE MAIN BEDROOM was equally orderly. Over the dark brown duvet was draped a white towelling bathrobe. Two red furry mules between the bed and the wardrobes, the usual woman's bric-a-brac of pots and flasks and jars on a mirrored dressing-unit. A pair of earrings that might be either diamond or paste. Some hair-grips in a china dish. It all looked newly decorated, and Roper thought he could still smell paint. The curtains were open. The cream-coloured carpet was as lush as the one downstairs.

Treading carefully, Roper drew back one of the sliding doors of the white wardrobe that lined the wall opposite the bed. Underwear, silk slinky stuff; tights in plastic bags, brassières, none of it cheap. A smell of old-fashioned lavender-bags. Behind another pair of doors were jammed enough dresses to last Roper's own wife a good five years. The shoes on rails beneath were mostly Italian, again quality. Mrs Blezard had clearly gone in for nothing tatty. One fur coat in a plastic bag was ermine; no mistake about that. Another was mink. Another was nylon fun-fur—but that was from somewhere in Bond Street, too.

The soap was still damp on the handbasin in the bathroom, and so was the face-flannel draped over a ring beside it. The electric towel-rail was switched on, the two Turkish towels over it bone dry. A soggy unflushed paper tissue floated in the lavatory pan.

The two rear bedrooms looked as if they had not been

used in some time. From both, Roper could see straight down into the conservatory.

But there were no signs of violence anywhere.

IT WAS ONE O'CLOCK. Roper and Butcher sat in a corner of the saloon bar of the Duke of Wellington near the town gate, the market-day hubbub of farmers and traders going on all about them. For Roper there would be few more snatched lunches of cheese rolls and halves of bitter—and that was on the better days. It was little wonder that policemen ranked high on the statistics for stomach ulcers. Talk was of retirement.

'When are you going?' asked Butcher around a bite of his roll.

'Christmas,' said Roper.

'Got any plans? Or are you just putting your feet up?'

'Antiques,' said Roper. 'Sheila and me. We've got a shop staked out along at Bournemouth.'

'I've got another couple of years to do,' said Butcher. 'I'm changing the scrap metal on my shoulders after Christmas. Super. HQ. It'll help the pension along.'

'Congratulations,' said Roper.

'There's a fair bit of enquiry work in antiques these days,' said Butcher. He wore a raincoat and muffler over his uniform, but he still looked like a copper in mufti, eyes everywhere among the press at the bar, weighing, tagging, sizing up. 'Could bring in the odd shekel or two.'

'I might,' said Roper. 'We'll see how it goes.'

'Old coppers never die,' Butcher smiled knowingly. 'That's what the old saw says, eh, Douglas? And a lot can happen between now and Christmas.'

Roper smiled back and sipped at his beer and stayed noncommittal. Coppering these days was for the youngsters like Price, hi-tech fast-lane whizzkids with a university degree under their belts. Price had a degree in physics from Cardiff, and he was already earning more as a detective inspector than industry or teaching would have paid him. Twenty years younger than Butcher, Price would be a chief superintendent long before he was forty. Roper and Butcher were of the old breed that had worn out half a dozen pairs of boots on the beat before it could even look at promotion.

'This skipper you've lent me, Phil—seems a bright feller.'

'He is,' said Butcher.

'And he's got to be forty.'

'Yesterday,' said Butcher.

'So why's he still a DS?'

Butcher shrugged and drained his mug. 'Because I've blocked him,' he said.

'Good coppers are hard to find,' said Roper. 'And you said he was a good copper.'

'And he is,' said Butcher. 'Most of the time.'

'What about the rest of the time?'

'He thinks he's a one-man band. Won't delegate. And there've been a couple of occasions lately when I think he's bent the rules a bit.'

'How come?'

Butcher shrugged again. 'I don't know,' he said. 'Not for sure.... For instance, a couple of weeks back, we had two handbag-snatches in the one morning. Two old girls lost their pensions. In the afternoon, Clark sailed in with the two handbags. Intact. And about an hour afterwards the charge nurse along at the infirmary rang me up. She'd got a couple of young lads in the outpatients' department. They'd both come in to get their teeth straightened. Said they'd done it to each other. That was their story.'

'And you reckon there was a connection between the recovery of the handbags and the split lips?'

'I went along to the infirmary and had words with the two lads; they kept to their story. And Clark swore he'd found the bags in the alley beside the post office.'

'Not much to go on,' observed Roper.

'There've been a few other times,' said Butcher. 'I just can't hang them on Clark. But if I ever catch him out I'll have the bugger.'

But, for all his suspicions, Butcher still swore that Clark had the best nose in the county.

FOUR

THE MORTUARY ATTENDANT drew back the white sheet. The naked body of Mrs Blezard was already laid out on a stainless-steel trolley, ready for Wilson at two o'clock, a cardboard tag like a luggage-label tied to its left big toe. Marshall had arrived late by almost a quarter of an hour because of heavy market traffic.

'Yes,' he said. 'That's her.'

'Who, sir?' asked Roper, as the rule-book decreed.

'Mrs. Blezard,' said Marshall.

Roper nodded to the attendant, who folded the sheet back over the face.

'I think I'd like to go outside, if you don't mind,' said Marshall, shakily plucking off his rimless spectacles. He looked distinctly queasy. Tall, bronzed and fit, and just going grey at the temples, he wore a natty dark business-suit and a flamboyant yellow tie knotted under an immaculate white shirt-collar. Roper put him in his late thirties, and guessed he could cut quite a dash with the women if he put his mind to it.

The trolley was wheeled into the examination-theatre next door. One of its wheels had a squeak in it. The rubber doors flapped shut behind it.

In the passage outside, Marshall was slipping his spectacles back into their case with a tremulous hand.

'Sorry about that,' he said. 'I've never been in one of these places before. Do drowned bodies always look like that?'

'She'd been in the water a long time, sir,' said Roper.

'Yes,' said Marshall, fumbling his spectacle-case into the upper pocket of his square-cut waistcoat. 'Yes.... Quite.... But she was a bloody good-looking woman. I never expected her to look like that—even dead.'

They reached the door and the three stone steps down to the yard outside where Marshall's black BMW was parked in front of Roper's grey Sierra. Marshall took several deep breaths. Across the carpark an ambulance was backing towards the hospital emergency entrance, and from the sudden bustle of activity that erupted around it—a doctor, a couple of nurses, a porter with an oxygen-trolley—it looked as if somebody had been brought in with a heart-attack. Marshall slowly exhaled, drew himself upright and braced his shoulders.

'Feeling better, sir?'

'Yes. Thank you,' said Marshall. His wavy dark hair was newly barbered. A set of long slim fingers plucked a silver cigarette-case from inside his jacket. He flipped it open and proffered it to Roper. Roper shook his head and took out his cheroots.

'All right if I ask you a few questions, Mr Marshall?'

Marshall struck his lighter and shielded it against a sudden bluster from the direction of the infirmary.

'Can we do it on the hoof?' he said as he snapped his lighter shut and tucked it away. 'Frankly, I could do with a breath of fresh air.'

He collected a smart white raincoat from the back seat of the BMW and put it on. He and Roper started walking, parting about a couple of blue-caped nurses hurrying off duty, then converging again once they had gone by. Steam rose from a nearby manhole-cover.

'How long had you known Mrs Blezard, Mr Marshall?'

'Five years. More or less.'

'Know her well?' They passed the steaming manhole-cover. The steam had the smell of a laundry in it.

'Yes,' said Marshall. 'I suppose I did.'

'Socially?'

'Yes. In a way, I suppose. I visited her at home fairly often. I advised her financially.' For a few paces, Marshall seemed to find something absorbing about the polished black toes of his shoes. 'But I wasn't a friend, exactly.'

'How about enemies? Did she have any of those?'

Marshall considered that. 'Difficult to say,' he said. 'Is it ever that black and white? I can think of plenty of people who disliked her. Is that the same thing?'

'Did *you* dislike her, Mr Marshall?'

'I neither liked nor disliked her,' said Marshall. 'I work for Blezard's. Mrs Blezard was on the board of directors. That was the extent of our relationship.'

'How about friends?'

'I wouldn't know,' said Marshall. 'Her private life was nothing to do with the firm.'

They had reached the end of the cul-de-sac path and the entrance to the single-storey maternity department. They slowly turned about.

'When did you last see her, sir?'

'Monday,' said Marshall. 'I had lunch with her. A business lunch. She was getting her bank account into the red and wanted a few hundred to tide her over. I wrote her a personal cheque for two-fifty.'

'Risky,' observed Roper, surprised that someone of Mrs Blezard's apparent standing should be short of two hundred and fifty pounds.

'I'd done it before,' said Marshall. 'She always paid me back. Usually later than she'd promised, mind; but she paid in the end.'

'And later you telephoned her, I believe.'

'Why, yes.' Marshall's forehead corrugated attractively in surprise. Yes, Roper thought again, in the right circumstances Mr Marshall would be a more than competent charmer. 'So I did. Monday evening. But she wasn't in.'

'Can you remember what time that was, sir? When you made that call?'

'Yes,' said Marshall. He broke stride to drop the end of his cigarette on the path and heel it out. 'It was twenty to midnight. I rang her from home. About tomorrow morning's board meeting—which in the circumstances we cancelled.'

'And you've no doubt about the time?'

'None,' said Marshall. 'While I was waiting for her to answer, I looked at my watch. It was exactly twenty to twelve.'

Which meant, at a guess, that Mrs Blezard was either dead before twenty to twelve or busy entertaining whoever had shared her coffee-cups and her night-music.

'How did Mrs Blezard figure in the firm's hierarchy, Mr Marshall?'

'A ten-per-cent holding,' said Marshall to Roper's further surprise. 'Her late husband's. He'd owned seventy per cent, but he'd made over the other sixty per cent to the other three directors a few months before he died. He was a sick man. Dicky ticker. We all think he'd got wind of what she'd been up to, you see. I think he was frightened she might take over and ruin the business.'

'Wind of what, exactly?' asked Roper, breaking in. 'You said her husband got wind of something.'

'She'd had several affairs,' said Marshall distastefully, 'and she hadn't exactly been discreet about them. That's the story.'

'Story? So *you* don't know for sure?'

'No,' said Marshall. 'Sorry.'

'You didn't have an affair with her yourself, for instance.' Roper dropped it in like an aside, with a smile.

'God, no,' retorted Marshall. 'I'm long past messing on my own doorstep. I'm salaried; she could have had me out with a word.'

Roper doubted that. Marshall wore an air of shrewd efficiency, looked the kind of smart operator who could conjure facts and figures out of thin air at board meetings. And if he had been the company secretary at Blezard's for five years he would not be a man who could be replaced overnight, even at the whim of a ten-per-cent stockholder.

They had passed the steaming manhole-cover again and were approaching their cars beside the mortuary.

'Do you know if Mrs Blezard was engaged in some kind of liaison recently, Mr Marshall?'

'I don't know,' said Marshall. 'Like I said, I wasn't privy to her private life. Only her bills.'

'Which reminds me....' Roper reached inside his jacket and brought out the three envelopes that Butcher's constable had collected that morning from the postman. 'I wonder if you'd mind opening these, sir? I believe Mrs Blezard had no next of kin.'

'Yes. That's true.' Marshall took the three envelopes and slit their flaps. The first was an overdue telephone bill, the second from the County Council—a bill for the second half-year's rates for the house.

The third, at first glance, looked like a letter. But it was clear from the puzzled expression on Marshall's face that it was not.

'May I, sir?'

Marshall handed over the single sheet of folded blue notepaper.

No date. No signature. And just three words, cut from a glossy magazine and pasted on.

where is it

A question, without a question mark.

Roper turned the sheet over. The back was blank. The three words had each been cut from a different portion of whatever the text had been. A powdery band of paste bordered each of them. Roper held out his hand for the envelope. It had definitely been posted here in King's Minster yesterday, and caught the early-afternoon collection.

where is it

A blackmail note. That was Roper's first thought. Or, rather, a follow-up to a blackmail note. It wasn't impossible. It was even probable. Because, for all its crudeness, there was a hint of the sinister about it. It was a frightener of some sort. Ergo: whoever had pasted it together could not have been a friend of Hannah Blezard's.

'I'd like to keep this, if may, sir.'

'Yes. Of course,' said Marshall. He still looked bewildered. 'Strange, that.'

'Yes, sir,' agreed Roper, folding the cryptic note and tucking it into his wallet.

'And I'll arrange whatever has to be done with these,' said Marshall. 'I'll see that Mrs Blezard's solicitor gets them.'

'Yes, sir. Do that.' Roper slid his wallet inside his jacket, while Marshall did the same inside his with the two bills. His fingers came out with a visiting-card, the Blezard's Electronics logo across its top, Marshall's name in black underneath. B.L. MARSHALL, MA(Oxon), FCA—and several other earned or honorary qualifications which were further evidence that B. L. Marshall was nobody's fool.

'My home address and telephone number are on the back,' he said. 'If there's anything else I can do to help....'

'I'm obliged, Mr Marshall. I'd like to talk to Mrs Blezard's co-directors as well. Perhaps you could let them know that.'

'I shall,' said Marshall. He extended his hand. Took it slowly back again when Roper appeared not to notice it. Roper was still not sure about Mr Marshall.

'I'll—er—bid you good-day, then, Superintendent.'

'Yes, sir,' said Roper. 'And thanks for coming along.' He stretched a smile.

He climbed into his Sierra, drew the door to quietly and stubbed out his cheroot as he watched through the windscreen. Marshall took off his expensive raincoat and tossed it carelessly across his back seat, then half-turned and raised a hand in curt salute as he opened his driving-door and climbed in. In his driving-mirror, he checked the knot of his yellow necktie, and his wavy locks, seemingly unaware that he was being observed. Then tipped the mirror again and adjusted it, and switched on his engine.

Roper had earlier categorised Marshall as natty. Now he decided that Mr Marshall might also be a bit on the flashy side.

PRICE ANSWERED the door.

'How goes it?' asked Roper, stepping in and carefully wiping his shoes on the coconut mat. Price closed the door again behind him.

'The fingerprint crew's just finishing off down here,' said Price. 'And the photographer's arrived.'

As he spoke, the two fingerprint men came out of the dining-room with their hand-lamps, brushes, and trays of powder, and started work on the newel-post and hand-rail of the stairs.

'Have they found anything?'

'Too much,' said Price. So far, the two of them had identified over a dozen quite different samples of prints. Excluding the ones on the cups and saucers in the sitting-room. 'The ones on the saucers are grade one,' said Price. 'One set female, the other male.'

It was safe to assume the female set was Mrs Blezard's. Which was not, at this stage, exactly a great leap forward.

Several sets of sole- and shoe-prints had been found around the pool. The sole-prints, left by damp feet, were size six and unlikely to be anyone's but Mrs Blezard's own. The shoe-prints, just inside the door to the garden, had been made, at a guess, by a pair of fairly new train-ing-shoes with rubber soles. Size eleven. The pattern of fine dust they had left behind showed them entering the conservatory. But not leaving it.

'How about the prints in the sitting-room carpet?'

'They're mostly size six. Probably Mrs Blezard's again,' said Price. 'But there are three other sets for sure. Two different styles of size eight—and Mr Size Eleven again. And it looks as though it was Size Eleven who sat near the coffee-table as well. And, with any luck, left his dabs on that other cup and saucer.'

'Bully,' said Roper. It wasn't much to go on, but two hours ago they had had next to nothing. Mr Size Eleven would be a six-footer at least. Finding him, of course, would be a needle-in-a-haystack job, even with a set of his fingerprints available—unless he already had a record of some sort. And even then he still might be the wrong man. Because, if he was the right man, and had had his wits about him, at least he would have wiped the cup and saucer he had used clean of his dabs. Unless—hopefully—he had panicked, lost his head; in which case he was the right man and ultimately identifiable. At this stage, however, the less identifiable owners of the size eights were equally likely suspects.

'What else?'

'Nothing,' said Price. 'No signs of a forced entry, no signs of violence. Dead end, you might say.'

Clark came from the sitting-room. He was running a finger and thumb along the patent seal of an evidence-bag to close it.

'Just found this, sir,' he said. 'Tucked down beside the cushion of an armchair near the front window.'

Roper took the bag. It contained a gold bracelet. Heavy. Hinged at one side and fitted with a wisp of a safety-chain.

'It's eighteen-carat, sir,' said Clark assuredly. 'London hallmark. Last year.'

'You're a mine of information, Sergeant.' The bracelet was intricately engraved—by hand. But its finding meant nothing. If it had been found out at the pool, or even outside in the garden, it might have meant something else altogether.

'Do you know if Mrs Blezard's solicitor was a local man?'

'Crawley and Bohun's,' said Clark. 'I've often seen her going in and out. They're over the bank in the High Street.'

'Telephone them,' said Roper. 'Tell them they'd better send someone around here to keep us company, and to make an inventory of the goodies.'

'Right,' said Clark and went straightway across the parquet floor to the telephone-table and sorted out a directory. Price raised a questioning or perhaps an appre-

ciative eyebrow at Roper. Roper raised one back. Clark
was certainly putting on a brisk show of efficiency, even
if this was his manor.

IN A PORK-PIE tweed hat, frayed green pullover, stained
white riding-breeches and a pair of battered riding-boots,
Ailsa Crispin stood athwart the entrance to her stableyard
like a watchful Grenadier, a shovel in one hand, a steaming bucket in the other, until her short-sighted eyes recognised Sergeant Clark and her body relaxed—as much,
that is, as Ailsa Crispin ever permitted it to relax.

'Hah....' Her weatherbeaten handsome face creased.
'Mr Clark. Afternoon to you. It's going to rain, y'know.
Smell it?' She lifted her nose and sniffed with flared nostrils. All Roper could smell was the odours of horse that
rose in the vapour from her bucket. 'And who's this gentleman?'

Clark effected the introduction, and Roper showed her
his warrant-card.

Ailsa Crispin was impressed.

'Superintendent, eh? Must be serious.' She jerked her
head sideways towards Mrs Blezard's house on the far
side of her paddock. 'To do with her, is it? Hannah?' She
returned the card and sniffed again, much as she had
sniffed for the rain. 'Seen all the comings and goings,'
she said. 'Knew *something* was up. None of my business,
of course, but I couldn't help noticing.'

Roper smiled, already won over. Mrs—for she was a
Mrs—Mrs Crispin was certainly a touch larger than life,
big and bluff and cheery, as her voice had sounded on
Mrs Blezard's answering machine.

'Perhaps we could go inside, Mrs Crispin.'

'Yes. 'Course.' She dumped her bucket down on the
stone setts with a clatter, and plunged the working end

of her shovel into it. 'Can rustle you up a cuppa if you fancy. This way.'

She preceded them across the front of her yard. Her cottage was of Portland stone and its woodwork badly in need of a coat of paint, a green plastic water-butt and a well-used iron boot-scraper beside the front door.

The cramped untidy kitchen seemed barely large enough to contain her as she busied herself with kettle and matches at an elderly gas-stove. Three mugs, milk in a bottle, sugar in a tin. A couple of account-books lay open on the white-wood table, a pair of reading-glasses beside them, and a vintage pocket calculator with a cracked window over its display panel.

'Have a pew,' she said. 'Apologies for the clutter, by the way. Wasn't expecting company.'

Hefty measures of sugar were spooned into each of the mugs; milk was tipped in after it with prodigal abandon.

'What's the gel done? Disappeared?'

'What makes you think that, Mrs Crispin?' The four wheelback chairs were hand-made country-style. Even in here, the smell of horses pervaded.

'Lights,' she said. 'Been burning for two days. Thought the gel might be ill.'

'I'm afraid she's dead, Mrs Crispin,' said Roper.

Ailsa Crispin's healthy red face paled distinctly. The milk-bottle froze an inch from the table. She hadn't known. That much was certain.

'Great God in heaven. So she *was* ill.' With a creak of leather, she subsided into the chair beside her. The bottle she was still holding went belatedly down to the table. The kettle had begun to hiss on the stove. A soft whinny and the scrape of a hoof on a stone flag came through the open window above the sink.

Then, in the subsequent silence, an expression of slow dawning crossed her face.

'I was in town. Lunch-time. Heard they'd fished a gel out of the river this morning....' She broke off, fixed Roper with a look of horrified consternation. 'Not Hannah, was it?'

'It was, I'm afraid, Mrs Crispin,' said Roper.

'Great God.'

The kettle started to bubble out water from around its lid. Clark rose quickly and lifted it off the flames, and tilted it over the waiting china teapot.

'I'm sorry.' Mrs Crispin recovered herself quickly. 'Thank you, Mr Clark.' Then to Roper she said: 'Of course, I didn't know. Had no idea. I'd seen all the lights.... I'm so sorry....'

'When, Mrs Crispin? When did you first notice the lights?'

She frowned. 'Monday,' she said. 'Late. About midnight. When I got out of bed to open the curtains. I saw the lights over the trees.'

'Unusual, was it? For Mrs Blezard to have her lights on that late?'

'Well, no,' she said. 'Not exactly. I just *happened* to notice. Then yesterday, when I was out in the paddock— in the morning—I saw that the lights were still on in that glasshouse contraption. And in the afternoon, too. And all last evening. And again this morning, as I said.'

'And that was unusual?'

'Yes,' she conceded. 'I suppose it was.'

Clark had sat down and was opening his notebook on the table.

'You *suppose*, Mrs Crispin? What does that mean exactly? The lights have been on all night before, have they?'

'Well, yes. I have noticed them. On occasions.' Something in Mrs Crispin's voice, a hint of unspoken deprecation.

Roper waited for her to continue. But Ailsa Crispin was clearly not the kind for gratuitous gossip about her neighbours.

'She had visitors?' he prompted, more in hope than in certainty. 'Men friends, perhaps?'

'Well, yes.' Ailsa Crispin plucked off her battered tweed hat and stood it on the table beside her. She shook out her wiry grey hair. Despite the warhorse exterior, Roper suspected that she was not so tough underneath it. '*Mostly* men friends, I'm afraid.'

'Do you happen to know any of them? Would you recognise them? Any of them?'

Clark's ballpoint pen had stilled over his notebook.

'I don't keep watch, Superintendent.'

'No, madam,' said Roper. 'I never said that.'

Ailsa Crispin had not bridled, merely stated her position as a matter of fact.

'I saw one last Thursday,' she said eventually and reluctantly. 'Dark-haired. Fortyish. Very smart. A black car. Late in the afternoon. He came often.'

Mr Marshall perhaps.

'Any others?'

'A younger one. On Friday. I'd seen him before.'

'You say younger. Can you describe him?'

'Tall. On the hefty side. Had a bicycle.'

'How old?'

'A chit. A lad. Young enough to be her son, I should think.'

'And you'd seen him visit the house before?'

'Yes,' she said. 'Not that I'd exactly recognise him again if I saw him; it was simply that he always arrived at about the same time—and leaped off his bicycle like a spring chicken and carried it up Hannah's front path. He started coming in the summer. Late summer. I often saw him working in the garden. He came on Monday, too, now I come to think of it, but I don't think Hannah was in. He came out again a minute or so afterwards and hopped back on his bicycle.'

'And which way did he go?'

'That way.' She gave a flick of her head. 'Towards the town.'

'Had you seen him cycle off that way before, Mrs Crispin?'

She shook her head. 'I usually only saw him arrive. I'd never seen him leaving before.'

Roper gave her a breather. He had pressed her hard over the last minute or so; and perhaps she didn't keep watch on her neighbours, but she seemed to be a reliable observer all the same. Except, as Roper recalled, she had appeared not to recognise Sergeant Clark just now until he and Roper were within half a dozen paces from her.

'You wear glasses, Mrs Crispin?'

'Yes. Damn things. Dropped me distance ones in the yard this morning and trod on 'em.'

'So you *were* wearing them last week, and on Monday, when you saw this young lad?'

'Yes. Without 'em, I'm as blind as a bat. Anno Domini. Did without 'em for sixty-odd years, too, dammit.'

SHE HAD FILLED the three mugs with tea. Roper stirred his.

'You told us this lad usually arrived at about the same time, Mrs Crispin. What time was that exactly?'

'Can't be sure. Quarter to five. Give or take.'

'It would have been nearly dark by then,' Clark interrupted. But he was right. It was half-past three now, and already the afternoon was drawing in.

'It was the way he got off his bike,' she countered. 'Nimble. Youngster.'

'Perhaps he was a paper-boy, Mrs Crispin,' Clark broke in again.

'Thought he was. First time.'

'Why was that, Mrs Crispin?' asked Roper.

'He had a bag. Slung across his back.'

'Like a newspaper-sack?'

'Thought so. At first. But it was one of those things the youngsters use for satchels these days.'

'You mean a duffel-bag, Mrs Crispin? Something of that sort?'

'That's it. Duffel-bag. Dark. Could have been a blue one.'

Roper sipped at his tea. Earl Grey. Muscularly brewed and as thick as molasses, the spoon still in the mug. There wasn't a saucer in sight. One plate in the wooden rack over the sink, one knife and one fork on the draining-board. Two saucepans. Mrs Crispin was clearly a widow. Some nice pieces of old pottery about, probably family heirlooms. The teapot, whence had come the Earl Grey, looked like Staffordshire-ware if its wet-looking glaze was anything to go by. A chipped spout had depreciated its value by half.

According to Mrs Crispin, on both Friday and Monday when she had seen the young man she had been riding or, as she called it, walking back her string. Now that the afternoons were pulling in earlier she liked to see her little gels home. Both on Friday and on Monday, riding one horse and leading back her other three, she had seen the youth from no more than fifty yards away. And opposite Mrs Blezard's front gate was a street-lamp. There was no mistaking him. It had been the same boy each time.

'Boy, Mrs Crispin?' said Roper. 'With respect to you, he seems to be getting younger.'

'At my age, Superintendent, if they're under twenty they're either boys or gels.'

Clark was holding his ballpoint between white-knuckled hands. It was bending and looked in imminent danger of snapping in half.

'What was he wearing, Mrs Crispin? D'you remember?' he interrupted again, to Roper's displeasure.

'Black jacket. And light trousers. The bicycle was white.'

'It could have been yellow,' snapped Clark. 'They're sodium lamps in the lane. Sodium lamps alter colours.'

'Well, perhaps. But it did *look* white.'

'So he *could* have been the paper-boy, couldn't he?'

His fusillade of questions had followed each other too quickly, pushing Mrs Crispin into momentary confusion. 'Couldn't he?' persisted Clark.

'Well, yes…I suppose.…'

'You only suppose?'

Roper put his mug down heavily enough to make it thump on the table and let Clark know he was out of order. The message was unmistakable. Clark shrank back into his shell.

'How well did you know Mrs Blezard, Mrs Crispin?' Roper asked quietly in the ensuing silence.

'She was just a neighbour.'

'You didn't know her socially?'

Ailsa Crispin shook her head. 'No. Sorry. Can't help you there.'

And, again, Roper thought he detected that tiny grace note of disapproval.

'How *long* had you known her, Mrs Crispin?'

'Since the house was built. Eight years. Knew her husband. Lovely man.' But not like her. She was a cow. Not that Ailsa Crispin had said that, but the stress on the 'lovely man' was so loaded with innuendo that it was obvious that Mrs Blezard was not a 'lovely woman'. 'It was our land. Had to sell it when my old boy died.'

'You wouldn't know if Mrs Blezard had any enemies?'

'Enemies? Good God, I shouldn't think so.'

'Did you hear anything unusual late on Monday night, Mrs Crispin? Voices? The sound of a car? Anything out of the ordinary?'

Ailsa Crispin considered that. Then a finger sprang upwards from the handle of her mug.

'A car,' she said. 'Or, rather, car doors—and before that the rattle of her garage door. It's one of those modern metal things. Sounds like a bloody battleship being launched.'

'D'you remember the time?'

'Ten o'clock. On the dot.'

'You sound very sure.'

'I am,' she said. 'I was in the stables. Saying goodnight to my nags. Ten o'clock. Every night. On the dot. They're like us, y'know. Feed 'em, love 'em, and they're yours for life.'

People like Ailsa Crispin came close to restoring Roper's faith in human nature, even if she couldn't make tea. Clark had stopped jotting and was looking at his watch, as if he were in a hurry to be away.

'You telephoned Mrs Blezard recently, Mrs Crispin—and got her answering machine. When did you do that exactly? D'you remember?'

'This morning,' she said. 'Oh'—she flapped a hand—'nine-ish.'

'Ish?'

'Perhaps it was later. Nearer half-past. Yes, it must have been. Minster clock was striking ten as I parked in the High Street.'

'So half-past nine? You're sure? It's important, Mrs Crispin.'

Yes. She was sure.

And the young lad on the bicycle, it suddenly came to her, wore white shoes. Of that she was equally sure.

ROPER AND CLARK marched in step up Mrs Blezard's front path in the gathering dusk. There were now two more cars parked on the grass verge, and from within the house enough shadows moved behind the net curtains to make it evident that Price had called in more personnel from County.

They reached the porch. Clark gave a tug on the bell-pull.

Roper said quietly, regarding the letter-flap: 'When I'm asking questions, Sergeant, you'll do yourself a favour by just taking notes, unless I give you the nod. Follow?'

Clark stared blazingly at the door, said nothing. Roper's anger surfaced despite himself.

'Did you hear me, Sergeant?'

'It won't happen again, sir,' said Clark, but so that Roper could not only hear his resentment but also feel it, like another palpable presence, in the little space between them as they stood on the doorstep.

'Good,' said Roper. 'Now, we'll both forget I had to say that, shall we?'

FIVE

IT WAS DS MAKINS who let them in. He and DS Rodgers had arrived from County about half an hour ago, together with a couple of DCs. Price was upstairs with a Mr Bohun, Mrs Blezard's solicitor, who had brought an inventory of Mrs Blezard's valuables with him. The two Forensic men were up in the bedrooms; the two DCs were in the sitting-room and methodically taking it apart.

'This is Sergeant Clark, George,' said Roper. 'Local CID.'

Makins smiled cheerily and stuck out a hand. 'Howdy,' he said.

Clark said nothing, and Makins's hand was on the point of dropping away again before Clark took off his right glove and proffered the hand that had been inside it. The handshake was as brief as courtesy permitted. It was obvious that Clark was still rankling over the muttered exchange on the doorstep and, even if Roper forgot it, Clark would not.

'Anybody looked for documents yet?' asked Roper.

'Not yet, sir,' said Makins.

'You do that, then,' Roper told Clark.

Clark jerked a sullen nod.

'Scout about. You're looking for documents. Marriage lines, driving licence, passport, National Insurance number—whatever you can find.'

'Spare gloves in the case in the hall,' said Makins helpfully.

Clark slouched off without a word.

'Charmer,' observed Makins, when Clark was out of earshot.

'We've had words,' said Roper.

'Ah,' said Makins, with honest sympathy. Makins had occasionally been on the rough end of Roper's tongue himself.

'Anything new?' asked Roper.

'No,' said Makins. 'Not a lot. A few drink-stains on the carpets, especially in the lounge. I've just been going through her cheque-stubs. She spent more on clothes and hairdressers in a month than a copper earns in six—and drew a lot of cheques on Cash. Three or four hundred quid a time. Her paying-in slips show two thousand a month, and her current account only shows eighty quid—which for somebody who lived in a place like this was pretty close to being broke, I reckon.'

'I reckon, too,' said Roper. 'What are you doing now?'

'I was on my way upstairs to see Dave Price—find out what he wanted me on next.'

'Tell him you're coming out for a while with me. Pocketbook job. Tell him we'll be along at Mr West-lake's place. For about an hour.'

'A TOUCH OF the Hansel and Gretels,' observed Makins as he and Roper approached Florian Westlake's bright orange front door.

'Ay,' said Roper. Even in the late dusk, the rambling old cottage certainly looked that way. The windows were leaded, its roof thatched, its window-boxes downstairs colourful splashes of plastic flowers in defiance of the season, its drawn curtains chintzy-pretty with the lights shining through them. The white stucco looked freshly painted, and the car under the Perspex-roofed carport was a vintage black Rolls-Royce limousine, perhaps even older than Roper was, but immaculately kept.

The door-knocker was a grinning brass goblin squatting on a toadstool. Makins lifted it and rapped it down twice. The afternoon had turned chilly, and the breeze had stiffened enough to scurry a few leaves on the flagged front path and stir the shrubbery round about. Mrs Crispin was right; it would rain soon.

A bolt was drawn on the door as a shadow fell across its net-curtained window. A triangle of light pushed back the dusk. Somewhere at the back of the cottage a type-writer clattered.

'Yes?' A man. Sixtyish, well preserved, softly spoken, dark hair slicked down, and with too fine a set of teeth for a man of his age. He might have been handsome once.

'Detective Superintendent Roper, sir.' Roper held his card to the light. The man's glance was brief, a little nervous through the smile. 'And Detective Sergeant Makins. County CID.'

'Yes, of course,' he said. 'You're the gentleman who rang. Do come in, won't you?'

He stepped aside, taking the edge of the door with him. He was about Roper's height and wore a loose yellow cardigan that had seen better days, a crisp white shirt and well-cut khaki slacks. Roper smelt steak and kidney pie cooking—or something very like it.

'Mr Westlake?'

'No.' The diffident smile was put back. 'Roland Hollister. Mr. Westlake and I share the house.'

'I know your face, sir.' Not quite true, but in the light of the warm narrow passage the face certainly had a nostalgic familiarity about it.

The face dipped modestly. In the better light it sagged here and there around the jawbone.

'I used to be an actor. Films. Not good ones, I'm afraid.'

'Rollie?' A fruity male voice called loudly from a back room. 'Who is it? Who've you got out there? Who're you flirting with?'

'It's the police, Flo. Where do you want to see them?'

'Sitting-room,' the voice shouted back. And the type-writer keys clattered again.

'He won't be a moment,' said Hollister. He extended a hand towards a door on the left beside the staircase. 'Please,' he said, ushering them ahead of him. 'Do go in.'

The room was snug. Oak-beamed. An electric fire with fake logs and flickering flames; buttoned leather arm-chairs, brown and capacious and silk-cushioned. A brass pot of chrysanthemums stood on a half-moon side-table near the curtained window, and more brass glistened on the fender around the hearth and the set of decorative fire-irons that lay across it. A standard lamp in a tasselled pink silk shade glowed softly in each recess beside the chimney-breast. The wallpaper, a pale pastel green, had the sheen of satin. The hearthrug looked like a Bokhara.

Hollister snatched a newspaper from the settee to make a place for Roper.

'A mess,' he said. 'I'm sorry.'

Hardly a mess—unless Hollister was obsessively tidy—but definitely snug; and just a touch womanish, only off-set by the masculine solidity of the leather chairs.

Roper and Makins lowered themselves to the settee and unbuttoned their raincoats.

'Would you like a cup of tea?' asked Hollister, still hovering nervously.

'No, sir, thank you,' said Roper. Makins took out his

notebook. Hollister perched himself on the arm of the chair furthest from the window.

The typewriter keys continued to clatter. Hollister leaned forward and plucked a packet of cigarettes and a lighter from the top of the bookcase beside him. He offered the open packet. Roper and Makins both declined.

'We're making a few routine enquiries, sir,' said Roper. 'We won't keep you long.' Hollister's extended hand had had a distinct stiffness; his dark eyes behind the courteous smile were wary. But in Roper's experience most people were on their guard when the police came calling, the innocent ones as much as the villains. 'Perhaps we could start with you, sir.'

'Yes, of course,' said Hollister around his cigarette as he struck his lighter. After one draw and puff, the cigarette was lifted away between two fingers and the hand went to rest on Hollister's knee. 'I presume all this is about Hannah—Mrs Blezard. Mr Westlake and I are devastated. Utterly.'

'Perhaps I might have your name, sir?' asked Makins, glancing at his watch and writing the date and time in his notebook.

'Hollister. Roland Jervis Hollister.' The cigarette was briefly lifted, glowed, fell again. 'That's my real name, by the way.'

'Thank you, sir,' said Makins, head down again and writing.

'How well did you know Mrs Blezard, Mr Hollister?' asked Roper.

'Very well,' said Hollister. The typewriter had stopped.

'Socially, too?'

'You *could* say that. We popped in and out of each other's house from time to time. Borrowed the odd cup of sugar from each other. Not friends exactly, but good neighbours, you know?'

'For how long, sir?'

'Since Mr Westlake and I came down from London. Three years.' Hollister reached forward to the mantelshelf for a pretty china ashtray and held it cupped on his knee while he knocked ash from his cigarette. He had slim flexile fingers, a few incipient liver spots dotting the backs of his palms. In the gentle glow of the fake logs and the standard lamps he again managed to give an illusion of youth.

'When did you last see her, sir?'

'Monday,' said Hollister. 'In town. About one-thirty.'

'In company, sir?'

'Why, yes. She was, in fact.'

'Man or woman, sir?'

'Man. Young-old. Dark-haired, going grey. Very *distingué*—if you know what I mean. A friend, I think; I'd seen Mrs Blezard with him before. I saw him calling at the house several times. A black car.'

'A BMW, sir?'

Hollister sketched a shrug with the hand that held his cigarette. 'Sorry. I wouldn't know a BMW from a bicycle. But it was a *smart* car. This year's registration-plates. I remember that.'

That sounded like Mr Marshall again, and confirmed Marshall's statement that he had lunched with Mrs Blezard on Monday.

'And you didn't see her after that, sir? Not yesterday?'

Hollister shook his head as floorboards creaked in the passage outside; and Florian Westlake puffed in heavily from his study, breasting the air like an overfed pasha. A jowly face flewed like a bloodhound; silver hair that looked blow-waved; yellow-shirted and green-chokered under a multitude of chins. Hollister had risen from the arm of his chair.

'These gentlemen are policemen, Flo…er… Oh, I'm so sorry—I've forgotten.…'

'Roper, Mr Westlake,' said Roper, rising. 'Detective Superintendent. And this is Detective Sergeant Makins. County CID, sir.'

'Welcome, gentlemen—or perhaps not, in the circumstances,' Westlake wheezed gravely. 'We heard about it on the wireless at lunch-time. Devastated, weren't we, Rollie? Utterly.'

With some difficulty, he skirted the coffee-table, lowered himself the first few inches into the armchair opposite Hollister, and flopped the last foot or so, making air gasp from the leather cushion like a rush of gas.

Roper and Makins both sat down again. Hollister resumed the arm of his chair.

'When did *you* last see Mrs Blezard, Mr Westlake?'

'Monday,' he said, his eyes slowly opening again. 'Yes. Monday.'

'When, sir?'

Florian Westlake closed his eyes again to contemplate. Mr Westlake was obviously going to be heavy weather. A massive belly hung over the waistband of his baggy grey trousers, and ellipses of white undervest peeked out between each of his strained shirt-buttons. He had brought a potent waft of aftershave in with him.

'It was tea-time, Flo,' said Hollister quietly. 'You were in the garden.'

'Yes. So I was.' Westlake slowly opened his eyes and beamed. 'Quite right. Thank you, Rollie.'

'Did you speak to her, sir?'

'No. We waved to each other.'

'What was she doing, sir?'

'Clearing up leaves, as I recall.'

'And the time, sir?'

There was another somnolent pause. Hollister broke it.

'It was half-past three, Flo,' he said, this time with a touch of impatience. 'For God's sake—you *always* take your walk at half-past three. We live to a timetable here, Superintendent,' he explained to Roper. 'Mr Westlake writes. He *also* likes to prevaricate.'

'It's a matter of *details,* Rollie,' protested Westlake peevishly. 'A matter of getting things *right.* There's *no* call to get waspish. You do want it *exactly* right, don't you, Superintendent?'

'Yes, indeed, sir,' said Roper.

'And I remember exactly. It was *twenty* to four. I *went* for my stroll at half-past three. And when I waved to Hannah I was on my way *back* to the house. Which would make it twenty to four.'

'Alone was she, sir?'

'Definitely.'

'And cheerful?'

'Oh dear, yes. Hannah was *always* cheerful. Isn't that right, Rollie?'

Rollie agreed. Yes, Mrs Blezard was always cheerful.

'How about callers?' Roper addressed the question to the middle air between them. 'On Monday—after four o'clock say.'

'I wouldn't have seen,' said Westlake. 'After tea I go *straight* back to the study—where I stay until dinner-time. Half-past seven.'

'There *was* a boy,' ventured Hollister. 'A lad on a bicycle. *Not* that he stayed. I saw him wheel his bicycle up the path. And a minute or so later I saw him wheeling it out again. I'd been washing the flowers in the window-boxes,' he explained.

'He's trying to tell you he isn't a Nosey Parker.' West-lake cackled mischievously, the upper half of his body momentarily taking on the quality of a quivering mass of jelly in a yellow bag. 'Which he is. Terribly. Aren't you, Rolls—mm?'

Makins smiled dutifully, Hollister thinly as he stubbed out his cigarette in the china ashtray on his knee.

'What was the time when you saw this lad, Mr Hollister?'

'It was almost dark,' said Hollister. 'It must have been twenty…quarter to five. Something like that.'

'Had you seen him before, sir?'

'Yes,' said Hollister. 'Often. I *first* saw him during the school holidays. He did a spot of gardening for her.'

'And what sort of bicycle did he have, sir?'

'The sort they all have. A racer. Dropped handlebars. White, I think, or it might have been yellow. And lately he's had a bag slung over his back. I think it was a blue one.'

'And the boy, sir—can you describe him?'

'Tall,' said Hollister. 'On the dark side, I think. Well built. Eighteen or nineteen, perhaps. But a schoolboy. On Monday, I'm sure he was wearing a blazer with a badge on it.'

'And *we* wondered if he was her toy-boy, didn't we, Rollie?' Florian Westlake broke in. 'Come for his little bit of tea and sympathy.'

Roper's ears pricked.

'Really, sir? And why would you wonder that?'

'*We* didn't,' said Hollister tiredly. '*Florian* did. He lets his imagination run away with him sometimes.'

'Rot,' snorted Westlake. 'Several times we've seen the bedroom lights go on when he's been there. Haven't we?'

'Well, yes,' Hollister agreed tetchily. 'But it didn't signify anything, did it? My God....'

Roper didn't pursue it. It sounded possible. And that anguished voice on the answering machine this morning might just have been that same young lad. And certainly the same young lad that Mrs Crispin had seen. The cycle was right—yellow and white looked much the same under sodium lamps. The bag was right. Crispin's and Hollister's times agreed to within a few minutes. Perhaps the same young lad had received no answer on Monday evening, and returned later, and wore a size-eleven training-shoe, and entered by way of Mrs Blezard's swimming-pool.

So FAR AS Westlake and Hollister were aware, Mrs Blezard had had no enemies. But plenty of visitors. She entertained a great deal. On Saturday night, there was a car parked in her drive all evening; and it was quite late, so Hollister told them, two or even three o'clock in the morning, before it was driven away again. But Hollister did not know the make of the car. He thought that it might have been orange, or pale red, or even pale brown.

'How about Monday night, gentlemen? About ten o'clock. Didn't happen to hear a car door then, did you?'

Westlake had not. But Hollister had.

'Not a car door exactly,' he said. He was lighting another cigarette, his third, from the stub of his last. 'But I got the impression she might have been going out in her car—or had just come back, perhaps. I was out at the dustbin. I heard the door of her garage opening—or closing. It could have been either. It creaks. The door. You couldn't miss it. Ten o'clock. The news had just started on the television.'

And that, too, tallied with Mrs Crispin's time.

'But you didn't hear it, Mr Westlake?'

'I hear *nothing* after half-past nine,' sighed Westlake with infinite weariness. 'I plug my ears and take my pills. If I don't have at least *ten* hours sleep each night, it's *hardly* worth sleeping at all. I write a book every eight weeks.' He passed a hand tiredly across his broad raked-back forehead, presumably to demonstrate what a tedious business writing was. 'It drains me. Doesn't it, Rollie?'

'Utterly,' said Rollie, with such saccharine sweetness that it could not be mistaken for anything but irony. Westlake appeared not to notice it. 'It drains him.'

A proper little cabaret act, thought Roper. But what they were not, in his considered opinion, were the two old gays he had thought they were. Because Westlake was hamming it up and going too far over the top; and Hollister didn't like it one bit. Westlake was a deliberate caricature of himself, Hollister the earthy one. And Roper wasn't even sure now that they even liked each other.

'You rang Mrs Blezard recently, Mr Hollister,' said Roper, 'and got her answering machine. D'you remember when that was?'

'Monday,' said Hollister. 'Afternoon. About three o'clock, I suppose.'

'Did she reply? Later?'

'No,' said Hollister. 'If she had, Mr Westlake had intended walking across after dinner. But she didn't.'

'It didn't occur to you to ring her back?'

'There was no hurry.' This was from Westlake, still sprawled exhaustedly like a latter-day Buddha in the depths of his chair. 'I merely wanted to borrow some magazines from her. Fashion magazines. I write for the ladies. I have to get the details just so.'

'But Mrs Blezard's lights were on all day yesterday, sir,' said Roper. 'Didn't that concern you?'

'Why should it?' enquired Hollister. 'So far as we knew, there was nothing wrong.'

'But she hadn't replied to your phone call of Monday afternoon, sir.'

Westlake stirred ponderously and flapped an airy hand.

'It wasn't important,' he said. 'She would have replied eventually.'

'She was dead, sir,' Roper reminded him.

'Quite,' agreed Westlake. 'But, as Mr Hollister says, we weren't to know that, were we? And we often didn't see her for days at a time. Why should we?' Westlake shrugged hugely. 'We keep ourselves very much to ourselves. Don't we, Rollie?'

ROPER HAD RISEN and was buttoning his raincoat. Apart from the time when Hollister had spoken into Mrs Blezard's answering machine and the confirmation of the lad on the bicycle, the case was really no further forward. The smell of steak and kidney pie baking had grown mouth-wateringly stronger.

'If I could have your full name, sir,' Makins was saying to Westlake, who was struggling to his feet with some assistance from Hollister.

'Westlake. Florian Westlake.'

'We may have to ask you to sign an official statement, sir,' said Makins, politely but firmly.

'It's Hawkins, Sergeant,' said Hollister, and perhaps with a touch of malice. 'Ernest George Hawkins.' And Westlake looked balefully at him.

ROPER AND MAKINS wiped the wet soles of their shoes on the late Mrs Blezard's doormat. It was half-past five, dark outside, and raining.

The house was still a hive of activity, voices rose and

fell, a photographic flash flared briefly in the sitting-room. Price was coming down the stairs with a fair-haired and fragile young man in a dark suit and with a clipboard tucked under one arm. Nicholas Bohun, Mrs Blezard's solicitor—well, almost. He assisted his father actually. His frail handshake was moist and limp.

On his clipboard were three sets of inventories, one of Mrs Blezard's furniture, one of her antique collection and the third of her jewellery; all that he could not account for were two diamond rings.

'Which Mr Price here tells me are still on the body.'

'So there's nothing missing, Mr Bohun?'

'No. Apparently.'

In which case robbery could be safely disposed of as a motive.

Roper moved away briefly to hang up his damp rain-coat on the coat-stand beside the telephone-table.

'Mrs Blezard leave a will, did she, Mr Bohun?'

'Yes,' said Bohun. 'My father drafted her a new one last year.'

'D'you know the substance of it?'

'No,' said Bohun. 'Not exactly. The house, of course, wasn't Mrs Blezard's. The company owns it. Blezard's Electronics, that is. Actually, as I understand it, Mrs Blezard's estate was simply her jewellery, the furniture, and her collection of antiques.'

'Worth?' asked Roper.

As young Mr Bohun recalled, at their last valuations for insurance purposes, the jewellery was worth some hundred thousand pounds, the bits and pieces—as he called them—of china were worth another thirty-five thousand. The furniture and carpets, although of good quality and insured for some twenty thousand pounds, would only fetch perhaps some two thousand pounds at auction—and then only on a good day.

'So quite a modest amount, actually,' added Bohun. 'Say a hundred and fifty thousand at the very outside.'

'How about liquid assets—cash?'

'Ah.'

Solicitors, even fledgling ones, could, in Roper's experience, like doctors, drum up a great deal of mileage from a professionally murmured 'ah'. Nicholas Bohun's hand rose to sweep back the blond wisp of his forelock. He glanced over his shoulder and drew closer.

'In confidence, of course, Mr Roper, Mrs Blezard was not *good* with money—especially of late. Not good at all.'

'We've found her cheque-stubs, Mr Bohun. Unless she had another account somewhere else she was down to eighty pounds.'

'Really? Well, of course, we didn't handle her *immediate* financial affairs,' said Bohun, beating a hasty retreat on his father's behalf. 'I think Blezard's own accountant saw to those. A Mr Marshall, I believe.'

'Just now, Mr Bohun, you said "of late". Not good with money—especially *of late*. D'you mean she was able to handle it competently before—and then suddenly couldn't? Or what?'

It wasn't quite as simple as that, actually. It had been a sort of slow drift. From comparative wealth to comparative penury.

'She had a new car, Mr Bohun. A Daimler Sovereign Double Six. Not exactly cheapo-cheapo.'

'No. Quite,' agreed Bohun. 'But that was a company car. Tax-deductible, I suspect. You'll have to ask them about that.'

'So when did you first notice this slide, Mr Bohun?'

It had been Mr Bohun senior, actually. The last time
the insurance premium had been reviewed. Last July.
About. Several items on the inventory of antiques had
been no longer in the house. Mrs Blezard had sold them.
At auction in London. They had fetched some five or six
thousand pounds. Which had embarrassed Mr Bohun senior because he had told the insurance company that the
inventory had remained unchanged since last time.

'Perhaps she didn't like the pieces, Mr Bohun,' Roper
suggested. 'So she sold them.'

'Well, no, actually. When my father taxed her, Mrs
Blezard told him that her finances were desperate. So,
you see....' Young Bohun shrugged his narrow shoulders.
'Her word, Superintendent. *Desperate.*'

He could add no more, perhaps because he knew no
more or had been briefed by his father not to say too
much for some reason or other. Mr Bohun senior, however, was fully cognisant of the seriousness of this matter,
and should Roper care to avail himself of the invitation,
then he would gladly give the Superintendent the half-
hour between eight and eight-thirty tomorrow morning.
Actually.

SIX

AND THEN, all too quickly, it was nine o'clock of the evening and thirteen hours since Hannah Blezard's body had floated up-river on the morning tide; and Roper was aware of the loss of momentum. He sat in one of the late Mrs Blezard's white kid armchairs with a pad on his knee. Price sat across the hearth from him, Makins beside Price, and Clark on the settee. One of the DCs was still upstairs with the two technicians from Forensic. The other DC and DS Rodgers were out interviewing Mrs Blezard's three co-directors in the hope of dredging up something new about her or, rather, practically anything at all about her.

Because Sergeant Clark had been through every drawer, cupboard and handbag in the house—twice—and located not a single piece of official paper with Mrs Blezard's name on it. No wedding certificate, no passport, no driving licence and no National Insurance number; not even her National Health card with her doctor's name on it.

Nor, as Price pointed out, had there been an address-book anywhere, or a notebook of telephone numbers out in the hall. Nor, it appeared, had Mrs Blezard kept any personal correspondence.

'How about a photo-album? Snapshots? Anything of that sort?'

Price, Makins and even Clark met Roper's enquiring glance. None replied.

'Perhaps she kept it all under the floorboards,' proposed Makins.

But Roper was not, at the moment, in a mood for whimsy.

Everybody had documents of some sort or other. Everybody was on a computer somewhere, even if they didn't know it, and a picture of Mrs Blezard would be put together eventually. Her year of birth would be encoded in her driving licence, her maiden name and the date and place of her wedding would be on her wedding certificate at St Catherine's House. And somewhere there would be a will—and perhaps the will might even provide a motive. But not now, not tonight. Tonight, Mrs Blezard's background was as obscure as it had been at eight o'clock this morning when Hawkesley had hauled her on to his ramp.

AT TEN TO TEN, the bleary-eyed technicians from Forensic came downstairs. With Roper's permission they would call it a day. If anyone had touched it, then they, the technicians, had lifted fingerprints from it. Tomorrow, at the crack, the lifted prints would be sent for comparison checks at Central Records; although that, in Roper's opinion, was a strict no-hoper. Murder was mostly a one-off villainy, and murderers' prints were rarely on record anywhere.

'How about that patch of cleaned window at the back of the pool?'

'No prints,' said the senior man. 'But there was a thread of material snagged up in a crack in the paint.' He dipped into his case and brought out a small polythene envelope. 'It's probably from the cloth it was cleaned with—if we're lucky.'

It wasn't much. A fragment of what looked like red cotton, about an eighth of an inch long.

Roper handed it back.

'Not exactly the stuff a window-cleaner would use, is it?'

'No, sir.' The envelope was dropped back into the bag. 'But we'll burn the midnight oil on it just the same.'

'Thanks,' said Roper. 'Obliged to you.'

At a few minutes after ten, he decided to shut up shop for the day. Everyone was tired, himself included, and the sheer frustration of looking hard and finding nothing was bad for morale. And it was still possible that Mrs Blezard had drowned accidentally; and if she had, then Roper would find himself swiftly called to account to the Assistant Chief Constable, because a lot of valuable time would have been wasted today, and the new ACC fancied himself as a business-efficiency expert.

IT WAS A typical office tucked away in a typical provincial police station, painted in institutional cream, cramped for space, two of its walls hidden behind racks of metal shelving jammed with dusty lever-arch files, lino on the floor, a few fly-specked notices on the wall beside the window, a calendar still showing last month's dates hanging from a hook behind the door. And temporarily Roper's operations room.

On the desk lay a pile of newly processed photographs. Ordinarily, Roper would have referred to them as scene-of-crime photographs—except that on this occasion he suspected that they were not. They were more scene-of-find photographs. Some showed Mrs Blezard's naked torso, some her face, a couple the whitish-purple patches where the switches of hair had been yanked from her scalp. They were photographs of unwarrantable intimacy, of a woman's life snuffed out long before her allotted span. Whatever she had done in life, no woman ever deserved to look like that in death. Roper was of the old school. Violence of any kind was anathema to him, and wreaked upon women even more so. He had been brought up that way, and he was too old now to change his spots.

Another set of photographs showed Mrs Blezard's plum-coloured Daimler Sovereign, some taken in the open air of Witling Lane, some taken in the more revealing light of laboratory floodlamps. A tight close-up of the driver's door-handle with a fragment of white thread snagged on it. A wide-angle shot of the back seat; and a duplicate of that same print worked over with a Chinagraph pencil, to show how the damp-stains on the seat and back might be linked together in the shape of a body with its knees drawn up. And it looked right, had that certain ring of authenticity. If Mrs Blezard's wet body had not been across that back seat, then someone else's had. And wet bodies rarely came in pairs. Ergo: if the Forensic artist was right—and he usually was—Mrs Blezard, alive or dead, but certainly wet, had been taken for a ride on Monday night on the back seat of her own Daimler Sovereign. Because…? Because of *what*…?

Of course because!

Roper tossed down the pencil he had been doodling with.

Because she had drowned in her own pool!

Of course!

RELAXED FOR a while, a plastic cup of coffee in one hand and a cheroot in the other, he stood by the window overlooking the High Street. It was twenty-five to eleven. A few minutes ago Wilson had telephoned to say that he had finished his post-mortem examination and would soon be on his way over. Well, now Roper had something to tell Wilson.

Under the sodium lamps, the wide stone-setted street still glistened with rain. Human shadows joined and parted. Market-day had left its toll of litter. Lifted in a momentary breeze, a page of newspaper cartwheeled desultorily and came to rest against the steps of the monument to Queen Victoria. A Cavalier that nosed out of the arch beneath the window looked like Sergeant Clark's. With a squeal of rubber it quickly turned left towards the town gate. Clark was obviously in a hurry. Roper was still not quite sure what to make of Detective Sergeant Clark. He was a shrewd observer, he thought on his feet and, according to Butcher, was more than willing to put in the hours. Except....

His thoughts wandered no further. The brisk rap at the door was followed by Wilson's familiar face peering around the edge of it.

'Hah! Here you are,' he said cheerily. A plastic cup in one hand and his document-case in the other, he backed against the door to shut it. Roper resumed his chair.

'Got anything interesting?'

'Plenty,' said Wilson enthusiastically. The coffee-cup went down on the desk and Wilson into the spare chair. He swung his case on to his knees and clicked the catches. 'How about you?'

'Next to nothing,' said Roper. 'Just a few ideas, that's all.'

'Well, for a start,' said Wilson, head down over his open case. 'Mrs Blezard *didn't* drown in the sea.'

Roper sipped at his coffee. 'I'm not exactly surprised,' he said.

Wilson, about to toss his draft report across to Roper, was plainly disappointed that Roper was not surprised.

'According to the biologist, the diatoms in her bloodstream were freshwater ones. And the water we drained from her lungs was approximately three parts per million chlorine. The kind of concentration you find in a swimming-pool.'

'She had her own. It stank of the stuff.'

'I see.' Wilson, now slightly deflated, laid the report on Roper's blotter. 'The lab did *suggest* a swimming-pool.'

'Well, now they can take it for fact,' said Roper. He drew the report closer. Terrible handwriting Wilson had. Spider's legs dipped in ink and left to roam at will. Female—he read with some difficulty—1 m. 75 cm. tall (5' 9''); body weight 55 kilos (126 lb.); well nourished. No distinguishing features. Caucasian type.... Aged approximately 35 years...something or other...

Roper conceded defeat and slid the report back to Wilson.

'I'll read it when it's typed, Mr Wilson. Just tell me— and not in words more than a foot long, if you can manage it, eh?'

'Asphyxia by drowning,' said Wilson. 'Quite simply. I can only guess when she died. Some time between six o'clock and midnight on Monday. But I can only base *that* assumption on the state of rigor.'

'Which isn't reliable,' said Roper.

'Quite,' agreed Wilson, hooking his spectacles down his nose and peering at Roper over the top of them. 'Wholemeal biscuits, whisky and highly sugared coffee. That's what I found inside her. If you can tell me when she swallowed 'em, I can tell you when she died to within a quarter of an hour.'

Roper spread his hands. 'Sorry,' he said. 'I don't know.'

'When you find out, then,' said Wilson, 'just add an hour to the time. That's when she died.'

Roper noted that. He or she might not be Mrs Blezard's murderer, but there was someone somewhere who would know exactly when that time was.

'How about sexual activity?' asked Roper. 'Any signs?'

'Can't say,' said Wilson. 'She'd been more or less irrigated during the time she was in the sea. But her *blood* samples show she was on the Pill, so there was very likely a man about somewhere.'

'How about her face? How did that happen, d'you think?'

'Something hard, something sharp.'

'Tiles, perhaps? The edge of her pool?'

'Now, that,' agreed Wilson, in the appreciative manner of a man suddenly presented with an irrefutable proposition, 'is *highly* likely.'

'What about nail-scrapings?'

'Clean as a whistle,' said Wilson. 'The sea had seen to that.'

'Could she have been dead, then pumped full of water afterwards? A cover-up job?'

'Definitely not,' said Wilson. Death by drowning, he explained, involved not only the inhalation of water but also of the numerous microscopic organisms that lived in it. During the course of the victim's struggles, some of these organisms—specifically diatoms—were caused to enter the bloodstream. If the water had been pumped in afterwards, the diatoms would *not* enter the bloodstream. And there were diatoms recognisable as marine organisms and others that only existed in fresh water. The diatoms in the blood sample from Mrs Blezard were the kind that lived in fresh water. There had also been traces of inhaled chlorine in the *bloodstream* of Mrs Blezard—more so than was ever likely to be found in drinking-water.

'So she was murdered,' said Roper, 'by accident or by design, and taken down to either the sea or the river and dumped.'

'Yes, Mr Roper,' said Wilson. 'I'd say that was highly likely.'

'Another coffee…?'

'Please,' said Wilson.

AS ROPER and Wilson settled down to their second cup of coffee, Detective Sergeant Clark was shooting the bolts shut on his garage door, while his wife waited in some trepidation in the kitchen. She recognised the signs. The way the car door had been slammed, then the garage doors slammed, the *crash-crash-crash* of the bolts. And when he was late he usually rang to tell her when he was about to leave the station. He had not rung her tonight. And that was ominous, too.

His footsteps on the path by the back door. The smile she had hitched on froze off her face. He was deathly white, standing in the doorway with his fists clenched.

'Where's Stephen?' he said. 'I want 'im.'

'Upstairs,' she said. 'But….' She put out a hand to stop him. She was frightened; in twenty years she had seen him lose his temper often enough, but *never* like this. He struck her hand aside—he had never hit her before, never—stormed past, out to the hall, up the stairs. Two paces along the landing.

She heard him barge into Stephen's bedroom, the door crash shut behind him, her husband's raised voice, then

Stephen's in protest, then the two of them together. Then a thud, like a body hitting a wall, and then another, and yet another. And Julie Clark felt her legs buckle as she started after him.

God forbid, it sounded like a fight to the death up there.

ROPER HEADED the sheet 'Summary of Evidence', and underlined it; then lit his last cheroot of the day and took a sip of his coffee. Outside in the High Street, a steady tattoo of slamming car doors and a couple of drunks singing out of tune evidenced that it was well past eleven o'clock and the pubs were turning out. Somewhere downstairs two fingers pecked hesitantly at a typewriter.

He wrote at random, writing as the facts came to mind. Mrs Blezard's garage doors had been heard by two reliable witnesses being opened, or closed, or both, at some time around ten o'clock on Monday night.

Two or perhaps three voices on Mrs Blezard's answering machine had still to be identified: one heavy breather who might have called twice, and one lovelorn male.

Mrs Blezard's Daimler Sovereign found by a field-gate a quarter of a mile from where she lived.

One cryptic note. In brackets Roper wrote 'blackmail', and followed it with a question mark before he closed the brackets. The note and its envelope were presently across at Forensic. They would both undergo an iodine-fume test on the faint chance that they might bear fingerprints other than sundry postmen, Butcher's constable's, Ben Marshall's and Roper's own.

Hairs torn from Mrs Blezard's scalp. Wilson had carried out a few experiments this afternoon. And, according to his subsequent calculations, a pull of some eight kilos, roughly seventeen and a half pounds, would have been needed to tug out the largest switch.

Fingerprints on the coffee-cups and their saucers in the sitting-room. Another needle-in-a-haystack job, that. According to Butcher, the total population of King's Minster was around six thousand. Of which, say, a thousand might be males over the age of fourteen. They could all be fingerprinted—it had been done before in bigger towns than King's Minster—but such an exercise relied on public goodwill, it was expensive, and in the end it might turn out that the murderer was not a local man—although statistics showed that murderers usually lived within a few miles of their victims, and frequently in the same house. But it still wasn't foolproof.

A young lad on a bicycle.

A couple of shoe-prints, size eleven, just inside the doorway of Mrs Blezard's conservatory. Probably left by a pair of training-shoes. And the most prolific wearers of training-shoes were young lads. Roper bracketed those shoe-prints with the lad on the bicycle. Then added a line with an arrowhead at the end to connect that bracket with the line above it, because Mr Size Eleven might also be the donor of the set of male fingerprints on a cup and saucer.

Not much of a summary. Hardly a summary at all. As an afterthought, Roper leaned forward again and wrote: 'clean window-pane at rear of pool'. Which added little more flesh to the list than had been there before, and was even possibly nothing to do with the matter in hand. Clark's theory was probably right. Mrs Blezard had more than likely suffered the attentions of a peeper, who might be the murderer, although Roper doubted it. Few peepers, once observed, stayed on the scene and put up a fight.

He tossed down his ballpoint and sat back, his cheroot

still only a quarter smoked, the hands of his wristwatch advanced by only five minutes since he had first started writing. Two-thirds of a sheet of A4 paper he was using were still blank.

He could, at a push, drum up a possible scenario. Mr X had visited Mrs Blezard late on Monday evening. Perhaps parked his car outside the lane—if, that is, he owned a car. He was possibly Mrs Blezard's lover—or an ex-lover with an axe to grind. At some time a row had developed, its likely site the swimming-pool. X, in the extreme of his anger, had pushed Mrs Blezard into the pool, and held her head under by her hair. Then he found himself with the problem that all murderers eventually find themselves with: what to do with the body.

The adrenalin overflows, the blood pressure rises, the heart flaps around in the ribs and the brain scurries about in a hundred directions at once. It was called panic.

He could have left the body where it was. It might not have been found for a week or more, unless Mrs Blezard's milkman or charlady had become suspicious—but no, Mr X, whoever he was, decided to complicate matters. He had carried the body to Mrs Blezard's car and dumped it across the back seat—thereby staining its upholstery; the boot would have served him better, but he still wasn't thinking straight or perhaps he hadn't been able to open the boot. Then, if Hawkesley was right, X had driven the body along the coast and dumped it in the sea somewhere to the north of King's Minster in the hope that it would be swept away on the tide. Or he had a boat of some sort, and had taken the body well out to sea and dumped it there. That was likelier. According to Wilson, the body had definitely spent some considerable time in the sea. What had looked like encrustations of dandruff on Mrs Blezard's scalp were in fact patches of salt.

But Mr X was no mariner. Because, if he was, he would have known about the direction of the local predominant currents and the phenomenon of the whirlpool action where the river met the sea.

Then X, having, he assumed, disposed of the body, drove Mrs Blezard's car back. But not to its garage. Perhaps the garage was too close to the scene of his crime. Perhaps his nerve had finally gone—or whatever. In either event, he had driven on for another quarter-mile and parked it beside a farmer's gate. And disposed of its keys—or put them in his pocket out of habit. He had wiped the steering-wheel, and certainly the door-handles, and everything else he might have touched, clear of his fingerprints. And yet he *might* have left his prints behind on a coffee-cup and a saucer in the house. Had he, in his panic, not considered those? Or were he and the visitor who had been so prodigal with his fingerprints—and possibly training-shoe prints—two entirely different people?

Like the summary, the scenario was a ramshackle affair and at this time of night scarcely worthy of further consideration. Across the river the minster clock chimed the half after eleven. The town had gone quiet again. Roper was tempted to go home himself, but there was still one more straw to grasp at. He reached for his telephone and drew it closer.

'Duty sergeant, please.'

A click. A ringing tone. Another click.

'Sergeant Harper,' a cautious voice said.

'Roper, Sergeant. Does your interview room run to a tape-recorder?'

'Yes, sir.'

'And do you know who's got the key to the safe?'

'I have, sir.'

'Good,' said Roper. 'I'll be down.'

They opened the safe together. Harper was a tall flabby character, getting thin on top, and close enough to his pension to do everything by the book. Roper signed for the audio-tape in its polythene envelope while Harper locked the safe again. The signature above Roper's was DS Clark's.

'The interview room's along the passage and first door on the right, sir.'

'Thanks.'

Musty. A smell of wax floor-polish and stale cigarette-smoke. All interview rooms smelt the same. Roper found the light-switch, closed the door. The tape-deck was like his own back at County. He slipped in the tape from Mrs Blezard's answering machine. Pressed the PLAY button, turned the volume control most of the way to maximum, waited for Mrs Blezard's voice.

He did not hear it.

What came from the loudspeaker was barely recognisable as a human voice. A distorted spluttering gobble-dygook broken here and there by what sounded like a Tube train rushing out of its tunnel. He wound the tape forward a few revolutions and tried again. More gobble-dygook, like an old 78 record played at a quarter of its intended speed. Silence again. Then a few crackles, and then a prolonged whine that just might have had a voice muttering beneath it.

He checked the evidence bag. On it was the white self-adhesive label with Roper's signature on it, and Price's beneath as witness.

He wound the tape back to the beginning and played it through again, fiddled with the tape-deck's volume and tone controls. The result was the same. Noises. Just noises.

'Sergeant!'

Harper had probably not moved so fast since he'd come off the beat.

'Sir.'

'Your tape-deck—when was it last used?'

'About two hours ago, sir. Mr Butcher used it before he went off duty. He checked a tape that's going to court tomorrow.'

'Machine working, was it?'

Harper shrugged. 'Mr Butcher didn't say otherwise, sir.'

'Mr Butcher's tape still in the safe, is it?'

'Yes, sir.'

'Get it,' said Roper.

Harper shifted uncomfortably. 'I'm not supposed.... Mr Butcher's orders, sir.'

'Sorry, Sergeant,' said Roper, 'I'm pulling rank. I'll explain to Mr Butcher in the morning.'

And reluctantly Sergeant Harper went back up the passage. Keys jingled. The safe door closed with a muted thud. Harper returned, and grudgingly handed Roper Butcher's tape.

'A couple of shakes and you can put it back again,' said Roper.

He slipped the tape into the machine. Pressed the PLAY key.

There was no gobbledygook. Only Butcher's voice, loud and clear....

'The time is fourteen-thirty hours on the first of June. I am Chief Inspector Philip Butcher and I am about to interview John Arthur Singleton....'

Roper stopped the tape and wound it back to its beginning. There was nothing wrong with the tape-deck. He removed the cassette and returned it to Harper.

'Thank you, Sergeant.'

'That's all, sir?'

'That's all, Sergeant. You can put it away again. Thanks. And put the phone in here on an outside line, will you?'

'Yes, sir.'

WHILE THE telephone rang at the other end, Roper slipped the visiting-card back in his wallet. The telephone rang for a long time. Too long. Marshall was out.

'Hello?' a voice said at last as Roper had been about to put the telephone down again.

'Mr Marshall?'

'Yes.'

'Superintendent Roper, sir,' said Roper.

There was a long silence.

'Sorry to ring you so late, sir,' said Roper, filling the gap. 'I'm looking for an electronics man. A good one. Know where I can lay my hand on one at this late hour, sir? It's important.'

'An electronics engineer?' Marshall sounded half-asleep. 'Yes, I expect so. But what for exactly? The business of Mrs Blezard, is it?'

'Not exactly, sir, no,' said Roper. 'I've got an audio-tape here at the station. I'd like your man to listen to it and tell me what's wrong with it. That's all, sir.'

Another long silence followed. Or perhaps it was a yawn.

'It's terribly late, but I'll try. I doubt I can get one there before midnight, though.'

'Don't worry, Mr Marshall,' said Roper. 'I'll be here—at the police station.'

HE ARRIVED AT five to midnight. A short, plump, be-spectacled young man with wayward hair and boundless enthusiasm. His name was Blows. Second in command of Blezard's experimental laboratory. He looked a bright lad.

'Sorry if I got you out of bed, Mr Blows.'

'I wasn't in it.' Blows beamed around his spectacles. His shabby suit was perhaps a sign of how grossly underpaid he was. 'What's the problem?'

'This is.' Roper handed him the tape from Mrs Blezard's answering machine.

Blows lifted his spectacles into his hair and peered closely at the tape, this way, that way, turning it over. He hooked his spectacles down again.

'Looks all right to me. What are the symptoms exactly?'

'This morning it was working. Now it isn't.'

'How about your deck?'

'Working,' said Roper. 'I tried another tape on it about half an hour ago.'

'May I hear it?'

Roper slipped the tape into the machine and pressed the PLAY button. It seemed that young Mr Blows's hearing was also improved by lifting his spectacles into his hair.

'Can you turn it up, please?'

Roper swung the volume control to a deafening maximum. Blows listened intently.

'That'll do,' he shouted.

Roper backed the tape to its beginning and took it out of the machine. Still with his spectacles in his hair, Blows subjected it to another thorough scrutiny.

'What was on it?' Blows asked.

'Speech,' said Roper. 'It's from a telephone answering machine.'

'And you've *definitely* heard something on it?'

'Definitely,' said Roper.

Blows twitched down his spectacles, and perched himself thoughtfully on the edge of the interview-table.

'Well…it certainly hasn't been wiped…strictly speaking. Or we'd have just heard silence. And there *are* voices on it—of a sort. I'd say,' he hazarded, 'that someone's inadvertently dumped it down on a loudspeaker—or something else with a powerful electromagnet in it.'

'Is there a way of bringing the speech back?'

Blows stretched his mouth and shrugged his shoulders. 'Frankly, no. If there was just a steady hum on it, I could filter out the hum; but a lot of that garbage is what we call white noise—no specific frequency. Filter out white noise and you're left with nowt. Sorry. It boils down to the fact that the magnetic particles in the tape have been disorientated. And there ain't no way of putting them back the way they were. In a word, it's buggered.'

At twenty past twelve Sergeant Harper, feeling distinctly uneasy because he smelt trouble in the offing—and Superintendent Roper was still a devil he didn't know—adopted a posture that approximated to standing at attention in front of Roper's desk.

'When did you sign on duty, Sergeant?'

'Ten to ten, sir. With the night crew.'

Roper held up the audio-cassette, now back in its polythene bag. 'And you saw Sergeant Clark put this in the safe?'

'Yes, sir.'

'When?'

'Ten thirty-five, sir. On the dot. I saw DS Clark write it in the book.'

'And Clark put it in the safe himself? No one else touched it? Nobody else went to the safe afterwards until I did?'

'Yes, sir. Sergeant Clark put it in the safe himself. And nobody touched it afterwards, sir.'

'Did he go into the communications room first? Anywhere near the radio?'

'No, sir.'

According to Harper, Clark had come straight in from the street to the duty desk, booked himself in, signed the safe-book, seen the cassette into the safe, then signed himself off duty and gone home.

'You've got a side-entrance,' said Roper. Clark, as he recalled, had left Mrs Blezard's house, together with the tape, at five past ten. At that time of night, he ought to have made it back here to the station in five or six minutes. Instead, it appeared to have taken him nearer twenty.

'I heard his car pull up outside, sir,' said Harper. 'He came straight in.'

'And how long was he in here?'

'Ten minutes at most, sir,' said Harper. 'He said he was in a hurry. In and out like a flash he was.'

Something in Harper's voice, a subtle inflection that was perhaps not even intended. Harper didn't like Clark—that was the impression Roper got.

'Thank you, Sergeant,' said Roper. 'And we keep this conversation between ourselves. Right? And, for what it's worth, you can put this back in the safe.'

'Yes, sir,' said Harper, patently relieved that whatever the trouble was it had skirted him and left him unscathed. Sergeant Harper looked of the genus that spent most of its career doing its best to stay fireproof.

At half past midnight Roper climbed into his car and buckled his seat-belt.

It had not been an auspicious day. Sometimes it went like that.

Perhaps tomorrow would be more fruitful. And tomorrow, too, he was going to find out just what DS Clark had done with that tape, because he'd certainly done something with it. And with any luck, and a few door-to-doors, find out who was that schoolboy on the bicycle who had called so frequently at Mrs Blezard's.

Roper was beginning to set a lot of store by that boy, whoever he was.

SEVEN

THE SENIOR Mr Bohun sprawled back in his antiquated swivel-chair and steepled his fingers under his chin while he and Roper weighed each other up. Bohun was middle-fiftyish, with a well-fitted and expensively cut dark suit and a thatch of milk-white and immaculately barbered hair. And he was inevitably cautious. At a few minutes past eight on this Thursday morning it was raining again, and from the look of the sullen grey sky it seemed settled in for the rest of the day.

Bohun's smile was thin and without body.

'How can I help you, Superintendent?'

'For a start, sir, how well did you know Mrs Blezard?'

'Socially, not at all,' said Bohun. There was a cup of steaming coffee on his desk. He had not offered Roper one. 'She was a client.' The steepled fingers came apart and bobbed lightly to and fro against each other. 'Merely a client.'

'A good client?'

'I'm not sure what that means, exactly,' replied Bohun guardedly—or perhaps pedantically. The fingertips continued to bob. Plump hairless hands, an ostentatious gold signet ring on one of them. Gold-rimmed spectacles. A frayed carpet underfoot. Window-frames that hadn't had a fresh lick of paint in ten years or more. It was clear that Mr Bohun knew where his priorities lay when it came to spending his profits.

'Did she spend a lot of money on your services, Mr

Bohun? When did you first act for her? Did she pay her bills on time? That sort of thing.'

Bohun considered. The bobbing fingers came together and were stilled.

'She paid us a retainer,' he said at last. 'Annually. What we did for her occasionally exceeded that sum. She usually haggled when it did. And we first acted for her when she contested her late husband's will—some three years ago.'

'Why did she contest the will, Mr Bohun?'

'Some of the terms were not what she'd been led to believe,' said Bohun. He paused to stir his coffee and take a dainty sip of it. He dabbed fastidiously at his mouth with a handkerchief he plucked from his cuff. 'There had been a previous will totally in Mrs Blezard's favour. The last will was not—if you follow.'

'For instance, sir?' prompted Roper.

'For instance…' Bohun lay back in his chair, joined his hands contemplatively again. 'Mrs Blezard had been led to believe that the house had belonged to her late husband. It transpired, in fact, that it was the freehold solely of Blezard's Electronics. Mr Blezard had had it absorbed into the company's assets some eighteen months previously for purposes of collateral at the bank.

'There was also the matter of her late husband's holdings in the company. Seventy per cent.'

'What was the company worth?' asked Roper.

'As a piece of real estate'—Bohun's plump hands briefly parted again—'some three and a half million, I suppose.'

To which Roper's quick application of some mental arithmetic—knock two noughts off three million, add one nought back and multiply by seven—made Mrs Blezard's expected share in the estate something around two million one hundred thousand pounds—to say nothing of her share in the odd five hundred thousand. Which was not exactly, as the old expression had it, simply so much hay, even in these days of depressed coinage.

'Except,' continued Bohun, 'that Mr Blezard had already disposed of six-sevenths of those shares to his three codirectors shortly before he died. Which left Mrs Blezard a mere ten-per-cent holding.'

Which was still—another rough calculation—three hundred and fifty thousand pounds. Still a lot of money by most standards—except that Mrs Blezard had clearly expected a great deal more than that.

'So she went to law?'

'Quite,' said Bohun. 'Mind you, I warned her against it. The will was completely copper-bottomed. And of course her marital indiscretions were made a great deal of—the will, in fact, itemised them. The costs alone came to thirty thousand pounds. A hopeless case from the very beginning.'

'You say these affairs were itemised, Mr Bohun,' said Roper. 'Were names named, anything of that sort?'

'No,' replied Bohun. 'Simply dates, places. But they did tie in with certain of Mrs Blezard's unexplained absences from home—and some dates on her passport. She could not deny them—eventually. It was also revealed by Mr Blezard's own solicitor that the two of them had discussed—tentatively, I hasten to add—the possibility of Mr Blezard instituting divorce proceedings. But of course Mr Blezard died. Quite suddenly. Heart. Went to the works one morning—and *poof!*' Bohun softly clicked finger and thumb together. 'Thirty-eight years old. Stress, you see. Stress does it.'

Roper was still dwelling on the mention of Mrs Blezard's passport. So she *had* had such a thing.

'Mrs Blezard had no next of kin, Mr Bohun. Is that right?'

'So we understood.'

'But last year, according to your son, your firm prepared a new will for her.'

'Yes,' agreed Bohun. 'We did. I did, in fact. Personally.'

'Who was the main beneficiary, Mr Bohun?'

'There *was* only one beneficiary, Superintendent,' said Bohun, smiling smugly, relishing his little moment of procrastination. Because Roper knew that Bohun knew damned well what Roper was after. A name, or even a hint of a name.

'And who was that, sir?' asked Roper, smiling winsomely.

'Ah,' said Bohun, joining his hands together again under his chin. 'Now, that I *can't* tell you.'

Roper let the winsome smile dissolve. At this hour of the morning, especially after only six hours' sleep, his sense of humour had still got a lot of catching-up to do. At this rate, he might have to do without it all day.

'With respect to you, Mr Bohun,' he said, 'I'm conducting a murder inquiry. And Mrs Blezard was *your* client, sir.'

'I've answered your question, Superintendent,' said Bohun equably. 'You asked me to name Mrs Blezard's beneficiary, and I answer again: I have no idea *who* is Mrs Blezard's beneficiary.'

'But *you* prepared the will, Mr Bohun,' insisted Roper.

'All bar the *name* of the beneficiary, Superintendent,' said Bohun, equally insistently, hunching forward abruptly with his hands clasped on his leather-bound blotter. 'And his—or her—address. Mrs Blezard filled those in herself. So....' He leaned back again and spread his hands expansively. 'There you have it, Superintendent. I have no idea who he—or she—is. You see?'

'And that's legal, is it, Mr Bohun?'

'One can scratch a will on the side of a car with a screwdriver, Superintendent,' said Bohun. 'And with the proviso that two people witness your signature it is—I'm afraid—perfectly legal.'

It was one dead end after another after that. Mr Bohun had no copy of the will. He did not know where Mrs Blezard had put the will for safe keeping; he suggested a bank deposit-box—but which bank? Perhaps her own here in King's Minster. Or perhaps not. Neither did he know if Mrs Blezard had once been Mrs Someone Else, nor her maiden name, nor her place of birth.

'But I can tell you one thing, Superintendent.'

Roper was on his way to the door by now, had his fist about the loose brass knob that felt in imminent danger of falling off in his hand. Bohun had remained at his desk and was sipping at his by now cold coffee.

'And what's that, Mr Bohun?'

'God forbid that I should speak ill of the dead, Superintendent, but I have a strong feeling that Mrs Blezard let a sight more money go out of her hands than was ever coming into them. But you didn't hear me say that—mm?'

AT TWENTY PAST EIGHT, Roper was walking the fifty or so yards back to the police station in the drizzling rain. For some reason best known to herself, Mrs Blezard had been keen to cover her financial tracks, and possibly her personal ones as well.

Why?

Somewhere, there was a deed-box, or whatever, with possibly a will in it; and perhaps a marriage certificate and even a passport, and all the other documents that folk needed these days to substantiate themselves.

Where was it?

Someone knew. The beneficiary of her will would know, surely. He—or she.

Who were they?

Mrs Blezard's death had been widely reported in the national newspapers this morning, and on Radio Solent. So the beneficiary would probably know by now, and be licking his—or her—lips.

Would he or she come forward? Yes, surely. If only because Mrs Blezard's holding in Blezard's Electronics, on paper at least, was worth a third of a million. And that, equally surely, had to be irresistible to someone or other.

Unless they had murdered her, that beneficiary, that someone or other. In which case, if they had any sense, Mrs Blezard's estate would remain unclaimed....

Roper strode up the six shallow steps two at a time and pushed through the swing-doors. Phil Butcher was behind the public counter, talking quietly with a shirt-sleeved constable and looking harassed. He lifted the counter-flap for Roper to come through, broke off his conversation with the constable, touched a hand to Roper's arm.

'Morning, Douglas. If you can spare a moment, I'd like a word.'

'Now, if you like,' said Roper.

They went up the stairs together and turned into Butcher's office. Butcher closed the door and hung his cap on his coat-stand.

'Flap?' asked Roper.

Butcher gestured to a visitor's chair.

'Bloody Clark,' he said, as he skirted his desk and dropped into his seat.

'The very gentleman I was going to bring up,' said Roper.

'What's *your* problem?'

'Buggered evidence,' said Roper. 'What's yours?'

'He hasn't reported for duty this morning,' said Butcher. 'We haven't seen him, and his wife hasn't seen him; she rang in at half-past seven this morning to ask if we knew where he was. He usually takes her up a cup of tea before he goes out. This morning he didn't. And when she checked he wasn't in the house. And he'd left the garage doors open—which is something he *never* does, so she says. And their lad's taken off, too. Left a note on the kitchen table. She thinks Clark read the note when he got up this morning and took off after him. All very fraught.'

'How old's the boy?'

'Eighteen after Christmas.'

'Then, he's entitled to take off,' said Roper. 'Not our problem.'

Butcher looked haggard this morning, his eyes redrimmed. King's Minster was only the core of his parish; he was responsible for close on a hundred and fifty square miles of the surrounding countryside as well, and Phil Butcher took his job more seriously than most.

And then Butcher came to the point.

'There was a fight at the Clarks' house last night, Douglas,' he said. 'A chair got broken and a wardrobe door was stove in.'

'Who was hurt?'

'Clark and his lad. Both of them.'

'Anyone else involved?'

Butcher shook his head.

'Domestic,' said Roper. 'Not our business, Phil.'

'Not that easy,' said Butcher. 'I know the family. Julie Clark's a bloody nice woman. And according to the PC who took her phone call she sounded pretty frantic. I can't just leave it, Douglas. And I've got two County Court appearances today. One at eleven and one at two-thirty. So I can't give you a hand with the Blezard business. Sorry.'

'We'll manage,' said Roper, levering himself out of his chair. 'But keep me in touch with the Clark affair, will you? And if Clark turns up here I want someone to remind him he's working for me, and say I want 'im. In the flesh—and as quick as he likes.'

'Will do,' said Butcher. 'But, if I get hold of him first, there might not be much of him left.'

'The part that talks is the only piece I want, Phil,' said Roper grimly. 'You can have the rest of him.'

Roper's office looked a little less temporary this morning. Makins and Rodgers had hauled the metal shelves and the dusty files out to the passage and annexed another old desk from somewhere for Price to work at. The two of them were still in shirt-sleeves. Price was fixing the photographs taken yesterday on the wall with blobs of Blue Tack.

'You look well and truly knackered again this morning, my son,' Roper remarked appreciatively to Makins, as he hung up his raincoat behind the door. 'You sure you're fit for work?'

'Late night, sir,' confessed Makins, yawning. 'But I'll manage somehow.'

'He found out there was a WDC working next door,' Price said over his shoulder. 'You know how it is with Makins.'

'Hell's teeth,' said Roper to Makins. How long were you in this place last night?'

'About twenty minutes, sir,' said Makins, whose prowess with the ladies was a legend back at County. 'That's all it takes.'

'He's a very slick operator is our George, sir,' observed Rodgers drily. 'He's the only bloke I know who can chat up a bird while she's jogging.'

'I have heard,' said Roper, easing himself into the narrow space between his desk and the window. Two messages already on his pad. *DS Clark AWOL. Ring Mr Hawkesley at boatyard.*

'I know about Clark,' he said. 'What does Hawkesley want?'

'I took that one, Super,' said Rodgers. 'About twenty past eight. He was a bit coy, as if he didn't want to make a fool of himself, but he says he's got a boat in for some work on its electrics. He'd like us to take a look at it. He was definitely cautious, sir.'

'Go round and see him,' said Roper. 'Ring if it's important.'

'Right.' Rodgers got back into his jacket and raincoat.

Roper gestured for Price and Makins to sit. Price took a chair, Makins the corner of Price's desk. The door closed behind DS Rodgers.

'Either of you notice Clark taking that tape out of Mrs Blezard's answering machine yesterday?' asked Roper.

Neither had. Price had only seen it bagged up and lying on the table beside the telephone in Mrs Blezard's hall.

'There's a problem?' asked Price.

'I decided to run it through before I went home last night,' said Roper. 'All that came out was a load of garbage.' He sketched a brief account of Blows's midnight visit and his subsequent conversation with the night sergeant.

'Clark brought the tape straight back here,' said Price. 'I saw him leave the house with it.'

'Did you tell him to?' asked Roper.

'No,' said Price. 'Sorry. But I thought you had.'

And Roper had thought that Price had.

'Either of you got any idea how long it took you last night to drive here from Mrs Blezard's place?'

'About five minutes,' said Makins.

Price thought the same. Perhaps six, at a push, but he'd caught two sets of traffic lights.

'It took Clark nearly half an hour,' said Roper, and left a long pause for thought.

'I can't be following this,' said Makins, puzzled. 'I don't see the connection. Clark brings the tape back here. Clark puts tape in safe. Tape later found to be rubbished.' Makins's scowl gave way to a look of dawning realisation. 'You reckon *Clark* buggered it?'

'Nobody else touched it,' said Roper.

'But not deliberately, eh?' said Makins.

'I'm not even sure about that,' said Roper. Driving home late last night in the car he had thought a lot about Sergeant Clark, mainly about casting the Sergeant to eternal perdition. And amongst those thoughts a couple of memories had surfaced: the way Clark's face had gone blank yesterday morning over Mrs Blezard's answering machine and his subsequent fluffing over its switches; his sudden burst of hostile questioning across Mrs Crispin's kitchen table yesterday afternoon.

'That WDC you chatted up,' Roper said to Makins. 'I presume she works for Clark. Did she talk about him at all?'

Makins shrugged. 'From time to time. Nothing important—except that he pushes 'em hard. There's just her and a young DC and Clark at the moment. He expects a sixty-per-cent clear-up rate. Plus.'

'Does he indeed?' said Roper. 'And does he get it?'

'We didn't exactly spend the small hours discussing crime statistics, Super.'

The telephone rang. Roper leaned forward and reached for it.

'Roper.'

'Regional Forensic here, Mr Roper.' A sing-song female voice rose and fell. 'I have the Director for you.'

A few crackles and splutters on the line. Roper drew a pad closer, and a ballpoint pen from his inside pocket.

Then Guthrie was on the line. A man of limitless good cheer was Mr Guthrie, even at half-past eight on a cold wet autumn morning.

'What have you got for us, Mr Guthrie?'

'Plenty. Got your notebook handy?' Paper rustled at the other end. 'The size-eleven shoe-prints—definitely rubber-soled training-shoes. And, equally definitely, the depressions in the sitting-room carpet—including the two by the coffee-table—match them.

'And the fragment of red thread from the conservatory window-frame—that's a cotton and nylon mixture. Possibly from a shirt. And the piece of white thread from Mrs Blezard's car-door handle—that's pure cotton. More than likely from a fabric handkerchief.'

Roper jotted down only the salient words. So far, nothing the Director had said was exactly exciting. The chance of finding remnants of an old red shirt was remote. And how many white cotton handkerchiefs there were about was mind-numbing.

'I hope you're saving the good news till last, Mr Guthrie,' said Roper, stabbing a full stop on his pad.

'Oh, yes. Indeed. Fingerprints. The nitty gritty. You ready…?'

On the handles of the cups and on the saucers found in Mrs Blezard's lounge one set of prints was indubitably hers, the other set, from their size, definitely male.

'I'm in a fever of excitement, Mr Guthrie,' said Roper.

'You will be,' said Guthrie, warming to his task. 'Hearken to this.'

'I'm hearkening,' said Roper.

'That curious letter you picked up yesterday. Addressed to Mrs Blezard. An absolute plethora of prints on it.'

'I don't doubt it,' said Roper. An absolute plethora. Sundry Post Office sorting staff, a postman or two, the constable who had collected it yesterday, Ben Marshall, and Roper himself; all had handled the envelope and/or the letter with total abandon.

'*And* Mrs Blezard herself,' added the Director dramatically. 'Now, how come *that?* I wonder. Since she was dead before it arrived.'

Roper felt the skin prickle on the backs of his hands. When he wasn't sure of anything, Guthrie wore his caution like an overcoat.

'*And* those of the gentleman who shared her coffee-cups, Mr Roper,' said Guthrie, in the ensuing silence. 'But *he'd* only touched the envelope. You've gone very quiet, Mr Roper.'

'Thinking,' said Roper. 'Tell me, were Mrs Blezard's dabs on the note *and* the envelope?'

'Definitely. Oh, and the paper was Basildon Bond, and the adhesive used to put the note together was Pritt Stick. Leaves a splendid print behind, does Pritt Stick. Her right thumb. A classic example of what a fingerprint ought to be.'

Roper glanced across at Price and Makins.

'Anybody see a tube of Pritt Stick at Mrs Blezard's yesterday?'

Makins nodded. 'In the kitchen cabinet.'

'Go on, Mr Guthrie.'

'It's a fair chance that she licked the envelope, too,' said Guthrie. 'We did a saliva test. She was group AB, and that's a rare one.'

And, like Roper, Guthrie had had a feeling in his gut that the note had borne all the trademarks of a blackmail letter. Until, that is, late last night when his technician had completed the tests in the iodine-fume cabinet and the ultraviolet checks. And then, beyond all reasonable doubt, it had transpired that Mrs Blezard had sent the note to herself. And Mr Size Eleven, whoever he was, had most likely slipped it into the postbox for her.

'Now, there's a thing,' said Roper.

'Quite,' said Guthrie. 'And that frond of seaweed between her fingers was bladder-wrack. But it thrives inshore, so it doesn't indicate she went far out to sea. And, sad to say, that's all I can do for you at the moment, but I'll keep in touch.'

'Greatly obliged,' said Roper, although he was not too sure now that he was. 'Thanks, Mr Guthrie.'

The receiver went back on its rest, Roper to the depths of his uncomfortable chair.

'How about this, then?' he said tossing his ballpoint on to the pad. 'If anybody was blackmailing Mrs Blezard, it was Mrs Blezard. Any ideas?' He swivelled his hastily scrawled notes so that Price and Makins could read them. 'And that's the rest of it. For what it's worth.'

Both scanned the few lines with deepening gloom on their faces.

'Add that to the botched-up tape,' observed Price, 'and we're back to square one.'

'Right,' said Roper, impatiently reaching for the telephone as it rang stridently again. 'Hello.'

This time it was DS Rodgers. He was along at Hawkesley's boatyard.

'I think you ought to come down, sir.' The usually dour Rodgers was patently excited about something. 'Mr Hawkesley's got a boat up in his shed. Electric trouble. Only it isn't. It looks as if somebody's hot-wired it. And there are hairs wound round a couple of washers where the propeller shaft comes out of its tube.' Roper heard Hawkesley's voice muttering a correction in the background. 'Mr Hawkesley says it's called the propeller gland, sir. But the point is, sir, they're black hairs—like Mrs Blezard's—and they're long. So they're definitely a woman's hairs, sir.'

'Don't move,' said Roper. 'I'll be there.'

EIGHT

THE SMART LITTLE white cabin cruiser had been winched up into Hawkesley's workshop and presently sat on a towing-trolley between the twin hulls of a glass-fibre catamaran that took up the rest of the shed. Beyond the open doors the steadily falling rain took the sheen off the river.

'It's here, Super.' Dropping to a crouch, DS Rodgers shone Hawkesley's torch at the propeller gland on the cabin cruiser's underside. Roper went down on his heels beside him. Behind the propeller, between it and the tube that housed its shaft, were three greased and corroding washers. And caught up between them, and wound tightly around them, were thick strands of what definitely looked like hair.

'I managed to unwind one,' said Rodgers. From his raincoat pocket he brought out a polythene envelope.

Roper took it and held it up to the light. A human hair. No mistake. Black as ink.

'How long is it?'

'About eighteen inches,' said Rodgers. 'Too long for a bloke.'

Roper stood up. Rodgers rose with him and switched off the torch.

'Who does the boat belong to, Mr Hawkesley?'

'Arthur Chaucer,' he said. 'Next door.'

'And he's asked you to look at it?'

'He thought he'd got a duff starter motor, asked me to check it over for him.'

'And you found it hot-wired, did you, Mr Hawkesley?'

'Yes,' agreed Hawkesley. 'If that's the expression. The live lead on the ignition switch had been ripped off and twisted around the other terminal; the live lead to the starter motor was the same.'

'In other words, sir,' said Roper, starting to circle the boat in what little space there was around it, 'somebody had used the boat who didn't have the ignition key for it.'

'I'd say so,' said Hawkesley.

It was an expensive-looking artefact—white glass-fibre hull, chrome-plated fittings, a directional-loop radio aerial on top of the stub of mast above the cabin—although as cabin cruisers went it was a relatively modest affair. A glance into the cabin showed only two upholstered berths that doubled as seats and a narrow folding table between them. Fifteen feet from prow to stern, certainly no more. But certainly big enough and obviously stealable enough, if what you wanted it for was to carry a body out to sea in the dead of night and lose it. The wheelhouse was merely a weather-canopy over the wheel and the dashboard. A square of plywood cladding beneath the sloping dashboard had at some time been levered off and only crudely put back again.

'Did you do that, Mr Hawkesley?'

'That's the way whoever used it got to the wiring,' said Hawkesley. 'I haven't got around to repairing that yet. It needs a new piece of ply.'

'What made you look underneath the boat, sir?'

'Pure fluke,' said Hawkesley. 'If it hadn't been raining, I'd have worked on it on the river. But it was, and in case it turned out to be a long job I winched it up here in the dry. And since I had I decided to go over the propeller with a wire brush. End of story.'

'But you did repair the electrical leads?'

'Yes,' said Hawkesley. 'I'm sorry. I should have rung your people when I found them ripped off the switch. But boats get borrowed all the time. Kids mostly. Joy riders. I didn't think it was important. The boat was back, relatively undamaged.' Hawkesley shrugged. 'No harm done, you might say.'

'In your place I'd probably have done the same, sir,' said Roper, to Hawkesley's obvious relief. 'And you did spot the hairs around the propeller.'

'I had second thoughts about those, too,' said Hawkesley ruefully. 'I almost put the wire brush to 'em.'

'Glad you didn't, Mr Hawkesley,' said Roper. If those hairs tangled around the propeller shaft were Mrs Blezard's, then it was clear now how Mrs Blezard had lost so much. It also accounted for the sudden snatch which Wilson had calculated necessary to pull so many out at once. But, of course, it had yet to be proved that the hairs *were* Mrs Blezard's, although Roper's inner voice was already telling him they were. It was too much of a coincidence to be otherwise. The body of Mrs Blezard had been dumped out at sea. Mrs Blezard had jet-black hair. Strands of jet-black hair were wound around the propeller gland of a seaworthy cabin cruiser that had recently been borrowed and put back again where it had been. As logic it wasn't exactly irrefutable; but for the time being it was logic enough. The simplest explanation of the facts was usually the right one.

'You said the owner was a Mr Chaucer, sir?'

MR CHAUCER led the way through his shop, his black-beamed Tudor restaurant-cum-tearoom and thence up a wrought-iron spiral staircase to his palatial office on the first floor. A framed certificate on the wall proclaimed the premises to be the registered offices of Chaucer's

Bakeries, and a map on the wall opposite showed the disposition of the other branches around the county. Businesslike and brisk, Chaucer swivelled one chair closer to his desk for Roper and pulled another one away from the wall for Rodgers. Then he seated himself in his own chair on the other side of the desk and made himself comfortable on its studded green leather. He drew his tooled-leather blotter closer and clasped his hands on it.

'I take it this visit's about the boat, gentlemen.' A frank youthful smile seemed to be permanently moulded into the smooth fabric of his face. Gold figured prominently on his wrists and fingers. 'To be frank, I wasn't even going to bother you about it. Boats get stolen from around here all the time.'

'I think it's a little more serious than a temporary theft, Mr Chaucer,' said Roper. He put Chaucer somewhere in his early forties, his grey suit hand-stitched, the ostentatious watch on his right wrist a waterproof Rolex. There was obviously a lot of money in bread. 'Did you know about the damage under the dashboard, sir?'

'Yes,' said Chaucer. 'Sam Hawkesley rang me as soon as he found it, and told me that the boat had probably been stolen.'

'But you didn't notice it yourself?'

'No,' said Chaucer. 'Frankly, I didn't look. I went down to the boat last night to give the engine a run-up. I couldn't get it started, so I contacted Sam first thing this morning. And that's it. All I know.' He spread his hands in a gesture of artless sincerity. 'And the boat—if it *was* stolen—has been brought back again. So I'm really not bothered.'

More like a prosperous bookmaker than a baker, well fed and squeaky clean, and with the whitest hands Roper had seen in years. Like most plump men on the verge of

running to seed, Chaucer's pink bland face was wider at
the bottom than it was at the top.

'Was the boat padlocked to its moorings, Mr Chaucer?'

'Just tied.'

'And you hadn't noticed it missing?'

'It had been there all the time,' said Chaucer. 'So far
as I was aware.' He jerked a thumb over his shoulder
towards the window behind him. 'I can see it from here.'

'Unless it went missing at night.'

'Yes, that's possible,' agreed Chaucer. 'But I'm here
most nights until well after ten o'clock. So it would have
had to be stolen quite late.'

'Much petrol in the tank, was there?'

'A couple of gallons,' said Chaucer, shrugging. 'That's
all. I keep it low for that very reason. In case it ever gets
stolen, that is.'

'How far would a couple of gallons take you?'

'About twenty miles. To Poole, say.'

Which, to Roper's mind, was *more* than far enough.
About six times more than far enough. Chaucer's leather-
topped reproduction—and very expensive—desk was immaculately tidy, his filing-trays of smoky-grey plastic
suitably trendy and almost empty. The business was obviously profitable enough to run to a desk-top computer,
on a trolley near the window, and an Olivetti electric
typewriter on a table nearby. A new navy-blue raincoat
with a silk lining hung on the coat-stand beside the door.
In the next room someone was using a typewriter.

The castors of Chaucer's luxurious executive-chair
creaked as he shuffled it closer to his desk, folded his
arms on his tooled-leather blotter, and did his courteous
best to mask his impatience.

'I don't intend making a formal complaint, Superintendent.' Another smooth smile for Roper and another one in the direction of Rodgers—a salesman's smile, drawing in their confidence like a net full of fat fish. 'And I'm sure you're busy enough already.'

'When did you last use the boat, sir?' asked Roper.

'Sunday,' said Chaucer, settling back again, and clearly irritated that Roper was going to be persistent. 'Afternoon. I took it out around the sandbar and back again. With the youngsters.'

'Youngsters, sir?'

'I'm divorced,' said Chaucer. 'It was my weekend to have the children.'

'And you didn't use it after Sunday?'

'No,' said Chaucer.

'You didn't use it late on Monday, sir? A couple of hours either side of midnight, say?'

Chaucer's expression revealed nothing. 'No,' he said. 'Definitely not.'

'Did you know a Mrs Hannah Blezard, sir?'

'Yes,' said Chaucer. 'Not well. But, yes, I knew her. Chamber of Commerce, Yacht Club, all the usual things. You know how it is in business.'

'What sort of lady was she, Mr Chaucer, in your opinion?'

'Oh,' said Chaucer, searching for the apt words with his forehead puckered, 'intelligent, charming…good-looking…not short of a few shillings. She was a director of Blezard's Electronics on the industrial estate. Widowed about three years ago. A damned nice woman.'

Not quite the way Mrs Crispin had seen her, but still….

'Did you ever take her out in your cruiser, sir? Any time?'

'No,' said Chaucer. 'Well, not exactly. We didn't go

out together, but she did borrow it once. Back in the summer that was. The tail end. Early September.'

'Went out alone in it, did she?'

'No,' said Chaucer. 'With her nephew.'

Which brought Roper up short. Because if Mrs Blezard had had no next of kin, then she could not possibly have had a nephew. Or everyone he and his team had spoken to so far was lying in his teeth.

'Met this nephew, did you, sir?'

'Yes, of course,' said Chaucer. 'I had to show him how to operate the cruiser.'

'Could you describe him, sir?'

'Yes, I think so.'

Chaucer pushed his blotter fractionally away, and for a few moments stared down at it like a crystal ball.

'Tall,' he said. 'Dark. About twenty. Could have been younger—I'm not very good at guessing ages. Shorts and a T-shirt. Well-built sort of lad. Nicely spoken.'

'Local accent, d'you think?'

'Definitely a touch,' said Chaucer. 'Not markedly so; but, yes, I'd say he was definitely a Dorset lad.'

'Did you ever see him before, sir—or since?'

'Since,' said Chaucer. 'Or, rather, someone very like him,' he added cautiously. 'I couldn't be sure.'

'This someone very like him,' prompted Roper. 'How was he like him?'

Chaucer considered that, clearly not wishing to make a fool of himself. 'It's probably only a passing resemblance,' he said, 'but there's a lad from the local boys' school comes in here from time to time with a few of his friends. Lunchtimes. They pick up sandwiches. I think they take them across to the park.'

Roper felt the presence of that schoolboy again. Mrs

Crispin had seen him, Hollister and Westlake had seen him. Was Chaucer talking about that same boy?

'Could he possibly have been the *same* lad, sir?'

Chaucer pondered. 'Well, of course,' he said, 'the school uniform *might* have made the difference. Stripped down, he *could* have looked older.'

'He didn't seem to recognise you, sir, whenever it was he came into the shop?'

'Deadpan,' said Chaucer. 'That's why I thought it wasn't the same lad.'

And the lad would, thought Roper, have stayed deadpan, and certainly if he hadn't been Mrs Blezard's nephew, and certainly if he had been party to the deception of Mr Chaucer on the day the cruiser was borrowed. To have done otherwise would have given the game away.

He sized up Chaucer again. That suit, those rings and that watch, the green carpet on the floor and the expensive desk with its green leather top. Chaucer did, so the parlance had it, foot the bill. He was the right age, moderately wealthy, a local big-shot; and, more relevantly, he owned the cabin cruiser that very likely had carried Mrs Blezard's body out to sea before it was tipped over the side. And as for the hot-wiring of the starter motor and the ignition—well, Roper had come across faked evidence all too often before.

Roper lifted his elbows to the arms of his chair and propped his chin on his clasped hands. 'Do you mind telling us where you were on Monday night, sir? Between nine o'clock and midnight, say.'

Chaucer remained imperturbable. 'I was here,' he said. 'Working.'

'Alone, sir?'

'Quite alone.'

'Until when, sir?'

For the first time a twitch of irritability passed across the smooth plump face.

'About ten forty-five,' said Chaucer.

Which, if Roper's current theories were on the right lines, meant that Mr Chaucer must have been up here in his office when the cruiser was stolen. He rose from his chair and went to the window. It was double-glazed, so perhaps Chaucer might not have heard anything; but he could see clearly the gap in the moorings where the cruiser had been until Hawkesley had winched it up to his workshop.

'And after ten forty-five, sir? What then?'

From the back view he now had Roper noticed Chaucer's shoulders stiffen distinctly.

'I went along to the Wellington.' Chaucer glanced up sideways. The sticking-plaster smile was gone. 'And, if all this is leading up to a suggestion that I might have killed Mrs Blezard, you're barking up the wrong bloody tree.'

He and Roper were eye to eye.

'Well, did you, sir?' Roper asked equably.

'No, of course I bloody didn't,' retorted Chaucer, slowly coming to the boil now. 'What the hell reason would I have?'

'I don't know, sir,' said Roper. 'You tell me.'

'Are *you* bloody accusing me, Superintendent?'

'Of course not, sir,' said Roper. He returned to his chair. 'But supposing I told you that Mrs Blezard was out in your boat on Monday night.'

'Then, I know nothing about it,' snapped Chaucer. 'Absolutely nothing. I was up here. I called into the Wellington. I went home.'

No, he could not remember the time he had gone along

to the Duke of Wellington. Not exactly. But it was between the first and second bells.

'Did you meet anyone you know, sir?'

'No,' said Chaucer, still testy. 'But I expect the barmaid'll remember me.'

'Good,' said Roper. Thinking about it, Chaucer could have done it. Killed Mrs Blezard. Driven the Sovereign with her body in it, to the front door of his shop. Carried it through to the backyard. Dumped it aboard the cruiser, taken it out to sea and got back again and still have been in the Wellington by a few minutes to eleven on Monday night. Chaucer might look soft, but he wasn't. He was short and stocky, and the bulk under that smart suit wasn't all tailor's padding. He could have slung Mrs Blezard's body over his shoulder with comparative ease....

Slipping his own smile back into place and causing Chaucer to drop his guard, Roper asked: 'Do you know anybody who disliked her enough to kill her, Mr Chaucer? A lover perhaps?'

It happened sometimes. What Roper called a magic moment, a question pulled out of the bag for no better reason than that it happened to be lying about on top, and being rewarded with a physical response that was definitely on the shifty side. In Chaucer's case, it was the eyes. Too steady.

'I can't think of anyone. I didn't know her that well. I told you.'

'And yet you lent her that very expensive boat, sir,' Roper reminded him, smiling beguilingly. 'Surprises me, that does, sir. A few thousand pounds' worth of boat, lent to a lady and her nephew on the off-chance.'

Chaucer tried to hold the stare, but Roper held it the longer. If ever there was a man sinking fast, it was Arthur Chaucer.

Chaucer toyed uncomfortably with the corners of his blotter. Buying time.

'We were lovers,' he said. 'A long time ago. You'd have found that out in the end anyway.'

Roper waited.

Chaucer glanced up from the blotter, probably expecting a censorious eye looking back. But Roper had learned not to be censorious a long, long time ago. The human race was no longer capable of surprising him in any way.

'A few months,' volunteered Chaucer. 'It was shortly after her husband died. She was widowed, I was just divorced. Then I met someone else, and I think she did, too.'

'So you did know her that well, Mr Chaucer. Despite what you said just now?'

Chaucer nodded tiredly. 'Yes,' he said. 'I'm sorry.' He passed a weary thumb and forefinger across his eyebrows. 'But it really was all over before it got started.'

'But you stayed friends?'

'Yes,' said Chaucer. 'Difficult to do otherwise. But we parted amicably enough. I certainly had no reason to kill her.'

Roper measured him again. He certainly didn't look as if he'd killed somebody within the last few days; but by the same token he didn't look much like a lover, either. Although Roper had long since stopped trying to account for people's tastes in bedmates.

'Anything else you'd like to tell us, Mr Chaucer?'

There clearly was. The set of the shoulders said it, the downward gaze at the blotter said it. All the signs of a man who wants to get the last of the dirty water off his chest once and for all.

'Well, Mr Chaucer?'

Chaucer stirred uncomfortably in his captain's chair.

On his desk the back of his right thumb was being massaged by the front of his left with great concentration. Beyond the window behind him, the spire of the minster was veiled by the rain again.

'I lent her money,' he said. He spoke as if the words had been squeezed from him. 'Quite a lot. She told me she would pay me back within the month. She didn't.'

'How much, sir?'

A long pause. Roper could hear the rain through it.

Chaucer's gaze lifted at last, the stroking thumb stilled. 'Ten thousand,' he said. 'Cash. She told me she wanted it for a bridging loan.'

Folly upon folly, thought Roper. Another of Mrs Blezard's lapses of liquidity.

'IOU, sir? Did she give you one?'

Chaucer shook his head. 'I trusted her. No reason to do otherwise.'

'When was this, sir?'

'About six weeks ago. Soon after she and her nephew borrowed the boat. I called on her last Saturday night. She promised to pay me back at least half of it by this Wednesday—yesterday, that is.'

'What time did you *leave* her house, sir? On Saturday.'

'It was Sunday when I left, as a matter of fact. About three in the morning.'

So it must have been Chaucer's car that Hollister had seen and heard.

According to Chaucer, Mrs Blezard had told him that she intended to sell her house in Witling Lane and needed the ten thousand as a bridging loan for the one she had intended to purchase. And from the conversation subsequently it was obvious that Chaucer believed that Mrs B had in fact owned the property in Witling Lane. Mr Chaucer had, it seemed, been conned. And perhaps had

come to realise it. And, if he had, he had had a motive
to kill her; that much was certain. And he had spent most
of Monday evening alone and unobserved. He had a boat.

But these were early days, and Chaucer was unlikely
to go far. As Roper rose and buttoned his raincoat, it was
evident that Chaucer was relieved, loosing another bright
shaft of his salesman's sunshine to embrace both Roper
and Rodgers in his pinchbeck warmth as he showed them
out.

RODGERS CLOSED the door with the side of his foot, a
steaming plastic cup depending from the thumb and forefinger of each hand. He passed one across the desk to
Roper and sipped from the other.

Roper lit a cheroot.

'I didn't exactly fall for him,' said Rodgers, 'but he
wouldn't have needed to hot-wire his own boat, would
he?'

'Depends,' said Roper, tucking his lighter away. 'If
you'd wanted to spirit a dead body away in your boat,
you might tell the same story.' He reached for an ashtray.
'How did you get on with the Blezard's Electronics people last night, by the way?'

'They were all fairly normal,' said Rodgers. He rested
his behind against the edge of Price's desk and took out
his notebook, licked a thumb to flip through a few pages.

'Mr de Souza—he was an Anglo-Indian. Very bright.
He's in charge of design and development. Married. Two
youngsters. He and Blezard started the business together—twelve years ago. Blezard was the cash and the
contacts, and de Souza was the ideas man. I got the impression they started off in a lock-up garage with a couple
of coils of wire and a soldering-iron and a lot of navy-

surplus navigation equipment, which they got working and then sold off to little boatyards like Hawkesley's.'

'How did he get on with Mrs Blezard?' asked Roper over his coffee.

'He didn't,' said Rodgers. 'Nor did the other two directors I spoke to. The Blezards got married in Brighton, by the way, sir. Registry office. About ten years ago.'

'Good lad,' said Roper, making a note. That at least would save the lengthy search in St Catherine's House. 'Look into that later, will you?'

'Will do.' Rodgers turned another page. 'And Mr de Souza can account for his movements on Monday night. He was up in London with his wife. Theatre. They stayed the night with her sister in Dulwich and caught the train back here on Tuesday morning.'

Rodgers turned to another page.

'Mr Oliver Dexter. Single. With a living-in lady friend. Runs a souped-up Lotus. About thirty-five to forty. The lady friend says he was with her all Monday evening. A bit flash, I thought. Both of 'em.' Rodgers rocked his left hand, palm downward. 'Like that, sir. Dodgy. He's Blezard's sales director. Always nipping abroad. And he didn't like Mrs Blezard, either; and said that none of the others did if only they were honest about it.'

'Did he say why?'

'She showed no interest in the company at all, sir. She often didn't show up at board meetings, and when she did she was usually late. And the directors all take a regular salary, which is based on their holding in the company. Which means she takes home ten per cent for doing nothing. And they all knew she was two-timing Mr Blezard when he was alive. Which is another reason they didn't like her.'

'Who's the last one?'

'Mr Tiptree. Laurence Tiptree. He's the Managing Director. Looks after the works and the day-to-day running of things. Married. Forty-five-ish. Looks the kind of bloke who's run off his feet. He was at the factory on Monday night until eight-thirty. Then drove straight home. He lives at Wareham. But his wife was at her bridge club until midnight, so there's nobody to confirm. And he thought the sun shone out of Jack Blezard, by the way, like de Souza. Tiptree joined the company about a year after Blezard and de Souza got started. So they all go back a long way together—except Dexter.'

Roper sipped at his coffee.

'Did any of them mention Marshall?'

'Only Tiptree, sir. In passing. Said he was a solid reliable bloke. Works like a Trojan and never takes a holiday. Keeps a tight rein on the money, and if any of the other directors comes up with an idea that's a bit on the airy-fairy side Marshall brings him back to earth with a wallop.'

'Any likely villains among them?'

Rodgers shook his head.

'No, sir,' he said. 'I'd say they'd all got too much to lose—and they're all a bit worried about who Mrs B's left her shares to.'

'None of them knows, then?'

'No, sir,' said Rodgers. 'It's a bit of a mystery to them, too.'

'Right,' said Roper. 'Get in touch with Brighton CID first. See if they can sort out Mrs Blezard's marriage lines and ask them to send us a photocopy of the relevant page of the register or a copy of the certificate. Then phone County and ask them to rustle up a posse of cadets and get them here by lunch-time. Door to door. They're looking for a white bicycle with dropped handlebars. They'll

want street-maps. You take charge of all that, and give
me a buzz if you find anything. And you'd better have a
chat with Mrs Blezard's cleaning woman. She might
know something.'

Rodgers went, glad to be doing something construc-
tive.

ELEVEN O'CLOCK. Still the morning of Day Two and very
little accomplished. A few minutes ago a motorcyclist
had ridden off to Forensic with a couple of hair samples
carefully unwound from the propeller gland of Arthur
Chaucer's cabin cruiser. Although it was already Roper's
certain hunch that those hairs had come from the scalp
of Mrs Blezard. By noon, the cruiser itself would also be
across in the vehicle shed at Forensic. Which might, or
might not, turn the hunch into unassailable fact. And if
it did, then Roper was going to pay another visit to Chaucer the baker.

He sat on the edge of his desk, an unlit cheroot in his
hand, and cast a slow and hopeful eye over the mosaic
of photographs stuck to the wall. But they revealed no
more than they had last night. A drowned woman. A
jetty. A slipway. A row of moored boats. Including Chaucer's white cruiser.

Sex was involved somewhere. When a woman was
murdered, eight times out of ten sex was at the root of
it. An obsession with sex, or a lack of it, on someone's
part. A lover. Or an ex-lover. Like Arthur Chaucer. Or a
psychopath lurking on the off-chance in a lonely lane
somewhere. Except that Mrs Blezard had been murdered
in her own house. And there had been no sign so far of
a forced entry; nor had there been a need to force because
she had left the conservatory door open, hadn't she? And
no burglar or housebreaker would have made such com-

plicated arrangements to dispose of a body. In, out, and away—that was the housebreaker's dictum. They would have left the body in the pool, where it was, and quit the scene as fast as their legs could carry them, and hoped to God they'd got away with it.

An invited visitor was more likely. Perhaps the conservatory door had been left open for him. Mr Size Eleven, perhaps. Or one of the Messrs Size Eights. Except that no size-eight prints had been found between the conservatory door and the door to the lounge. So perhaps the size eights had been let in through the front door, and left that way. But it *had* been Mr Size Eleven who had been invited to stay and chat over a cup of coffee. And he had worn training-shoes.

A jogger?

A cyclist?

Mrs Crispin had told Roper that the boy on the bicycle had worn white shoes. And the likeliest kind of white shoes that a boy would wear on a bicycle would be a pair of trainers. Ergo....

The telephone rang.

Roper reached behind him.... The likeliest villain was still the boy on the bicycle.... Because the two size eights must have come in through the front door. But the boy on the bicycle had crept in the back way....

'Roper.'

Except that he had been invited to stay for coffee....

'It's Sergeant Harvey, sir. Downstairs at the desk.'

'What do you want, Sergeant?'

'I've tried to get in touch with Mr Butcher, sir, but he's in court. WDC Anderson's just radioed in. She's up at Harbour End. A place called Rope Walk. Number thirty-one. She was looking into a peeping complaint, sir.

And she's found a body, sir. Says it looks like a stabbing. She needs assistance, sir. Preferably a senior officer.'

Something at the back of Roper's mind surfaced like a bubble of gas in a pond.

'A peeper, you say, Sergeant?'

'Yes, sir,' replied the Sergeant, unaware of the hare he had sent coursing.

'Who's the victim?'

'He is, sir. The peeper. Alleged; but Anderson's pretty sure he was.'

'Tell her I'll be there,' said Roper. 'And phone Mrs Blezard's house. Contact DS Makins and tell him to meet me at—where was it?' Roper reached hurriedly to his other side for a jotter.

'Rope Walk, sir. Number thirty-one. I'll have a constable ready down here to show you the way.'

'Good,' said Roper. 'Thank you.'

The phone went back on its rest. And the cheroot was finally lit with a feeling of getting somewhere at last.

Because a peeper, even a dead one, might be just what Roper was looking for.

NINE

ROPER SQUEEZED his way between the piles of cardboard cartons, old furniture, antiquated television sets, and God alone knew what other old rubbish littering the dingy and tomcat-smelling hallway. The house was a late-Victorian labourer's cottage in an advanced state of decay, slate-roofed, two up and two down, no shades on the electric lights and peeling brown wallpaper that hadn't been changed in thirty years. In the front room, the curtains were still closed on more mounds of junk, one shrouded by an old bedsheet.

WDC Anderson was sitting at the bottom of the stairs, in the shadows, her radio still in her hand and her head hanging loosely between her knees, obviously still in shock.

He crouched in front of her.

'DC Anderson?'

She lifted her head, whey-faced and doing her best to pull herself together. She nodded, started to rise. Roper reached out and stopped her. He could feel her still trembling.

'Stay where you are,' he said. 'Where is he?'

'The scullery,' she said.

He squeezed past more junk and boxes wedged against the stairs. He could smell it before he saw it. Even stronger than the stench of tomcats. A smell like a butcher's shop. Only sweeter and more ominous.

He stopped at the doorway into the scullery, a knot of bile rising in his gullet and lodging there, and a ball of sour gas following it and making him gag on it. He forced it all back with difficulty. Dear God in Heaven.

More travelled blood than he had seen in years. Over the walls, across the ceiling, on the sink, the gas-stove, the cupboards, the back door, even over a table with the makings of a bread and cheese and pickle meal on it. Everywhere; shiny blobs dried to the colour of rust. At their epicentre the kneeling body of a man propped against the china sink, his lustreless eyes wide open and his mouth gaped wide in a frozen scream that probably no one had heard except his killer.

'Jesus,' Roper muttered softly, and was glad to turn away and squeeze back past the boxes.

WDC Anderson was on her feet, a cigarette stuffed into her mouth, and shakily trying to strike a flame from her lighter.

Roper struck his and held it to the wavering tip of her cigarette. His own hand, he noticed, was not all that steady, either.

She exhaled smoke. Against the pallor of her face, her eye make-up looked like bruises, her lipstick a red wound.

'Thanks,' she said. She plucked a shred of tobacco from her underlip. 'I'm sorry,' she said. 'I was doing all right—then I just corpsed.'

'Did you touch him?'

She shook her head. 'Just to feel for a pulse. There wasn't one.'

'Did you see a likely-looking knife?'

She shook her head, still doing her best to fight off her shakes. She was only a youngster, twenty-two or -three at the most, and all the police courses and training colleges in the world never prepared anybody for a mess like that one in the scullery.

'It's OK if I smoke, is it?'

No, it wasn't, but still....

'I shouldn't think a bit more dust in this place'll do any harm, would you?' said Roper. A cardboard box beside him looked solid enough to take his weight. He sat himself tentatively on it. Anderson perched herself back on the second-to-bottom stair.

She drew on her cigarette again and exhaled luxuriously. Under her smart raincoat she was wearing a grey sweater and black slacks. Dark and slim, the sort Makins always made his bee-line for. A nice-looking girl.

'How come you found him?'

She snatched at another lungful of smoke, and blew it out again.

'Woman across the street. Her husband called into the station last evening. Said he wanted to lay a formal complaint. A peeper....' Her head tipped backward towards the kitchen. 'Him. Oates. Mr Butcher asked me to get a statement from the wife, just to be on the safe side, and I did. And she pointed the finger *straight* at Oates, so I thought I'd come across and see him—Oates—and the front door was open—and I knocked and no one answered—so I came in. And found him. Like that.'

'Then what?' asked Roper.

'I radioed for assistance.'

'What time did you get here?'

'Eleven o'clock. I think. About twenty minutes after I first called on Mrs Cole across the street.'

'And Jack the lad in there was the peeper, was he?'

'Definitely.' Anderson jabbed upwards with her cigarette. 'I've had a quick look upstairs. He had all the gear. A sort of peri-telescope—an army-surplus thing—a bloody great pair of Japanese binoculars and enough cameras to open a shop with. And he did his own processing. The back bedroom's fitted out like a darkroom, with all the works.'

'And pictures?'

'Only a few. In an album.' Her mouth stretched in disgust. 'Kids mostly. Little girls; you know.' She was almost back in control of herself again. 'And his bedroom's the absolute pits. Centrefolds on the walls and fag-ash all over the floor. Like a pig in shit, sir, if you'll excuse the expression. But that's the picture.'

'Graphic,' said Roper. 'Thank you. How about the rest of the place?'

'Like a tip. He was a secondhand dealer—at least, that's what he calls himself on the side of his van—and he's got form, so Mr Butcher said. But I've only been on the patch six weeks, so I don't really know all the ins and outs.'

'And his name's Oates, you say?'

'Norman Oates.'

'Have you organized a doctor yet?'

'I radioed the station for the police doctor. About ten minutes ago.'

'Good,' said Roper. He weighed her carefully. A few minutes ago he had been in half a mind to send her back to the station, but she was clearly a young woman with her wits about her and what was in that scullery might be her first dead body but it certainly would not be her last.

'Feel like work?' he said.

'Yes, sir,' she said. 'Really. I'm fine.'

'Ever been on a murder inquiry before?'

'Not yet.'

Roper got up from his carton, Anderson from her uncarpeted wooden stair.

'Well, you're on one now,' he said. 'Radio in to the

station and get them to contact County. Tell them we
need Mr Wilson here—he's the Home Office pathologist.
Suspected foul play. We'll also need a couple of technicians to sort out the dabs. And a photographer. And the
Coroner's Officer. Can you remember all that?'

'Yes, sir.'

'And when you've done that take a good look around
upstairs, but touch nothing you don't have to. And you're
looking for a knife. All right?'

The colour was back in her face. She nodded. 'Got it,'
she said.

'Good,' said Roper. 'Off you go.'

ROPER HEARD Makins's stomach heave as they stood together in the scullery doorway.

'Bloody hell,' muttered Makins, briefly looking away
and closing his eyes, then forcing himself to look again.
'Bloody-bloody Nora.'

'My sentiments exactly,' agreed Roper. 'Poor sod.'

The police doctor, Evans, with his feet carefully astride
to avoid the puddles of congealed blood on the quarry
tiles, had a fingertip placed below Oates's right ear and
his stethoscope pressed between Oates's shoulderblades.
He shook his head and moved the stethoscope down a
little, then across a little. And listened. To no effect. He
straightened and took off his stethoscope.

'Yes,' he said. 'He's very dead, Superintendent. I'm
sorry. Multiple stab wounds to chest and stomach. Six
wounds that I can see without moving him.' Doctor or
not, even Evans was appalled. 'There must be three or
four pints of blood splashed about. My God.' He shud-
dered as he looked around and stepped carefully back to
the scullery doorway where Roper and Makins were.
They stood aside for him in what little space there was.

'How long, Doctor?' asked Roper. 'Any idea?'

Evans could only guess.

'Twelve, thirteen hours, perhaps. I can't hazard better than that. I'm afraid it's a specialist's job.'

AND THE SPECIALIST didn't like it, either. Wilson had arrived a few minutes ago. As yet he had touched nothing, on his face still a grimace of distaste.

Oates still lay propped as Roper had first seen him, his legs folded under him so that it looked as if he were kneeling, his left shoulder wedged under the sink and his left cheek pressed against its cold china like a dead lover. His right hand still clasped his belly; congealed oozed blood between his fingers and over the thighs of his greasy grey trousers. Five parallel stripes of blood down the front of the sink looked like smears left by a bloody hand, as if Oates had clung to the sink in his last extreme before subsiding to his knees on the tiles. There were a couple of handprints, too, on the chipped Formica top of the table, their smudged edges trailing off in the general direction of the sink. Oates had not died quickly.

Wilson stood aside.

'Front, back and profile, please.'

The photographer stepped forward. In the lightning stroke of his first flash, Oates's body seemed to jerk. But it was only a trick of the light.

ROPER FELT A TOUCH on his arm. He turned. It was Makins.

'Thought you ought to see this,' he said. 'DC Anderson's just found it upstairs.'

Pressing it open, he held out a notebook. Names and telephone numbers. 'Top right hand,' he said.

Roper took the notebook. Cheap. Red-covered. About

the size of a pocket diary. Years old and well thumbed. A lot of the early entries scratched through.

And Mrs Blezard's name and telephone number, illiterately scrawled on the top line of the right-hand page that Makins had been holding open.

'And there's a darkroom upstairs,' said Makins. 'All the gear.'

Roper was flipping backwards through the notebook. More names, more telephone numbers, a few addresses.

'How about photographs?'

'Someone's beaten us to it,' said Makins. 'The fireplace in the upstairs front bedroom is full of ashes. Photos *and* negatives. But from the few pictures up there I'd say he was into little girls.'

'Show me,' said Roper.

He followed Makins upstairs. WDC Anderson was in the front bedroom, kneeling in front of the cast-iron grate and turning over the feathery black ashes in it with the end of a ballpoint. Beside her, on the hearthrug, were a few scraps of less charred fragments she had so far managed to salvage and which might turn out later to mean something.

'Anything useful?' asked Roper.

'Nothing I can make anything of,' she said. 'They're mostly edges and corners.'

Roper's eyes slowly raked the room. Unmade bed, lurid centrefolds of overly endowed young women Sellotaped to the faded yellow wallpaper, a pair of expensive binoculars lying among a clutter of dusty knick-knacks and junk on top of the chest of drawers by the window. And leaning against the window-ledge, with its eyepiece on the floor, some kind of tubular optical gadget that looked like an old army periscope, or perhaps it had been part of an artillery gun sight. In either case, it was a peeper's tool of some sort or other. A Pentax camera on the bed had its back open; and the film that had been inside it had been ripped out of its cassette, which was still in the camera, perhaps by someone who didn't have the knack of taking that out, too. Several new cardboard boxes were wedged under a dressing-table with a cracked mirror, and another one was half-hidden under the bed.

'What's in the cartons?' asked Roper.

'Transistor radios,' said Makins. 'Hong Kong. With delivery notes addressed to Oates. I've checked with the supplier. They're legit.'

Roper considered. His resources were thinly stretched and, strictly speaking, this wasn't his murder—except for the tenuous connection of Mrs Blezard's name in Oates's notebook, which could mean anything or nothing.

'Leave that for now,' he said to Anderson. He held out Oates's notebook. 'Ring around some of these numbers. See what you come up with. Anything they've got in common. Use a public phone.'

Anderson went downstairs with the notebook, Roper and Makins to the rear bedroom.

The front bedroom had been merely disorderly. This one had been ransacked. Drawers and cupboard doors hung open, an old wardrobe had been pulled away from the wall. Spilled photographic equipment lay scattered on the floor, cameras, lenses, an electronic flashgun, bottles of chemicals. What looked like a new packet of ten-by-eight printing-paper had been ripped open and its contents shot to the floor. The window was blacked out with a sheet of hardboard. On a bench stood an expensive enlarger, a couple of trays of liquid chemicals beside it. There was no print paper in either of the trays, nor in the stainless-steel sink nearby.

With the toe of his shoe, Roper tipped over the yellow

Kodak envelope whence the print-paper had been spilled; there was a smear of blood on it. There was another smear on the white china knob of a drawer—and a few more rusty brown spots on the lino.

This havoc had not been created by Oates. It had been done by his killer. Afterwards.

Someone had been up here looking for something. Someone with blood, literally, on his hands. And perhaps, in his panic, he had run out of time, scooped up every picture and negative he was able to find and simply burned it all because looking for something in the very particular was taking too long.

'How does this grab you?' asked Makins.

It was a photo-album, bulging with prints between its red plastic covers. Black-and-white prints, all of school-girls. Little girls playing in swimming-pools, little girls playing netball in schoolyards, bigger girls playing hockey, school-girls in their uniforms queuing at bus-stops. The compressed perspective showed that most had been taken with a long-focus lens, and the murkiness of some—mostly the ones snapped out of doors—led Roper to guess that they had probably been taken behind the cover of a car windscreen.

'Nasty,' he said, handing it back to Makins, noticing distastefully as he did that there was a brown stain on the spine, which might be yet more dried blood.

LIKE A toppled waxwork, Oates lay on his side on a pink rubber sheet, still immovably in rigor, his knees drawn up, his head still locked to one side, a frozen hand still clutching his stomach. An outline in yellow chalk on the front of the sink and on the quarry tiles showed where he had drawn his last breath.

The blood-stained slashes in his shirt had been checked

to ensure that they all aligned with the wounds in the flesh beneath. The police surgeon had been right. Oates had been stabbed six times. There was also a deep gash across the palm of his left hand; Wilson had suggested that Oates had probably made a grab for the knife-blade.

'What about those bruises around his ribs?' asked Roper. There were three of them, yellow stains with pale green edges, low down on Oates's pale and skinny rib-cage.

'Probably got himself involved in a fight,' said Wilson. But, since the bruises had had time to develop, it was his considered opinion that the bruises were at least twelve to thirteen hours older than the stab wounds. Not, thought Roper, that that ruled out a connection between the two assaults. Oates might have been involved in a petty feud with another of his ilk, a running battle of some sort.

It was, however, a particularly clumsy killing.

'Certainly not a professional job, I'd say,' said Wilson. 'Whoever did this one had never handled a knife in his life—except at the dinner-table.' He thrust home the ther-mometer which would measure Oates's liver temperature. His guess at the moment was that Oates had been dead for twelve hours—give or take a couple. Which made the death a couple of hours either side of midnight. And it was very likely that Oates had died from none of the wounds in particular, but from all of them. He had bled to death; would have been unconscious inside five minutes and dead within another ten.

'What sort of weapon are we looking for?' asked Roper. 'Any ideas?'

Wilson took a magnifying glass from his case, and with a plastic-sheathed finger and thumb stretched one of the gashes wider to determine its shape more exactly. He peered through the glass. Then did the same to a wound lower down, a couple of inches below Oates's navel.

'Single-edged,' said Wilson, through his mask. 'Thin—and about an inch wide. Could have been a carving-knife. Something from in here, perhaps.'

Or equally, perhaps, thought Roper, this killing had been premeditated; in which case the killer would have brought his weapon with him and, if he was sensible, taken it away with him.

'And not a professional job?'

'Doubt it,' said Wilson. 'Too wild. Looks as if whoever did it just stuck the knife in wherever he could. Definitely an amateur.'

'There's a fair bit of blood about,' observed Roper.

'The killer would have been smothered in it,' said Wilson. 'Photograph, please.'

The photographer's electronic flash plopped over Oates's chest and stomach.

So Jack the lad, whoever he was, would have left here last night drenched with blood. Had he walked home, or driven home? Was he another petty villain like Oates? Someone Oates had double-crossed?

Wilson withdrew his thermometer from Oates's liver, carefully wiped it and tipped its graduations towards the window, then fed the reading into a pocket calculator together with a couple of constants. Then sat back on his heels and took a guess at Oates's bodyweight; because thin bodies cool quicker than obese ones, and a fit body more slowly than a decrepit one.

'Perhaps he's been dead longer than I thought,' he hazarded at last. 'Say thirteen or fourteen hours.'

Which put Oates's killing back nearer to ten o'clock last night. Plus or minus.

'Any other thoughts?' asked Roper.

'Not for certain.' Wilson was dropping the instruments he had used into a plastic bottle of sterilising liquid and capping it. He arranged the bottle in his case, then peeled off his gloves. 'But, by the looks of them, most of the blows were delivered underarm....' Wilson mimed an upward stroke with a fist closed about an imaginary knife-handle. 'So it was probably a close-combat job. And he'd recently had a good hiding from somebody else.'

Wilson dropped his gloves into a plastic bag and sealed it. The door-knocker thudded. Makins went to answer it. It was WDC Anderson.

'Any luck?' Roper asked her, as she came down the passage.

'I've only rung eight of the numbers so far, sir,' she said, 'but I might have come up with something important. They're all women who live on their own—and they've all had dirty phone calls. Three say they reported them to us.'

'Good,' said Roper. Because eight calls out of eight had made it pretty obvious why Oates had kept his little red notebook. It might also mean that Mrs Blezard had been the recipient of similar nasty calls; and might also account for one or two of the blank passages on the tape of her answering machine. 'Now I'd like you to go back to the station and ring all the others. And contact Records; see if Oates has got a form-sheet. And, if he has, get 'em to telex a copy of it. Then type up your report on the peeping business across the street, with a copy for me, please. Leave it on my desk.'

ONE O'CLOCK CAME with a rush. Oates's body was across at the mortuary, and Wilson had gone to see the District coroner to sort out the legal details of the post-mortem examination.

In the mean time, Oates's cramped little cottage was a hive of quiet and methodical activity. Three technicians from Forensic were beavering away amongst the mayhem upstairs. Another technician was painstakingly quartering the kitchen, lifting and photographing fingerprints and handprints. And where he had been Roper followed, opening drawers and cupboards, still looking for a likely knife, even though his intuition told him it would not be here. Makins had gone around to the alley at the back, with a set of assorted car keys, to look over Oates's van.

The loaf of wrapped bread on the table was open, the block of Cheddar cheese beside it in an unopened vac-uum-pack. A slice of bread on the plate; spots of blood on both. A table knife with a knob of butter on it—on the table but with the blade of the knife hanging over the edge. A half-pound packet of butter, newly opened, the paper peeled back and a corner of the block of butter cut away. The knob of butter on the knife looked as if it had been cut from the corner. And the table, pushed hard against the wall, had not always been where it presently was. Four indentations in the lino showed where it *had* stood: some three or four inches closer to the back door. Maybe it had got jolted in the scuffle last night, which was also perhaps why the blade of the knife and the knob of butter on it were hanging over the edge and not resting on the plate.

So, Roper guessed, Oates had been here in the scullery last night when his killer had called. Just about to spread butter on the slice of bread. His first slice—because the cheese was unopened, and so was the blood-spattered jar of mustard pickle beside it.

The lock on the door between the scullery and the walled backyard was broken. The two bolts on it were drawn back. And the wooden gate between the yard and the alley behind was neither open nor closed, strictly speaking. It hung from one rusting hinge, and looked as if it had for some long time; four of its wooden featherboard palings were missing. Which left a fifteen-inch gap through which anyone could have squeezed—anyone, that is, of average build.

And if the killer *had* crept in through that rear entry, then it was more than likely that Oates had been taken by surprise. Quietly and unsuspectingly starting on his supper.

But he *had* put up a fight. That much was certain. The splashed blood about the place had travelled from several directions. At some time between the beginning of the scuffle and the end, Oates had made a grab for the knife, had clutched the edge of his table, probably with that same left hand, and then the edge of the china sink. Whence he had subsided to his knees, become unconscious, and subsequently bled to death.

Vicious. What tomorrow's tabloids would call 'a frenzied attack', and for once with some justification.

MAKINS MADE the really important connection at a quarter past one. Roper had moved upstairs.

'They're all glove-prints, sir,' the senior technician was telling him. He pointed to the white china knob on the chest of drawers in Oates's darkroom. 'If you look closely, you can see the stitch marks—and the pores in the leather.' He offered Roper his magnifying glass for his closer scrutiny. Roper took it; and it was at that juncture that he heard Makins rush in downstairs and say to someone, 'Where's the Super?' in the kind of voice that sounded as if Makins had found something.

'Up here,' called Roper.

Makins bounded up the stairs. Roper met him on the landing.

'What's up?'

Makins held out a bundle of rag. Red rag. Only, shaken into shape, it was a red shirt. With a sleeve ripped off at the armpit.

'And he *was* a peeper, wasn't he, sir?' suggested Makins.

Roper turned the shirt over. Greasy. Dark stains in the armpits. A cigarette burn on the collar. A couple of broken white buttons. A smell of engine oil and stale human sweat.

'Where did you find it?'

'His van,' said Makins. 'Under the driving-seat.'

'Good enough,' said Roper. 'Radio in for a motorcyclist and get it across to the lab. And tell 'em we want an answer today.'

Because, if the fabric of that shirt matched the fragment tweezered out from Mrs Blezard's conservatory window-frame, Norman Oates had not only been a peeper, but *the* peeper. Who had wiped clean a spyhole in the glass of Mrs Blezard's conservatory—with a piece of red rag—the better to see her through, or even to photograph her through.

And, maybe, even had to kill her because of it, however unlikely that scenario presently seemed.

TEN

ROPER LUNCHED at his desk. A ham roll and a polystyrene cup of soup, both from Chaucer's snack-bar further along the street.

This was the waiting time, the sweating-out time during which even the most dedicated copper is powerless, and must remain so until something new—a scrap of fresh evidence, an idea, or even a mite of luck—drops fortuitously into his lap. And two murders doubled the feeling of frustration; because now there were two. Half an hour ago, when Roper had reported in to the Assistant Chief Constable, he had been instructed to pick up the tab on Oates's murder as well.

None of Oates's neighbours had heard anything untoward last night. None had seen an unfamiliar car parked in the street; none had seen a suspicious caller knocking at Oates's front door, or loitering in the alley at the rear of the garden. And none of them *knew* Oates, except a neighbour with whom they passed the time of day; not that Oates always replied. According to some he was a surly neighbour, to a few others a furtive one. He was rarely seen about in the daytime, except in his van. More often than not, his van was heard returning in the small hours of the night. What he did for a living no one seemed certain, even the two couples who lived either side of him.

According to Mrs Cole, the red-headed young lady across the street, what Oates definitely was was a peeping Tom. The watcher had been watched of late. Whenever a young woman walked down the street, so said Mrs Cole, Oates's upstairs net curtains twitched. Sometimes a black disc of a camera lens appeared at a gap in them. And on Monday afternoon, after a bath, Mrs Cole had sat momentarily naked on the edge of her bed preparatory to getting dressed—and in the angled side-mirror of her dressing-table noticed a gap in those curtains across the street. And not one black disc but two. Which meant, according to her husband's deduction, that if Mrs Cole could see the gap in Oates's curtains in her dressing-mirror, then Oates could probably have seen Mrs Cole sitting naked on the edge of her bed. An enraged Mr Cole had called on Oates several times during the course of Monday and Tuesday evening, but Oates had either not been in or wisely chosen not to open his front door. Last night, Mr Cole had sensibly laid a formal complaint with the police.

Roper finished the ham roll and replaced the cap on the empty soup-cup. Chaucer made good bread, and didn't stint on his York ham. Paper plate and cup went into the wastepaper-bin, his raincoat off the hook on the door. Two-fifteen of a grey afternoon and the next port of call was Hawkesley's boatyard to sort out a small problem of geography.

He was in the passage and closing the door when the telephone rang. He quickly turned about, leaving the door swinging behind him.

'Roper.'

'Guthrie, Mr Roper. Are you sitting comfortably? Slate and chalk ready?'

Roper reached across the desk for his jotter.

'If I didn't know you better, Mr Guthrie, I'd say you'd been at the juice.'

'Only the juice of wisdom, Mr Roper,' said Guthrie.

'First, that nice little boat you sent us. The wheel and gear-stick only have Mr Hawkesley's prints on them. So we have to presume that whoever used it on the sly wiped them clean. We found an espadrille jammed under the bench at the stern. A very soggy espadrille. Black and white. Size six. Italian. Might not have been Mrs Blezard's, of course, but one usually finds shoes in pairs, does one not? And she *was* size six, was that good lady.'

'Indeed she was, Mr Guthrie.'

'And the hair samples,' said Guthrie. 'As a rule, I could only say that they *matched* the clippings we cut from Mrs Blezard. But she *dyed* her hair, and our chromatograph printouts from the clippings show twelve identifiable chemical substances, *all* of them identical with the dye in the hair we unwound from the boat. Which makes it about ninety per cent certain that *that* hair was hers, too.'

'And how about that red shirt, Mr Guthrie?'

'It matches the thread sample you sent us yesterday,' said Guthrie. 'But it does *only* match. There could be another five thousand red shirts like that in the country— but I only add that as a caution. If I had to put money on it, given the circumstances, I'd put my shirt on it, so to speak; I'd say your Mr Oates had definitely cleaned Mrs Blezard's conservatory window.'

'Good on you, Mr Guthrie,' said Roper, with an enthusiasm that at last matched Guthrie's. Two murder investigations veering off in two totally different directions were bad for the digestion. 'Greatly obliged to you.'

He laid the phone back in its cradle, ripped the page on which he had just written from his jotter, folded it and slipped it into his notebook. However trifling the connection was, a connection now definitely existed, and from little acorns great oaks did occasionally spring forth.

ROPER STOOD with Hawkesley on the jetty behind the boatshed. For the first time since early this morning it had stopped raining, and the sun shone brightly although it did nothing to warm. It was coming up for three o'clock in the afternoon.

'I want to borrow a boat from your moorings, Mr Hawkesley. It's dark. And I've got a car that I need to park close to the river so that I can transfer something from the car to the boat where no one's likely to see me. How would I go about that?'

Hawkesley chewed thoughtfully on the stem of his old briar pipe.

'How's your geography?'

'Let's assume I'm a local.'

'Then, it wouldn't be difficult,' said Hawkesley. He took his pipe from his mouth and pointed across the river with it, a quarter of a mile or so downstream from the minster. 'There's a road behind those reeds,' he said. 'Used to lead to the old sewage works. These days it goes nowhere, and you could have hidden your car in the trees.' The pipe stem swung slowly to the right. 'Then you could have walked back—through the minster grave-yard, across the precinct and out the other side—to the bridge. Over there.' The pipe stem was pointing to the south end of the stone road-bridge that Roper had first seen yesterday morning. 'Cross it. That would bring you out here to the High Street and then East Street to the old jetty at Harbour End. Along there—where all those cars are parked—it used to be the old wool-jetty.'

Hawkesley had turned to face downstream again, and was pointing towards the stone jetty on this north bank of the river where several ranks of parked cars glittered in the sunshine. It was about another quarter-mile beyond the reeded south bank where Roper had parked his own hypothetical car.

'And from there,' said Hawkesley, 'you could have walked back along this bank relatively unobserved, and taken the boat across to where you'd left your car.'

'Are there any other ways through to the river on this bank? Side-streets, back-alleys?'

'Only through someone's side-entrance and over their garden fence,' said Hawkesley. 'Only we people at this end have riparian rights. All those fences you can see further down this bank are maintained by the local council, and they're pretty solid. So I'd say you could only have done the transfer on the opposite bank.'

'How about down on the wool-jetty? Could I have done it there?'

'It's lit at night,' said Hawkesley.

'Thank you, Mr Hawkesley,' said Roper. 'Grateful to you.'

HE PARKED HIS Sierra in the narrow lane, lit a cheroot and took up a six-inches-to-the-mile Ordnance Survey map from the passenger-seat beside him. He opened the map over the steering-wheel to orientate himself.

The two spiked-top green metal gates a hundred yards or so ahead of him would be the entrance to the old sewage works. Chained and padlocked together, they made the lane into a cul-de-sac. The minster graveyard lay roughly a quarter of a mile behind him, and was bounded on the river bank by a six-foot wall. No way to the river from the graveyard. The lawns of the minster were bounded by a brick wall with tall railings on top of it all the way back to the bridge, which was lit all night. And, according to Hawkesley, the minster was floodlit until midnight, so nobody was likely to carry a body that

way. Opposite Hawkesley's yard was the river entrance
to the minster—where the ghouls had tried to gather yesterday morning—which was open to the public. But since
the minster had been built the river level had dropped
and the little stone pier was now eight or nine feet above
the water; and it was railed off, and there was no ladder.
So that was an equally unlikely route.

The body could have been transferred from the car to
the boat somewhere *beyond* the sewage works. To the
east. But, according to the map, it was open country in
that direction all the way to the river mouth on that bank.
And the contours showed rough going for a vehicle, and
only a couple of footpaths. It would have been too open.
And too far. Because the essence of everything would
have been time. No man with a dead body on his hands
would have wanted to hang about too long.

He took a pair of binoculars from the glove compart-
ment and climbed from the car. A faint smell of decayed
sewage still hung in the air round about.

The south side of the lane, to the right of the sewage-
works gateway, was bordered by a stout wire fence with
a tangled hedge pushing through it. This side was grass,
shrub and a few trees, and with plenty of places to hide
a car off the road at night. Closer to the river on this
bank the landscape was taken over by a rampart of tall
reeds, four or five feet high and very nearly impenetrable.
They covered the bank from the minster graveyard to the
sewage works, and perhaps even beyond that.

And the key lay in their *apparent* impenetrability. The
only way to get to the river was through them. To trample
them down. If Hawkesley's hypothesis was right, there
was either a way through them somewhere—or someone
had *made* a way through them—and hopefully as recently
as Monday night.

But where?

Near a tree. A tree within arm's reach of the river, because if Jack the lad had crossed the river in a boat he would have needed to tie it up somewhere while he did his dirty work. A tree easily identifiable from the opposite bank, so that he could bring his boat in to the exact spot where his car was. Or vice versa.

There were several willows beyond the reeds, but their branches would be trailing in the water and would have made it difficult to tie up at one, and equally difficult to get a body through the tangle of twigs and branches. So not a willow.

Some other tree, the trunk of which would be more accessible, close to the water.

Roper went deeper into the shrubbery and undergrowth and slowly scanned from right to left with the binoculars.

A clump of alder trees to the left. About halfway between here and the minster. Three of them. And, by the looks of them, at the very edge of the river.

He returned to the Sierra and backed it up the lane as far as the alders, climbed out again, still with the binoculars. Above the reeds, he could see the corrugated roof of Hawkesley's boatshed only a couple of hundred yards to his left, and the back of Chaucer's shop beside it.

Somewhere here. Had to be.

He walked to within twenty paces of the clump of alders. He could see their tops clearly above the reeds— and from the north bank, even at night, they would be prominent enough against the sky for anybody in a boat to home in on from the other side.

Slowly, then, he continued towards the alder clump, following the ragged interface of grass and reeds. The ground was muddy. A pity it would not have been as soft on Monday, before the rain.

His first *frisson* of triumph was short-lived. A swath of reeds *had* been trodden down just here, but not recently, and not deeply enough into them to give access to the river. And at second glance there was a rusty tin bath full of junk further in and over to the right. The only villainy committed there had been rubbish-dumping.

He dawdled on, eyes half on the ground, half on the reeds. There might not be a footprint, but with any luck there might be tyre depressions about somewhere.

And then he found it.

A narrow path trampled through the reeds. And lately. The blurred shape of a shoe every foot or so, the reeds between them still standing upright. And, from what Roper could see, the weaving passage looked as if it went all the way down to the river bank and the alder trees.

Cautiously and painstakingly Roper trod a path of his own, a foot away and parallel with the one he had just found. The river bank steepened, and levelled off again as he made his way through to the alders. There were three of them, their taproots holding the wet soil of the bank together and so making a platform roughly a foot above the river level. On the middle alder, at its bole, one winding taproot had grown out of the soil and then back in again, or perhaps the river had washed away the earth around it over the years. But what made that taproot was, what it definitely was, was a ready-made and highly accessible mooring-cleat.

He edged closer to the original path, a hand outstretched for a branch to steady himself. The soil on the river side of the alder's bifurcated trunk had definitely been disturbed, close to the edge. A skid mark that might just have been made by a shoe-heel. Blades of grass sheared off and ground into the earth. Recently.

Hawkesley's hypothesis was growing less hypothetical by the minute.

Wedging a knee against the alder trunk, he scanned the other side of the river through the binoculars.

Hawkesley was right. Once past his yard and all the way to the old wool-jetty, all the back gardens were solidly fenced from the river. And to protect the bank from further scouring by the current on that side several hundred yards of sheet-steel piling had been installed, from the jetty to roughly two-thirds of the way to Hawkesley's yard. The ground behind it sloped up towards the wooden fences, but it was easily negotiable. From the end of the piling to Hawkesley's jetty was grass bank, equally negotiable.

He focused tighter on to Hawkesley's stone jetty and wooden slipway. There was a set of step-irons built into the stonework at the jetty's right-hand end, some six or seven feet above the natural bank. Access to the boats, other than by the slipway, was by means of wooden ladders—five, six, seven of them, each a few feet to one side of a well-worn wooden bollard.

Easy. If it had been done at all, it had been done that way.

Or Chaucer had hot-wired his boat himself to cover his tracks. Possibly even carried the body through his shop and out of the back of it, through the wooden gate that led straight on to the jetty. The body in a sack of some sort. A flour-sack. Nobody would think anything untoward about a baker carrying a sack into his own premises, even late at night. Far-fetched but not impossible.

And there was Chaucer himself, up at his office window and looking straight down into the binoculars. Then the net curtain dropped down again, and he was gone.

Roper took his own path back to the car. Inside it, he draped the map over the steering-wheel again and using a thumb-width as an approximate inch measured off the walking distance between here and the graveyard—and across it—and thence across the minster precinct and then the road bridge—and along the High Street, and its turn-off, to the jetty.

And, give or take, it was about three-quarters of a mile. At the regulated three miles an hour of a patrolling constable, such a walk would have taken, say, fifteen or sixteen minutes. But a man in a hurry could do it easily in—what?—ten, twelve, and perhaps even less if he broke into a run here and there.

Roper folded the map and reached to the seat beside him for his personal radio.

HE CONDUCTED the hastily convened briefing in the open, the map spread across the roof of the Sierra, his makeshift search-party a half-dozen cadets in boiler-suits and gum-boots, and the uniformed sergeant who had driven them here in the minibus from County.

'You two lads,' he said to the two pink-cheeked and unhewn boys who stood either side of him, 'hands and knees and magnifying glasses. That gap in the reeds over there. I don't care if you only find dead matchsticks—pick 'em up and drop 'em in a bag. And if you have the luck to find a shoe-print shout for Sergeant Graham here to come in and take a photograph. Got that?'

'Yes, sir.'

'And you four—form a line over there.' He pointed to the left, over the roof of the Sierra. 'About a yard apart. And scour the ground across that way.' His pointing finger swung to the right. 'As far as that dead elm. And *back* again. You're looking for signs of a car. Tyre prints. Exhaust soot on the grass. Anything that indicates a car might have parked off the road for a while. And you've only got half an hour before the light goes, so go to it.'

'Bloody hell, John,' he muttered sourly to Graham, as the cadets sorted themselves out and went from earshot. 'Are they even potty-trained yet, those youngsters?'

'I've heard the tall Scots lad's been seen buying razor blades,' said Graham. 'Only hearsay, though, sir. No proof as yet.'

'Well, keep 'em at it till dark. Anything important turns up, you'll find me at the station.'

Reliable was Sergeant Graham. Another old stager. If anything by way of evidence was lying about here, he would work those cadets until they found it.

HE DREW HIMSELF a coffee from the machine on the way to his office. It was ten past four.

More paper had landed on his desk while he'd been out. A photocopy of WDC Anderson's interview with Mrs Cole, three sheets of it stapled together. A scribbled message from Rodgers—he had spent half an hour with Mrs Leaf, Mrs Blezard's cleaning lady. Mrs L worked for Mrs B for two hours each Monday, Wednesday and Friday, from ten o'clock until midday. She knew nothing of Mrs Blezard's private life, but she had several times seen a photographic album lying about the house, *and* a passport. A telephoned message, again from Rodgers, timed in at four o'clock; to that hour, he and his crew had located six white bicycles in King's Minster, but none of them was ridden by anyone who also owned a blue duffel-bag. Another telephoned message from Price along at Mrs Blezard's house; nothing new there, either.

And yet another telephoned message, from Makins, who was still taking number thirty-one, Rope Walk to pieces in an effort to find the killer of Norman Oates. Equally negative so far.

And last, but by no means least, a telexed résumé of Oates's form-sheet from Central Records.

Roper hung up his raincoat and settled behind the desk.

WDC Anderson could type a lot better than most, was precise and articulate.

Mrs Cole alleged that on four separate occasions she had caught Oates spying on her. On numerous other occasions she had seen Oates photographing young women passing down the street. When asked how many of these latter occasions, Mrs Cole replied she could not remember. But there were *lots* of times.... She had discussed the matter with her husband....

But there had really been no case, thought Roper. It wasn't fair, it wasn't justice, but Norman Oates could never have been arraigned on such flimsy evidence. He turned to the third sheet. Anderson's subsequent interview with Mrs Cole after Oates's body had been found. No, Mrs Cole did not know of any associates of Norman Oates. She had seen few people ever go to the house, except the milkman and the postman, except on Wednesday. She had, she now recalled, seen a man knocking on Oates's front door on Wednesday morning. Soon after eight o'clock. Tallish. Broadish. Darkish. A dark blue raincoat. And a car. A grey one. And he *might* have had a moustache. She had been seeing Mr Cole off to work at the time....

Roper read the vague description again. Tall, broad, dark, navy raincoat. Grey car. And a moustache.

With only the slightest stretch of the imagination it was a description that fitted the absent Sergeant Clark.

He picked up the telex from Records. Norman Leonard Oates: d.o.b. 7/7/40. Charged in 1954 with theft. Three bicycles. Brighton Juvenile Court. Six months' probation. And in 1958 charged again with theft: exchanging one motorcycle engine of his own for another that wasn't. A twenty-pound fine and three months' probation. 1961: receiving a carton of cigarettes knowing them to be stolen. Fined fifty pounds. 1966: probation again, a year that time, for petty theft. 1968: driving a vehicle in a dangerous condition. Fined again. Forty pounds. 1972: intimidation—of a female. Remanded for a psychiatrist's report and subsequently given one year's probation conditional upon accepting psychiatric treatment.

And on. And on. Thirteen charges and convictions to date, the last of them as recently as February of this year. Charged with dealing in drugs, namely cannabis, but the charge had been later reduced to one of possession only. A two-hundred-pound fine and two years' probation.

So Oates had been a persistent petty criminal; or perhaps not so petty, because for every offence the average villain is collared for there are usually a dozen others that he gets away with. And Oates, by the looks of it, was a villain born and bred. He might have been killed by a brother villain, someone to whom he had owed money, or had double-crossed or threatened. The possibilities and permutations were endless. But what Oates had certainly been was a peeping Tom. And even a generous bookmaker would have given the shortest odds against Norman Oates *not* having cleaned Mrs Blezard's conservatory window.

BUTCHER WAS BACK from the County Court at half-past four. He sipped at a cup of tea while he read the tail end of WDC Anderson's report again.

'Yes,' he agreed. 'You're right, Douglas. The description fits Clark to a tee. And Rope Walk *is* along Harbour End. Where he went looking for those video-tapes. Could be significant.'

'Did you go along and see his wife after all?'

'She didn't know whether she was on her head or her heels, poor woman,' said Butcher sympathetically, setting his cup back on its saucer. 'According to the note the son left behind, he's gone for good. Told her he'd write as soon as he was settled in somewhere. And not to worry. Said he couldn't live in the same house as his father any more.'

'Why should he say that?' asked Roper. 'Do we know?'

'Clark was always nagging him, apparently. Mostly about his school work. Kept him at it, y'know. And didn't like the lad having girlfriends.'

'How about the row at the Clarks' place last night? What was that about?'

'When Julie Clark got upstairs, it was over. The lad was lying across the bed with a split lip, and Clark was leaning against the wall and getting his breath back. She went downstairs to ring for me, but Clark followed her down and stopped her. It was none of our business, he told her. Just between him and the boy. Then he went into the lounge and flopped into a chair. Didn't say a word for half an hour. Just stared. She went upstairs to talk to the boy, but he wouldn't say anything, either. And, between times, the daughter was having hysterics. All very fraught. I've put out a description of the boy and his bicycle, by the way. Unofficially, of course. Least I could do in the circumstances.'

In Roper's head, a little bell had rung at the joint mention of boy and bicycle. He asked, scarcely thinking about it: 'Don't suppose it was a white bicycle, was it, Phil?'

'Yes, it was, as a matter of fact,' Butcher replied equally casually, reaching into his tunic pocket for his notebook. He flipped through several pages. 'Hand-built. A firm called Moss—that's what Julie Clark remembers seeing written on the frame. Two red panniers missing from his cupboard, so they're probably on the bike as well.'

'How about a duffel-bag?' said Roper. 'A blue one.'

'What's this?' said Butcher, amused, dropping his notebook on his desk and picking up his tea again. 'A new party-trick? Yes, there's a blue duffel-bag missing from his room as well. What about it?'

The omission was Roper's own fault. He should have kept Butcher better-informed, and hadn't.

A few broad brush-strokes were all that Butcher needed. The finer details he was able to fill in for himself.

'I'd better make that search official, then,' he said grimly.

'Yes,' said Roper. 'I reckon you'd better. And for his father, too. Both of 'em.'

ELEVEN

It was a quarter to five, and dark outside now.

'He was a tea-leaf,' said Butcher. 'Dyed in the wool. I don't think half the time he even realised he was doing it.' The telex listing Oates's past misdeeds went down on his blotter.

'Cannabis, Phil,' Roper reminded him. 'That's serious.'

'Half an ounce,' said Butcher. 'In two packets. We were lucky to get a conviction at all. Clark swore in court that he'd seen Oates passing over another packet in a pub about a week before he finally charged him, but the other chap got away too quickly and Clark didn't have any witnesses. He works too much on his bloody own, that's Clark's trouble.'

'Clark was the arresting officer, then?'

'Oates was Clark's personalised villain,' said Butcher. 'Clark had a phobia about him. He brought him in twice after the cannabis business. I had to warn him about harassment, because that's the way it began to look.' Butcher broke off, and glanced past Roper as someone rapped on the door. 'Come in!'

It was Sergeant Graham, back from the river bank, with a cassette of 35-millimetre film, the map that Roper had left with him and a plastic bag of recovered litter. Beer-cans, cigarette-packets, cigarette-ends, dead matches, a few coins. And a tiny plastic envelope that he took with great care from the whistle-pocket of his tunic. It was the envelope he handed to Roper first.

'Looks like a piece of wool, sir.'

It was, indeed, a fragment of damp wool. Butcher pushed his desk-lamp closer to Roper. And Roper held the plastic envelope towards the light.

A hairy tuft of *black* wool. And Mrs Blezard's body had been wearing a black woollen sweater. It was too much to hope for....

'Where did you find it?'

'Snagged up on one of those alder trees. I took a couple of photos, and I drew a sketch—here, sir....' Graham unfolded the map and spread it out under the desk-lamp. 'X marks the spot. I took a couple of rough bearings, sir. And some measurements. And this is the sketch.' Graham folded half the map back on itself to show his drawing on its white reverse. A passable drawing of the bole and forked lower trunk of an alder. The tuft of wool had been found snagged on the bark sixty centimetres above the junction of the two forks, and between them. 'And we found a definite tyre depression, sir. Here....' The map was opened up again, and Graham's forefinger circled an 'X2' ballpointed close to the line that represented the gap in the reeds. 'Might not be connected, of course, sir, but whoever was driving took off in a hurry. And if he *had* tucked his car in there, sir, I'd have said it was well hidden; especially if it was dark.'

'Just the one depression?'

'Yes, sir.'

A pity, that. Two would have given the distance across the wheelbase. Four would have been perfect. Roper folded the map and looked at Graham's sketch again. The trunk of the alder forked as soon as it came out of the ground. The tuft of wool had snagged on the right-hand branch as it faced the river, sixty centimetres above the V.

'What does sixty centimetres look like?'

Graham took a metal tape-measure from his tunic pocket and extended it.

'A bit over twenty-three inches,' he said.

Roper took the tape from him and measured twenty-three inches upwards from the floor, then from the chair seat upon which he was sitting. The case of the tape came just past the halfway mark of his upper arm. Or, in Mrs Blezard's case, somewhere near her shoulder-level. Or between her shoulderblades. Perhaps her killer had wedged her dead body in the fork of the trunk preparatory to hauling it into the boat. It wasn't impossible; it was even likely.

'Call into Forensic on your way back, John. Get them to check that piece of wool against Mrs Blezard's sweater—and, if it matches, ask them to look over the sweater and see if they can find whereabouts it came from. And I'd like prints of the film you took back here before I go home tonight. And my thanks to your lads.'

'Think you're on to something?' asked Butcher, when Graham had gone.

'Not yet,' said Roper. It was all still too muddly, too many loose ends he couldn't tie together. He rose from his chair. 'If you want me, I'll be along with Dave Price at Mrs Blezard's. Not that I expect they've found anything new.'

Nor had they. But Price was a good sounding-board, and from the chaos of the day's events he came to a similar tentative conclusion as Roper.

Clark's son rode a white bicycle and carried a blue duffel-bag. Such a lad had been a frequent visitor to Mrs Blezard's, and as recently as Monday afternoon. And if he was the same young lad who had been out in Chaucer's boat back in the summer, then he would not have had too much trouble handling the cruiser on Monday night. And nobody needed a degree to hot-wire an engine. And a lad like that, still at school, would not have had a car of his own. Ergo: he had used his victim's car, with which, no doubt, he had been familiar. And if he was the same lad who had left that frantic message on Mrs Blezard's answering machine, then the conclusion could easily be drawn that Mrs Blezard had jilted him. Which was the sort of motive juries licked their lips over.

But neither Roper nor Price, at this stage, was able to string together a similar line of logic for the murder of Norman Oates. All they were able to do between them was to botch together a few disconnected facts with a somewhat dubious cement. Clark's son might have killed Mrs Blezard. Clark himself might have visited Oates on Wednesday morning. Oates's ribs had been bruised, but some hours before he had been murdered. According to Butcher, Clark, allegedly, was handy with his fists. And Oates, more than likely, had cleaned that patch of window at the back of Mrs Blezard's conservatory. But, as logic went, all that was shot through with too many flaws and perhapses and maybes, and probably, in the final analysis, there would be no connection at all between the death of Mrs Blezard and that of the small-time recidivist of Rope Walk.

At Oates's terraced cottage, Makins and his crew had exhausted all the possibilities of finding the knife that had killed its erstwhile tenant.

'How about the alley at the back?'

'Been all over it,' said Makins. 'Not there, either.'

So it was limbo-time again. Everybody ferreting and nothing happening, and none of them aware, as yet, that there had been a further development in the case of Mrs

Blezard in the shape of a buff envelope presently lying unregarded on Roper's office desk.

HE TOOK AN early dinner in the Duke of Wellington and a pint of bitter afterwards while he looked through the current edition of the *Antique Collector* in a quiet corner of the saloon bar. Prices, he observed with some satisfaction, were still on the up and up. A fruitwood lowboy, of which he and Sheila had a twin stowed away in the spare bedroom, and for which he had bid four and a half hundred at auction only six months ago, had recently gone at Sotheby's for half as much again.

At half-past eight he was walking back to the station and getting his mind into gear again. No rain, little cloud and the night sky pricked with stars, a few facts still nagging at him like a bad tooth. Clark's son had a white bicycle and carried a blue duffel-bag. Given that premiss, it was likely that he was the lad seen visiting Mrs Blezard's house by both Mrs Crispin and Roland Hollister. And perhaps, it suddenly occurred to Roper, Mrs Crispin's description of both boy and bicycle had been recognised by Clark as fitting his own son. And it was *that* which had accounted for his strenuous argument with her that the bicycle she had seen might have been yellow, and that the lad was Mrs Blezard's newspaper-boy.

Or something else—Roper had a blinding flash of insight as he turned up the station steps. Clark had already *known* his son had been seeing Mrs Blezard—*before* he and Roper had spoken to Ailsa Crispin.

And that is why the hitherto hyper-efficient Clark had suddenly fluffed the switches on Mrs Blezard's answering machine yesterday morning. Several hours *before* Mrs Crispin had mentioned the boy on the white bicycle.

Because Clark had recognised *his son's* voice.

What had momentarily knocked Clark off kilter had been hearing the sound of his own son coming out of that machine....

'DS Clark shown up yet?' he asked as he passed through the flap of the public counter.

'No, sir,' said the duty sergeant.

...and, if that was so, it led to an inescapable conclusion as to why Clark had messed up that tape on his way back here last night.

'Mr Butcher still about, is he?'

'Yes, sir. Up in his office.'

Butcher was sitting in the half-dark, his face lit by the pool of light cast by his desk-lamp and the desk a raft of paperwork that he was trying to catch up on before he went home.

'You busy, Phil?'

'Middling,' said Butcher, sitting back tiredly and laying down his ballpoint. 'Why?'

'Clark,' said Roper. 'I've just thought of a reason for his buggering up that tape from Mrs Blezard's answering machine.'

BUTCHER AGREED. It did all fit together.

'Julie Clark's been ringing here every half-hour,' he said, when Roper had finished. 'I didn't tell her any-thing—couldn't bring myself to, poor woman—but I managed to get a few more bits and pieces out of her on the basis that we're considering the boy a missing person.'

Mrs Clark had searched her son's bedroom again. His Post Office Savings Bank book was missing. And so, definitely, were two red panniers that fitted to the back bracket of his bicycle. And the blue duffel-bag. The boy's only relation outside his immediate family was Mrs

Clark's mother, who lived in Great Yarmouth; Butcher had already been in touch with the Norfolk Constabulary and given a description of both boy and bicycle.

Butcher passed over the desk a photocopy of the note that the lad left behind. 'Dear Mum, I'm off. Sorry, but I can't take any more of Dad. Don't worry. I'll look after myself. I'll be in touch when I've settled somewhere. Love, Stephen.'

'How about last night?' asked Roper. 'Did she say how that got started?'

Mrs Clark had attempted to telephone Butcher, but Clark had followed her downstairs and snatched the receiver out of her hand.

'It was none of our business, he told her,' said Butcher.

According to Mrs Clark, her husband had been acting strangely for the last few months. He fell asleep in an armchair after meals, did not always answer when she spoke to him but only looked blankly at her, as if he hadn't heard. He had also, of late, taken to talking in his sleep. She had put all this down to stress and overwork, and had been urging him to see the doctor. Which he still hadn't done.

And on Monday night, apparently, during dinner, Clark's daughter had made casual mention of seeing a man in a van taking photographs of her class netball team from outside the schoolyard. And with rising ire Clark had questioned the girl, about the van, about the man.

'And Terry went spare, so Julie said. Got up, put his coat on, and Julie had to grab him and hold on to him. Clark told her he knew who the guy in the van was and he was going round to kill the bastard.... It took her almost half an hour to talk him out of it.'

And Butcher had also had the wit to ask Mrs Clark if her son had been out late on Monday night.

'What did she say?' asked Roper.

Butcher looked graver than ever. 'So far as she remembers, he went out at about half-past seven—and
when he got home it was well after midnight.'

'Did she ask him why?'

'She didn't dare,' said Butcher. 'She was in bed at the
time, and Terry was asleep. The next time she saw the
boy was at breakfast on Tuesday morning, but Terry was
there, too, and it was his birthday and they were going
out that night to celebrate. She didn't want to start the
day with a row.'

It all sounded, to Roper, very ominous. Nor was
Butcher any more sanguine. No copper likes driving the
nails into another copper's coffin.

'Have you noticed any change in Clark lately, Phil?'

'Some,' said Butcher. 'A bit spikier than he used to
be. Avoids me when he can. But he's still the best copper
I've ever had working for me. He gets results. Can't ask
for more than that—unless he's bent. And I've never had
a formal complaint about him. No backhanders, nothing
of that sort.'

'How about the son?'

'Brilliant,' said Butcher. 'Well balanced. Nice lad. Before all this business, I'd have said he'd go a damn sight
further than his father has.'

Roper steepled his fingers under his chin. 'I'm going
to have to see Mrs Clark, Phil.'

Both of Mrs Clark's menfolk, husband and son, were
now witnesses at best, and suspects at worst, in a double
murder inquiry. By tomorrow morning a full-scale search
for both of them would be well under way throughout
the country. She would have to know.

For a whole hour, Roper and Butcher went painstakingly through all of it again, the way Roper had earlier

with Price except that more evidence had reared its head since then, the most damning of it that young Stephen Clark had been away from home, and so far unaccounted for, during the hours during which Mrs Blezard had probably been murdered. According to Butcher, Stephen Clark was a big lad, dark, six feet or more and hefty with it—which fitted Chaucer's description exactly—so it was likely that he had big feet to match. Size eleven, perhaps. And his father, according to Mrs. Clark, had threatened to kill a man who sounded very much like Norman Oates. And Norman Oates was now dead.

'Looks bad,' said Butcher.

'Ay,' said Roper.

'We'll go round and see her in the morning.'

'First thing,' said Roper. 'Get some photographs off her. Have some posters printed.' Tragedy was about to strike Mrs Clark like a mailed fist. It wasn't right, it wasn't fair, but that was the way of it.

The phone rang. Butcher picked it up, listened briefly, then said, 'Yours,' and passed it over the desk to Roper.

It was one of Guthrie's technicians at Regional Forensic.

'The Director asked me to give you a bell, Mr Roper. That piece of wool you sent in. I've had it up on the spectro. It matches the material of Mrs Blezard's sweater. And my assistant's just found the hole you asked us to look for.'

'Where is it?'

'At the back. Dead centre. About twelve centimetres down from where the collar's stitched on.'

Roper picked up a wooden ruler from Butcher's desk. Twelve centimetres was about five inches. Which, as he had earlier guessed, would have been between Mrs Blezard's shoulderblades. So perhaps her body had, after all, been wedged between the alder trunks while her killer had stepped aboard the cabin cruiser before hauling her on after him.

'That's all, I'm afraid, Mr Roper. So far as we're concerned, the bag of litter was just the usual old rubbish. Sorry.'

'Don't be sorry, old son. You've got a result. Thanks.'

Roper put the phone down with a feeling of satisfaction. What had started out as a whistle in the wind had become an established fact. It didn't often happen like that.

He and Butcher shared another brace of coffees, discussed the delicate tactics of tomorrow's visit to Julie Clark, to which neither of them looked forward, and at a quarter to ten Butcher went down to the parade room to see the night crew on duty and Roper went the other way to his temporary office. He was tired, his eyelids like leaden weights and the insides of them lined with grit. Tomorrow was Friday, the weekend looming up hard behind it. He had looked forward to the weekend off. That luxury no longer looked likely. He had married late, thank God; Sheila would not have to put up with a lifetime married to a copper the way Julie Clark had. The unsocial hours, the promise of an evening out that had to be cancelled at the last moment, the telephone ringing in the middle of the night, the husband coming home dead on his feet and bringing with him all the aggravations that he wasn't allowed to talk about. Any woman who could put up with all that, and not complain, was either a stoic or a gem.

As he passed the CID room he heard someone banging away at a typewriter. Probably WDC Anderson catching up on her lost morning's work. And a couple of paces on Roper stopped and turned about, because an encouraging word or two never came amiss and DC Anderson had more than done her bit this morning and she wouldn't get any medals for it. He rapped on the CID room door and put his head around the edge of it. But it wasn't WDC Anderson at the typewriter.

It was Detective Sergeant Clark.

TWELVE

HE WAS barely recognisable, dishevelled, unshaven; looked as if he hadn't been to bed for a week, and had aged ten years since yesterday. His fingers still poised over the typewriter keys, his wide red-rimmed eyes lifted bleakly and met Roper's over his desk-lamp. He was still in his raincoat, a white sweater underneath it. A man, Roper decided, well beyond the end of his tether.

'You look terrible,' said Roper.

Without a word Clark stood up, pushed the skirt of his raincoat aside and felt for the hip-pocket of his trousers. The hand reappeared with his wallet in it, and from the wallet he plucked out his warrant-card and reached across the desk to put it down in front of Roper.

'*And* your pocket-book,' said Roper.

Clark sat down wearily again and opened the top drawer of his desk. He took out his notebook and handed it across to Roper.

'You phoned your wife lately?'

Clark shook his head.

'Why not?'

'I don't know what to say to her,' said Clark, and Roper thought he heard a catch of despair in his voice. One wrong word and Clark would break in half.

'You eaten?'

Clark shook his head again.

Roper reached behind him for a chair and swung it in front of Clark's desk. Then he sat down, opened Clark's notebook on his knee and flipped slowly through the en-

tries of the last few days. There was no record of a visit
to Norman Oates on Wednesday morning. He regarded
Clark lengthily. If it was possible for a man to lose
enough weight in twenty-four hours for it to show, then
Clark had.

'You didn't report in this morning.'

'I know,' said Clark.

'Why not?'

Clark didn't answer. He ripped the sheet of paper he
had been working on from the typewriter and held it
across the desk. His resignation. It was addressed to
Butcher. Roper scanned it briefly.

'This won't get you off the hook, either,' said Roper,
laying it beside Clark's notebook. 'For the time it'll take
to process that, you're still a copper—and a bloody fool
into the bargain. You know that, don't you?'

Clark still didn't answer.

'Where have you been all day?'

Clark shrugged.

'About,' he said.

'About where?'

Another shrug. 'Lulworth.'

'Doing what?'

'Thinking.'

Perhaps a minute passed. Clark reached out a hand for
a couple of typed A4 sheets beside him. He passed them
across to Roper, then slumped back tiredly in his swivel-
chair, still without a word.

Roper found himself with two formal statement-sheets,
both of them dated, timed and signed by Clark.

At 1000 hours on Wednesday, 22 October, I was
detailed by Chief Inspector Philip Butcher to assist
Detective Superintendent D. Roper in the investi-

gation of the death of Mrs Hannah Blezard. At the house of the deceased, in company with these two officers, I was asked if I recognized a certain voice on the deceased's telephone answering machine. I replied that I did not recognise the voice in question. This reply was untrue. The voice I had just heard was that of my son, Stephen Terence Clark, and it was obvious to me from both his manner and the gist of his words that he had, unknown to either myself or my wife, been an acquaintance of the deceased, and perhaps been her lover, and that he spoke about visiting Mrs Blezard, perhaps on the night she had died, came as a shock to me. I realised immediately that my son was a possible suspect. It was for this reason that I lied about recognising his voice. Further evidence that my son was a frequent visitor to the house of the deceased was revealed later on this same day when I accompanied Det. Supt Roper at an interview with Mrs Ailsa Crispin, a neighbour of the deceased. During the course of this interview Mrs Crispin stated that on several recent occasions she had seen a boy riding a white bicycle and carrying a blue duffel-bag arriving at and leaving the house of the deceased. The description fitted my son, and the times Mrs Crispin stated fitted in with the times when my son finished school each day. Further to this, I was informed later by Detective Sergeant Makins that Mr Roland Hollister, another neighbour of the deceased, had also witnessed my son arriving at Mrs Blezard's house on several occasions, going back as far as last August. Bearing in mind my son's change of personality since August, I was now convinced that he had played a part in the death of Mrs Blezard, especially as a recent visitor to her house had left sole-prints of training-shoes in her conservatory. My son always wears training-shoes when riding his bicycle. I subsequently allowed my concern for my son to outweigh my duty as a police officer. Upon quitting the premises of the deceased at 2205 hours on the above date, I picked up the aforementioned message-tape, which I had not been instructed to do, with the full intention of destroying the evidence of my son's voice on it. This I did by removing the rear cover-plate of the loudspeaker of my car-radio, switching the radio to receive, turning the volume-control to its fullest extent and pressing the cassette against the speaker for several minutes. I did this on a layby on the Dorchester Road. I then continued on to King's Minster police station, which I managed to enter unobserved by the side-entrance. I ran the tape through the recording machine in the interview room to ensure that I had removed my son's voice from the tape. Then I returned, still unobserved as far as I was aware, to my car which I had left in Market Street. I then drove to the front entrance of the station, entered it, and in company with Sergeant George Harper placed the tape in the safe and signed that I had done so. I then signed off duty and went home. It was at this juncture, driving home, that I realised the seriousness of what I had just done, and that there was no going back on it. Arriving home, I taxed my son immediately. At first he denied knowing Mrs Blezard, then admitted that he had. His insolent attitude was such that I struck him. I also told him what his affair with Mrs Blezard had led me to do. He told me that I was stupid. I struck him again and asked him if he had killed Mrs Blezard and also if he had visited her on Monday night. He replied: 'Yes, I did go to see her. What about it?' I finally lost my temper and I remember no more except that several blows were exchanged between myself and my son and that we were eventually interrupted by my wife and daughter. My wife subsequently attempted to contact Chief Inspector Butcher, which I forbade her to do, although I now bitterly regret having done so. So far as I remember, I did not tell my wife later of my suspicions regarding our son. It was my intention this morning to bring my son to be interviewed by Det. Supt Roper. My son, however, when I entered his room at 0600 hours this morning, had already left the house. I found a note from him on the kitchen table declaring his intention of leaving home. I have not seen my son since last night. This to the best of my knowledge and belief is a true statement. There are no mitigating circumstances for my destruction of the evidence aforementioned and my resignation accompanies.

Clark had signed both sheets; beneath he had typed 'Terence David Clark, Detective Sergeant', and the date again.

Roper drew a long breath and slowly expelled it. If anything damned Clark, this statement did. It was precise, explicit, single-spaced, and all the words were crammed together into the one enormous paragraph, like a will, so that it could not be tampered with. There was not a single spelling mistake. It was orderly and, more, it was lucid; and yet at the moment Clark did not look like a man who was capable of lucidity, blue-chinned, bleary-eyed, hair awry, a bruise Roper saw now under his right eye. He held up the statement.

'You sure about this?'

'It's what happened,' said Clark.

'You think this lad of yours killed Mrs Blezard?'

'He could have.'

'What did he say when you asked him?'

'He told me not to be stupid.'

'Do you think he went to see her, on Monday night?'

'Sure of it,' said Clark.

A token rap came at the door. It was Butcher. At the sight of Clark, he came in all the way, his expression wooden, and closed the door quietly behind him. Roper handed up Clark's statement, and waited the two or three minutes it took Butcher to read it.

He handed it back to Roper.

'And this,' said Roper. He passed up Clark's resignation. Butcher read it briefly before putting it back on Clark's desk beside the typewriter.

'Phoned Julie?' Butcher asked Clark.

Clark shook his head. He would not, Roper thought, be able to hold himself together like this for very much longer.

Butcher leaned across the desk, picked up Clark's telephone and moved it closer to him. 'Do it now,' he said. 'That's a bloody order.'

'I can't,' said Clark, with that terrible catch in his voice again. 'I bloody *can't.*'

'Do it,' said Butcher. 'She's half out of her bloody mind, Terry.'

'I can't,' sobbed Clark. 'I don't know what to tell her, for Christ's sake.' Then, at last, he crumpled, his eyes brimming with tears and his head falling forward into his cupped hands.

BUTCHER CAME BACK from the machine with a cup of soup for Clark and a cup of coffee for himself. The last few minutes had given neither him nor Roper any pleasure.

'Here,' he said. 'Get this down you, and pull yourself together, for God's sake.'

And with a tremendous effort Clark did conjure up a semblance of pulling himself together, but even after wiping his eyes and blowing his nose and tucking his handkerchief away he still looked like death as he gratefully cupped his shaking hands around the soup and sipped at it.

Butcher pulled up another chair and sat down beside Roper.

'Right, Terry,' he said. 'Straight questions. Straight answers.' He picked up Clark's notebook and dropped it down by Clark's elbow. 'You visited Norman Oates yesterday. You didn't write it up. Why not?'

'I couldn't write it up,' said Clark. He shrugged hopelessly. 'I duffed him over.'

'Why, for God's sake?' railed Butcher.

Clark reached under his raincoat and brought out his wallet again. He took from it a much folded sheet of stiff white paper, unfolded it, and holding it down on his desk with one hand he flattened it out with the edge of the other before passing it across to Butcher. It was a photograph, black and white, Roper saw, of a mêlée of short-skirted schoolgirls playing netball. An eight-by-ten.

'Your Susan,' said Butcher, passing the creased photograph to Roper.

Clark nodded.

'Not a good enough reason, Terry,' said Butcher. 'Sorry.'

'I thought it was,' said Clark. 'At the time.'

'You should have brought him in.'

'And what would have happened?' asked Clark bitterly. 'Nothing. Another slap on the wrist and a fine. That little girl with the ball's *my* kid. The bastard took that from his van. She saw him.'

'You should have brought him in. Written up a charge-sheet.'

'I know,' said Clark.

'But you went along to Oates's place and beat him up instead. Right?'

'I wanted to kill the bastard.'

'He's dead, Terry,' said Butcher. 'Did you know?'

Clark's bloodshot eyes widened. It wasn't an act. He hadn't known. 'Christ…you don't think…?'

'We don't think anything, Sergeant,' said Roper. 'We're asking.'

Clark subsided like a deflating party balloon.

'I beat the shit out of him,' he said. 'But I left him alive and on his feet. Honest.' The bloodshot eyes swivelled from Roper to Butcher and back again. 'I didn't kill him, Mr Roper.'

'But you told your wife you wanted to, didn't you, Sergeant?'

'Yes,' conceded Clark. 'But that was only words, for Christ's sake.' He frowned as the deeper import of the question struck him. 'You've been to see my wife?'

'I did,' said Butcher. 'She's been ringing in here all day.'

Clark blinked tiredly. 'I'm sorry,' he said. 'I had to shove off on my own for a few hours. I had to think.'

'Think?' exploded Butcher. 'Terry, you've got a wife, kids; your son's a murder suspect; you've duffed over a ratepayer and cocked up evidence. When all this comes out, you won't even be back in uniform trying *shop doors,* for God's sake! Coppers get banged up for less than what you've done!'

'I know,' said Clark. 'I'm sorry.'

'Are you *sure* that was your son's voice on that answering machine, Sergeant?' asked Roper, breaking in.

'Yes,' said Clark.

'Beyond all reasonable doubt?'

'Yes,' said Clark. 'Everything ties up.'

'What's his shoe size? D'you know?'

'Big,' said Clark. 'Eleven. Twelve. I'm not sure.'

'And he rides a white bike and carries a blue duffel-bag?'

Clark nodded. 'Yes,' he said.

'Can he drive a car?'

'Yes,' said Clark. 'I taught him myself.'

Roper and Butcher exchanged glances. With each of Clark's weary utterances, his son sank a little deeper into the mire of suspicion.

'And those video-tapes are in the back of the car, Phil,' said Clark to Butcher. 'I found them at Oates's place.'

'I see,' said Butcher flatly. 'Anything else you ought to tell me about. Those two handbags, for instance?'

'The lads asked for it,' said Clark. 'All they'd have got from the beak was a slapped wrist. What I gave them was a proper lesson.'

'I see,' said Butcher again. 'And that'll be the subject of *another* statement, will it?'

'Yes,' said Clark. He was sinking fast. Once or twice in the last couple of minutes his eyes had closed. Now his head dropped forward.

'Terry?' said Butcher. 'Terry?'

There was no response. Clark had finally succumbed.

BUTCHER JOINED Roper in the passage and drew the door to quietly behind him.

'Think you'd better get a doctor to him, Phil.'

'You don't think he's pulling a fast one?'

'Sure of it,' said Roper. He had shaken Clark. Clark had opened his eyes for a moment and then fallen forward over his desk. Only just in time had Roper saved him from burying his face in his typewriter keys.

'Breakdown, you think?'

'I hope so,' said Roper. 'Indeed, I bloody hope so.'

Doctor Evans agreed. It was to Evans that Butcher had made his first telephone call. The second one, the more difficult, had been made to Clark's wife. She and the doctor had arrived within minutes of each other.

'Put in a lot of hours, does he, Mr Butcher?' asked Evans, while they waited for the ambulance.

'Seventy hours last week,' said Butcher. 'Not that I asked him to.'

'How about the week before?'

'The same,' said Butcher. 'But it's all under his own steam.'

'Any man who works like that has to be in overdrive,' said Evans gravely, putting his equipment away. He turned to Mrs Clark. 'It looks as if your husband's been winding himself up for some time, Mrs Clark. I'm sorry.'

BY ELEVEN O'CLOCK Mrs Clark had been told by Butcher as much as was meet for her to know, and she had been a policeman's wife long enough to guess what Butcher meant when he talked of her son being sought with a view to making routine enquiries of him. Considering her new circumstances, she remained remarkably composed.

'Do you really think he *might* have killed her, Philip?'

'I don't *think* anything, Julie,' said Butcher. 'Nor does

Mr Roper here. But evidence does point to your Stephen *being* there that night. And Terry drew the same conclusion when he heard the lad's voice on the tape.'

'He'll lose his pension, won't he? Everything he's worked for.'

'It depends what the doctor tells us, Mrs Clark,' said Roper. 'Your husband's got a good record. If he is in the middle of a nervous breakdown, the Chief Constable might regard that as a mitigating circumstance.'

'But he was working for you, Superintendent,' she said. 'You'll have to report him, won't you? You can't let it go?' She was fortyish, Roper guessed, blonde—perhaps dyed—and smartly dressed, and underneath it all worn out by the troubles of her day, poor woman. And she was asking the one favour that Roper couldn't grant her.

'I'll have to report him, Mrs Clark. I'm sorry. The matter will come up in court eventually; too many other officers know about it. But the tape's irrelevant as soon as we've talked to your son. If he tells the truth.'

'We'd like a photo of the lad, Julie,' said Butcher.

She knew what for. She reached into her handbag and delved about for a credit-card holder. Tucked inside, back to back, were two photographs. She took out one and handed it to Butcher.

'He didn't kill that woman, Philip,' she said. 'If you knew him better, you'd know he hadn't.'

'I hope so, Julie,' said Butcher. 'Believe me.'

Roper stayed silent. In other circumstances he would have questioned Mrs Clark, but she was tired like everyone else and was already harassed enough for one day. Perhaps after her son had been found he would talk to her again. For the time being there was little point.

At eleven-fifteen, stuffed with Valium and dead to the

world, Clark was driven across to the infirmary where he would spend the next forty-eight hours sedated and under observation. Doctor Evans had diagnosed a severe emotional disturbance.

'Thank God,' said Butcher fervently, and Roper was inclined to agree with him as the two watched from the window as Clark and his wife went aboard the ambulance and its doors closed behind them.

At twenty past eleven, Roper dragged himself along to his own office, feeling the strain of the day himself now and longing to crawl into bed before, like Clark, he fell asleep on his feet. There was yet more paper on his desk. The formal report from Forensic concerning the lab's findings on Mrs Blezard's car and other investigations carried out yesterday. Nothing there he hadn't already been told by Guthrie. A message from Wilson: the post-mortem examination of Norman Oates was scheduled for tomorrow, a.m. The photographs taken this morning at Rope Walk—as revolting at this late hour as the reality had been this morning; he put those aside until tomorrow. A buff envelope with the seal of the Sussex County Constabulary on the flap. He ripped it open, and wished afterwards that he had put that aside, too, until tomorrow, because it was late and he was tired and the investigations were convoluted enough already without Sussex chucking in yet another spanner. Because what was in the envelope, clipped to a compliments slip, was a photocopy of the formal registration of Mrs Blezard's marriage at Brighton Registry Office. And it seemed, despite all the verbals to the contrary, that Mrs Blezard *did* have a next of kin. And that he was very much alive. And living here in King's Minster.

THIRTEEN

ROPER PARKED HIS CAR beside Price's in the yard beside the station. It was nine o'clock on the morning of Day Three, Friday, and the weather forecast promising only rain for most of the weekend. It was drizzling now, a cold and penetrating wetness. He had overslept this morning, and treated himself to the luxury afterwards of not hurrying to make up the time.

He heard the scuffle at the public counter as soon as he turned in through the side-entrance. Butcher was in the thick of it, and four uniformed constables, and Sergeant Harper in a civilian raincoat and woollen muffler over his uniform, and a wild-eyed lout with his wrists manacled together behind his back and a grimace of pain on his face as he kicked out at all and sundry as they struggled to pin him against the wall outside the radio room.

'Get his bloody legs,' roared Butcher, and a beefy constable, who was already trying to, caught one of the lad's flying feet and jerked it forward some more so that the youth's other leg folded and he slid on his behind to the floor where his legs were swiftly sat on and his ankles buckled together with the belt of Harper's raincoat.

'Right, son,' gasped Butcher, standing over him as the boy still squirmed and struggled under the weight of four constables. 'Cool it. You're nicked. I'm charging you with assaulting several police officers—and me in the bloody particular—and possession of a weapon. And anything you bloody say from now on will be taken down and used in evidence. Got that? Have you? Eh? Have you?'

The youth stared up balefully at him. He was a big lad, six and a half feet of him and built like a barn, jeaned and T-shirted, dark-haired and needing a shave.

'And any more malarky and we strap you up in a jacket. Right? Now, lock him up and get him some breakfast.'

The lad was carried off past Roper and taken down to the cells, his body now inert but the rage still gleaming in his eyes. Only then did Butcher notice Roper. Butcher's tie was outside his tunic and the top button of that was missing and he looked as if he'd taken a mud-bath.

'Who the hell was that?' asked Roper.

'Terry Clark's boy,' said Butcher, tucking in his tie.

ROPER SAT BEHIND Butcher's desk, Sergeant Harper in front of it. Across the room Butcher, in his shirt and underpants, was taking his spare uniform out of his locker.

'How did you come to find him, Sergeant?' asked Roper.

'By accident, sir,' said Harper. 'I always give my whippets a run on the heath after I come off duty. I was up by the old Home Guard bunker on Cogden Heath and saw a white bike leaning against the back of it. And it had a couple of red panniers on the back bracket. So I guessed it was young Stephen Clark's.'

'Then what?'

'Well, sir, I didn't expect trouble, so I went towards the bunker. I was going to have a talk with him. I mean, I know him, he's a nice lad. I thought I could talk him into coming in. But when I got to about ten yards from the bunker, sir, he poked what I thought was a single-barrelled twelve-bore out of one of the slots and told me to piss off—or he'd bloody shoot me.'

'And was it a shotgun?'

'No,' replied Butcher from his locker, hauling up his trousers. 'But we all bloody thought it was, didn't we, George?'

'Ay, sir,' said Harper.

'How far's this heath?' asked Roper.

'About two miles, sir,' said Harper. He rose from his chair and went to a map hanging over Butcher's filing-cabinets. He pointed to a stretch of open country to the north of the town. 'And the bunker's here, sir. Just off the road to Wareham. It's on this hill, sir. Built during the war.'

'What did you do then?'

'Not a lot, sir,' said Harper, and Roper could not honestly blame him. 'I was worried he might do something stupid, like shooting one of the dogs. So I put 'em back on the leash, walked back to the road, and telephoned Mr Butcher. And I kept watch in case the lad hopped it in the mean time. Which he couldn't, although I didn't realise that until afterwards.'

'Why couldn't he?'

'His front wheel was buckled—and we think he's sprained an ankle.'

Freshly kitted out, Butcher pulled up a spare chair to the end of his desk and sat himself down.

'Did you question him, Phil?'

'Didn't get the chance,' said Butcher. 'It took all our time to get the cuffs on him and drag him into a car. He was a bloody maniac.'

'How about the shotgun?'

'It was a piece of rusty pipe he'd picked up some-

where. But, like George here said, we didn't know that
at the time. Ye bloody gods!'

'How long d'you think he'd been up at the bunker?'

'All night, I'd say,' said Butcher. 'And probably all
day yesterday as well. He'd got a sleeping-bag up there.
He'd made camp.'

According to Butcher, Clark's son had threatened him,
too, and his posse of constables, with the make-believe
shotgun poked out through an embrasure, until Butcher
had called his bluff by storming the bunker with one of
the constables and the other three hard behind him.
Which must have taken, Roper thought, a great deal more
by way of guts than Butcher would ever own to, whether
the gun had been a real one or not.

SHOELESS AND BELTLESS, Stephen Clark sat across the
interview-table from Roper. An egg-and-bacon breakfast
and an hour in the cells had made him somewhat more
amenable. His heavily bandaged right ankle was stretched
out beside the table leg.

'How did you manage to do that?' asked Roper.

'Came off the bike,' said Clark sullenly. 'It was raining. I skidded.'

'One balls-up after another, then.'

Silence. Clark stared sulkily back. Roper pushed a pair
of damp-stained training-shoes to the middle of the table.

'Yours, son?'

'You know bloody well they are,' said Clark, not even
bothering to look at them.

'Don't get cheeky, laddie,' warned Roper. 'If Mr
Butcher presses charges for the aggravation you caused
him this morning, you'll be doing a couple of years'
youth custody on the strength of that alone. So watch it.'

'They're lucky it wasn't a real one,' said Clark.

'And so are you, my son,' said Roper. 'Believe it.'

The boy averted his eyes. Taller than his father, but as dark and with the same lurking intensity; although without his father's Dorset drawl. If Roper had not known how old he was, he would have put him somewhere in his early twenties. And he was certainly brawny enough to have carried the dead Mrs Blezard as far as had been needed on Monday night.

Roper reached behind him and depressed the switch of the tape-recorder.

'The time is ten-o-five hours on October twenty-three. I am Detective Superintendent Douglas Roper and in company with Detective Inspector David Price I am interviewing Stephen Terence Clark, a minor, concerning the death of Mrs Hannah Blezard. He has been given medical attention.'

He turned to face Clark. 'Right, Stephen,' he said. 'You speak all answers. Any nods or shakes of the head will be recorded verbally by me and confirmed by Inspector Price. They will then become official evidence. Do you understand that?'

'Yes,' said Clark.

'Good,' said Roper. 'Did you know Mrs Hannah Blezard?'

Clark nodded.

Roper waited.

'Yes,' said Clark. Then sullenly: 'But I *didn't* kill her.'

'How long had you known her?'

'Summer. The holidays.'

'How did you meet her?'

'Does it matter?'

'Yes,' said Roper. 'It matters. How did you come to meet her?'

'She knocked me off my bike,' said Clark. 'In Witling

Lane. She was coming out of her drive, and I was taking the curve on the wrong side.'

'Did you report it?'

Clark shook his head. 'No,' he said. 'It was my fault. I finished up across her bonnet. The bike was a write-off. But I wasn't hurt.'

'Your bicycle was a write-off, and you didn't report it? Did you tell your father?'

'He's the last person I'd tell.'

'So how did you account for the smashed bicycle?'

Clark shrugged. 'I didn't have to. Hannah bought me another one. I told my parents I'd handed over the old one in part exchange.'

'And I presume you promised to keep quiet about the accident.'

'It wasn't like that,' retorted Clark.

'How was it, then?'

'You wouldn't understand,' sneered Clark. '*You're* a copper.'

'Try me,' said Roper.

'She carried the bike into her drive. She rang for a doctor, told him I'd fallen off my bike and wanted him to take a look at me.'

'And the doctor came, did he?'

'Yes.... I'd only got a few bruises.'

'Then what?'

'She made some coffee and sandwiches. And in the afternoon she drove us across to Bournemouth and bought me the new bike.'

'The one you were riding this afternoon.'

'Yes.'

'Expensive.'

'Yes,' said Clark. His head turned, and his eyes met Roper's. 'I told her it cost too much. But she insisted.'

'How did you account to your parents for the difference in price between that one and the old one?'

'I told them it was secondhand. Told them I'd made up the difference from my Post Office book.'

'You lie a lot, do you, Stephen?'

Clark shrugged the accusation off. 'If you knew my father, you'd know why.'

'You went to Bournemouth. She bought you a new bike. What then?'

'We went back to her place,' said Clark. 'We'd been talking about my getting a job after university. I'd told her I was into electronics and computers, and how there wasn't much hope these days of getting that kind of job unless you knew somebody who knew somebody. She told me she'd fix me up with an interview at Blezard's. I don't think I've ever talked so much,' said Clark vehemently. 'And *she* listened. Interested—you know? Not like home.'

Home was clearly not Stephen Clark's favourite place.

'What then, Stephen?'

'She got tea. She lent me a pair of trunks and we had a swim in the pool.'

'So you got friendly pretty quickly,' said Roper.

'No,' said Clark. 'Not exactly. I liked her, and I think she liked me.'

'When did you see her again?'

'On the next Saturday. The evening. She'd asked me to call in to tell her how the interview had gone.'

'And how had it gone?'

'I was promised a job,' said Clark. 'So long as I kept my head down and got at least a two-two degree.'

'And how about after that Saturday evening? Did you see her again?'

'Yes,' said Clark. 'Often.'

'How often?'

Clark thought about it. 'About once a week,' he said. 'Something like that. I helped her in her garden.'

'And that was all?' asked Roper. 'You just gave her a hand in the garden.'

Like his father, Stephen Clark was quick to smoulder. 'I told you. It wasn't *like* that. Not ever.'

'So you never went to bed with her?'

'No,' said Clark, a spot of bright colour rising to each cheek.

'Just platonic, then.'

'Yes,' said Clark.

'Were you in love with her?'

Clark nodded as he picked morosely at a patch of frayed blue denim over his knee.

'Were you in love with Mrs Blezard, Stephen?' Roper asked again.

'Yes,' said Clark grudgingly, still not meeting Roper's eyes. 'I suppose so.'

'How about the other way about?'

Clark shook his head. 'She said we could only be friends. That's all.'

'And you didn't mind that?'

Clark shrugged, still picking absently at the worn patch over his knee. 'It was better than nothing,' he said. 'Better than not seeing her at all.'

It was fairly obvious that Stephen Clark had been besotted and that Mrs Blezard, wittingly or otherwise, had led the lad on.

'Did you ever go out in a boat with her, Stephen?'

'Yes,' said Clark. 'During the summer holidays.'

'Her boat?'

'No,' said Clark. 'It was Mr Chaucer's. The baker.'

'Who took the wheel?'

'I did. We went around to Poole harbour and back.'

'If I put you on that boat now, would you know how to get it under way?'

Clark shrugged. 'Easy,' he said. 'Easier than a car.'

'How about without an ignition key?'

Clark looked blank. 'I'm not with you,' he said.

'Could you hot-wire the engine…get it started… without a key?'

'No,' said Clark. 'No idea. I don't even know what "hot-wiring" is.'

It sounded like the truth.

'Did you get together on the boat?'

Clark's mouth curled in disgust. 'That's all you can think about, isn't it? Bloody sex. It was never dirty. Whatever you're thinking. No. We didn't *get* together. Not *any* time.'

'Can you drive a car, Stephen?'

'Yes.'

'Mrs Blezard's, for instance. Did you ever drive that?'

Clark shrugged again. The gesture seemed to be the limit of his emotional display. As with his father, the last few days had worn him out. 'Once or twice,' he said. 'Up and down the drive.'

'Not outside?'

'Of course I didn't. If I'd bent it, it would have cost a small fortune to bend it straight again, wouldn't it?'

Roper lit a cheroot. Over the lighter-flame, before he snapped it shut, he said: 'This friendship, Stephen—still going on, was it?'

Clark shook his head. Roper snapped his lighter shut, waited.

'No,' said Clark.

'When did it finish, then? Lately?'

'Yes,' said Clark. 'Friday. I went there on Friday, after school.'

'Quarrel?'

'No.... She told me that I was a nice boy...that we could still be friends...but I wasn't to go to the house any more.'

'And what was your reaction to that?'

'I didn't like it.'

'Made you angry, did it? Upset you?'

Clark shook his head. 'No,' he said. 'Not angry. Just dead. Inside.'

'Got a girlfriend, have you, Stephen?'

'No,' said Clark. 'I don't like little girls. They're mostly stupid. That's why I liked Hannah. She wasn't stupid. She could talk about things.'

'Did you attempt to contact her again, Stephen? After Friday?'

Roper half-expected a denial.

'Yes,' said Clark. 'Monday. But all I got was her answering machine.'

'What time?'

'I don't know,' said Clark. 'I suppose about six o'clock.'

Roper opened his pocket book to a blank page, pretended to read it. 'And you said—I've noted here—"I know you're in". That so?'

'I might have done,' said Clark. 'I don't remember.'

'How did you know she was in?'

'Because I'd *seen* her,' said Clark. 'I cycled up there after school, and she pretended she wasn't in.'

'Pretended?'

'The sitting-room lights were all on. And I saw a curtain move in the bedroom. I knew she was watching me. And I *had* to see her. I knew she was older than me, but

I didn't care about that, either. I thought if I could talk to her face to face—get through to her....'

'What then? Did you go round to the back of the house?'

Clark shook his head.

'No,' he said. 'Not that time. I was too angry. I went home.'

Roper chanced his arm a little. 'But you went back *later* on Monday night, didn't you, Stephen?'

Clark looked back at Roper across the table, foursquare and for several long seconds.

'Yes,' he conceded at last with infinite weariness. 'I went back.'

'WHEN?' asked Roper.

'Half-past seven...about. I don't remember exactly. I'd been home and had my dinner.... I didn't ring the door-bell, because I thought she wouldn't answer.'

'So how did you get in?'

'The door to the pool.... It wasn't locked.'

'Where was Mrs Blezard?'

'Upstairs,' said Clark. 'I couldn't see her downstairs, so I called up.'

'And she came down?'

'Yes,' said Clark.

'Did she mind you creeping into her house like that?'

'No,' said Clark. 'Yes, she did. A bit.... But I think she was more scared of me than she was angry.... I was pretty upset. I think she thought I'd gone there for a row.'

'And had you?'

Clark shook his head. 'No.... I only wanted to see her. Talk.... I was angry, but I wouldn't have hurt her.'

'What was she wearing, Stephen? D'you remember?'

'A bathrobe,' said Clark. 'A white one.... But she went back upstairs again and changed.'

'Into what?'

'A sweater and trousers.... Black.'

'How about shoes?'

'Rope-soled things. The ones she always wore about the house.'

Espadrilles. So that shoe tucked under the stern seat of Chaucer's cruiser had, after all, been Mrs Blezard's.

'She went upstairs. She changed. What then, Stephen?'

'We talked. Just talked. Honestly.'

'About what?'

'Everything.' Clark shrugged despondently. 'Nothing.... It was about me, mostly. I don't remember half of it.... She said I could still have that job at the factory.... That we'd still be friends...although I mustn't ever come to the house again, or try to see her. I tried to tell her how I felt, but all the words got muddled up. We had to be adult, she said. We'd had good times together.... And now we had to be sensible. Stuff like that.'

'Did either of you have anything to eat or drink while all this was going on?'

'Yes. She made coffee. And we had some biscuits.'

'Can you remember when?'

Clark struggled to remember, but shook his head. 'No. Not exactly.... I left at about half-past nine. So it was before then. About half an hour I suppose.'

Which would have made it some time around nine o'clock. Wilson had told Roper to add an hour. Which made it nearer ten o'clock. And two witnesses had heard the up-and-over door of Mrs Blezard's garage being opened—or closed—at ten o'clock on Monday night.

'Did you see Mrs Blezard drink any alcohol?'

'Not while I was there.'

'You're sure?'

'Yes.'

Because it had suddenly occurred to Roper that he had seen no dirty drinking-glasses at Mrs Blezard's. And, according to Wilson, the whisky that Mrs Blezard had drunk had gone down her gullet *after* the coffee and biscuits. So either she had drunk alone, and then washed the glass and put it away—was she likely to have done that and yet not washed those two cups and saucers at the same time?—or there had been another visitor, her murderer. In which case *two* glasses may have been used, both of them subsequently washed and put away by that second visitor.

'Can you remember what time you got home, Stephen? On Monday night.'

'It was late,' said Clark. 'And I didn't go straight home. I didn't feel like it. I stopped off at the coffee-bar near the market.'

'Ten o'clock?' proposed Roper. 'Half-past? Eleven?'

'It must have been after midnight,' said Clark. 'I met another guy from school in there. We talked.'

'Was this schoolfriend in the coffee-bar when you arrived?'

'Yes.'

The schoolfriend's name was Christopher Garston. He, too, lived in Challow Street near the infirmary. Clark, to the best of his memory, thought he had reached the coffee-bar about twenty to ten; if young Garston could confirm that, then Clark very nearly had a cast-iron alibi—if only to the tune of twenty minutes.

'When you *left* Mrs Blezard's house, Stephen, which door did you use?'

'The front.'

'On your way out, did you notice if her garage door was open or shut?'

'I think it was shut. I'm sure it was shut.'

Roper gave the boy a rest. He stubbed out his cheroot and relaxed a little, fairly certain now that Stephen Clark was no murderer. The tape clicked to a stop. Price came across the room and turned it over.

'Did Mrs Blezard give you a letter to post on Monday night, Stephen?'

'Yes.'

'What colour was the envelope?'

'Blue.'

'And when did you post it?'

'I forgot,' said Clark irrelevantly. 'She asked me to post it on the way home on Monday night. But I forgot. I found it in my blazer after gym on Tuesday. I posted it at lunch-time.'

'Did she tell you what was in the letter?'

Clark shook his head.

'No,' he said.

'Had she asked you to post letters for her before?'

'Yes. Four…five times.'

'Do you remember who the letter was addressed to?'

'Yes,' said Clark. 'Herself. They all were.'

'Did you ever ask her why?'

'She said they were legal things. It was important to have a dated postmark on them.'

'Did you notice if the address on the envelope was handwritten or typed?'

'Typed,' said Clark. 'They were always typed.'

'Did you ever see a typewriter in Mrs Blezard's house, Stephen?'

No. Clark never had…. And nor, thinking about it—sloppy not to have before—had Roper. Mrs Blezard did *not* have a typewriter. And yet she sent typewritten envelopes to herself. How come?

'After Monday night, Stephen, did you attempt to contact Mrs Blezard again? Or was that the end of it?'

'I rang her Wednesday.... I was going to tell her that everything she'd said on Monday was right. And I wanted us to stay friends.'

'When, son?' asked Roper. 'What time on Wednesday?'

'Morning. About quarter to eleven. I had a double free-study period.'

'Where did you phone from?'

'School staff-room. There's a pay-phone in there. I had permission.'

'Anyone see you?'

'Southey. The art master. He left as I was dialling.'

'And what did you have to say to Mrs Blezard?'

'Nothing,' said Clark. 'I didn't say anything. I got the answering machine again. I supposed she was out. Shopping or something. I didn't know she was dead then. Not till Dad told me on Wednesday night.'

'So you left a message?' A trap, but young Clark didn't fall for it.

He shook his head. 'I was going to, but I didn't.'

Which sounded right, and made Stephen Clark the last mysterious caller on Mrs Blezard's answering machine on Wednesday morning, after that marker of Roper's. And he was unlikely to have made that call—and not spoken—if he had *known* that Mrs Blezard was dead. Unless he was very shrewd. Which Roper doubted. When Stephen Clark had left her house that night, Mrs Blezard had still been very much alive.

FOURTEEN

THEN ROPER took Stephen Clark over it all again, step by step, with a new tape in the machine behind him.

'When you went out that day in Mr Chaucer's cruiser, how did Mrs Blezard introduce you to him?'

'She said I was her nephew.'

'Which wasn't true, was it?'

Clark shrugged. 'That was her idea, not mine. Anyway, it didn't hurt anybody.'

'Added a bit of spice, did it? All these lies?'

'Yes, if you want to know.'

'And then she gave you the elbow, eh, son?' said Roper.

'It wasn't like that. I told you.'

Roper gave him a break for a few minutes. A constable brought in three coffees. Clark hadn't budged from his original answers. He had arrived uninvited at Mrs Blezard's house at roughly seven-thirty on Monday night. Entered by way of the conservatory door. He remembered seeing a towel draped over the back of one of the loungers beside the pool; and when Mrs Blezard had hurried downstairs in response to his call she had been in the robe she usually put on after a swim, and her hair was wet by her ears. He thought she was naked under the robe; which would account for Roper not having seen a swimming costume. She had seen him settled in the lounge, then returned upstairs to dress. For the best part of an hour, then, they had talked—or, rather, Mrs Blezard had, as whatever the feminine equivalent was of a Dutch uncle. Clark had insisted that there had been no quarrel between them, despite the circumstances. He had borne no grudge, so he had further insisted. Bitter disappointment, yes. But not a grudge. Mrs Blezard had been right. The friendship had been fun while it lasted, but there had been no future in it and, just lately, Clark's work at school had been slipping, and his A-levels were only just around the corner. He knew that he had to buckle to and get on with them.

Roper switched on the recorder again.

'What time did you leave Mrs Blezard's house on Monday evening, Stephen?'

'I told you. Half-past nine.'

'You seem very sure.'

'I am,' said Clark. 'She'd set a time-limit. Whatever happened, she said, I had to be gone by half-past nine. She had an appointment.'

That was new. So Mrs Blezard had *definitely* had another visitor, so there probably had been two dirty whisky-tumblers; and the murderer had washed both of them. But *not* the coffee-cups because he had realised that they would point the police in another direction entirely—or, rather, he had hoped so. And he had been very nearly right.

'Did she say who with?'

'No,' said Clark.

'When did she ask you to post that letter for her?'

'On my way out,' said Clark. 'It was lying beside the telephone in the hall. She said she'd meant to post it that afternoon, but she'd forgotten.'

'And you posted it at Tuesday lunch-time?'

'Yes,' said Clark. 'I forgot I'd got it.'

'And you didn't realise Mrs Blezard was dead until

you and your father had your row on Wednesday night. That right?'

'Yes,' said Clark. 'Honestly.'

THREE MORE COFFEES. Roper had lit another cheroot. The tape-recorder had been switched off.

'Care to tell us what happened at home on Wednesday night, Stephen?' asked Price.

'Is that your business, too?' asked Clark.

'No,' said Price. 'But it's put your father in the local infirmary for a couple of days, whatever it was.'

'Not what *I* did to him,' said Clark bitterly. 'I didn't get the chance. He went ape again.'

'Again?' queried Roper.

'He was always going spare lately,' said Clark. 'On Monday night, my sister told him two or three of the girls had seen a man outside the school in an old van. He looked as if he was taking photographs of them playing netball. The old man went bonkers. Asked her what the van was like. And when Sue told him he was up like a flash and putting his coat on. Mum practically had to beg him not to go out. He knew who the man in the van was. He was going round to wipe the floor with the bastard. At least, that's what he said he was going to do. He never stops being a copper, my dad.'

'How about Wednesday night?' asked Price.

'I was up in my bedroom revising. The next thing I knew he was there. He grabbed me...here'—Clark grabbed a fistful of T-shirt over his chest—'and hauled me up. I didn't know what love was, he said. A woman like that'd be screwed by anybody.... I didn't even know who he was talking about. Mrs Blezard, he said. He knew about it. He'd heard my voice on her answering machine...and he'd had to lie for me. I was dirty. Filth. And so was she. He went crazy after that. I couldn't hold him off, even though he's littler than me, and I still didn't really know what it was all about. I tried not to hit him back…but I had to. I thought he was going to kill me.'

'I can only see a thick lip,' said Roper.

'And the rest,' retorted Clark angrily. He hitched up the front of his red T-shirt. 'What about these, then?'

His ribs were daubed with pale yellow bruises, much as Norman Oates's had been.

'Then what happened?'

Clark dropped the hem of his shirt. 'I hit him,' he said. 'Hard. Then Mum came in…and Sue was screaming her head off on the landing. Honestly, it was a madhouse.'

It was at this juncture that the frightened Mrs Clark had gone downstairs to telephone Butcher. But Terence Clark had followed her down and taken the receiver out of her hand.

'Do you know what I heard him say? To Mum? "He'll live," he said. Just that. "He'll live." He really *was* like a bloody madman. Honestly. Mum thinks he's ill, but I think he's on the twist. When they'd all gone to bed, I packed my duffel-bag, left a note for Mum, and took off on the bike. I was going to put up for the night at the YMCA in Dorchester, and yesterday morning I was going to cycle on up to Norfolk, to my gran's. Only I'd come off the bike in the dark by Cogden Heath. The road was wet. I thought I'd broken my ankle. Then I remembered the old Home Guard place and crawled up there.'

Clark had spent two nights and a day in the bunker and lived on rainwater and a packet of biscuits he had filched from his mother's pantry on his way out of the house on Wednesday night. And it was not until yesterday morning, listening to Radio Solent on his Walkman radio in the bunker, that he had realised the full import

of his father's vituperative ramblings and that Hannah
Blezard was not only dead but murdered.

'I didn't mean to start a fuss. All I wanted to do was
to get away for a while, have a few weeks on my own
until I sorted everything out.' Then what Price had told
him earlier, about his father being in hospital, suddenly
recaptured his attention.

'Why's my father in hospital?' he said, and if Roper
read the abrupt digression rightly there was hope for the
boy and his father yet. 'Nothing I did to him, is it?'

THE REUNION between Clark and his mother took place
in Butcher's office, while he and Roper waited outside in
the passage. Writ large on Butcher's face was a relief
akin to Mrs Clark's.

'You're not charging him, then?' asked Roper, recall-
ing Butcher's wrath a couple of hours ago downstairs.

'We all deserve a second chance,' said Butcher. 'And
I don't think the poor little sod knew whether he was on
his backside or his elbow.'

'*And* his father's a copper.'

'Don't need the publicity, do we, Douglas? We take a
couple of stolen sheep back to a farmer and we're the
good guys. Pick him up the next day for crashing a set
of lights and we're the most evil sods on God's earth.
Can't win, can we?'

'No argument,' said Roper, because it was, alas, all
too irrefutable. And in all truth and for much the same
reason Roper was equally relieved to see the back of
young Clark as a suspect. No public organisation likes a
bad press, and few could afford it less.

Clark limped from the office with his mother behind
him. He was in carpet slippers and leaning on a stick. He
stuck out a hand to Butcher.

'I'm sorry, Mr Butcher,' he said, and looked as if he meant it.

'Good,' said Butcher, taking the hand and holding it fast. 'Now you can go downstairs and apologise for putting the boot in on my four lads. They're waiting for you in the parade room. And this afternoon I suggest you go along to the infirmary with your mother and chat up your father.'

'Yes, sir,' said Clark. 'And I really am sorry.'

'Good,' said Butcher, at last loosening his grip on Clark's hand. 'Now hop it before I change my mind and throw the bloody book at you.'

Mrs Clark was sensible enough to let her son precede her downstairs on his own. She took Butcher's hand. 'I can't thank you enough, Philip,' she said.

'Forget it, Julie,' said Butcher. 'It didn't happen.'

'And you, too, Mr Roper,' she said. 'Even though I know it's not all over yet.'

Her clasp was strong with emotion, her hand icy cold, her eyes still raw. But at least her troubles were halved now.

'I'll be writing to the Chief Constable, Mrs Clark. It may not go too badly.'

'Thank you,' she said again, smiled wanly, and turned and followed her son downstairs.

'You're getting soft, Douglas,' said Butcher, when she was gone from earshot.

'Me?' said Roper. 'Not on your bloody life.'

BY MIDDAY Roper, Price, Makins and Rodgers were crammed together in Roper's temporary office and back on the business of two murder inquiries. During the course of the morning, an enlarged photograph of the blue envelope which Mrs Blezard had addressed to herself had arrived post-haste from the laboratory. The type-written characters on its front had been blown up by some four or five times and several of them ringed with Chinagraph pencil. Because of the consistency of the pressure that had been applied to the keys, Guthrie's expert suggested the typewriter was an electric one. An old model, and much used. The dot over the lower-case *i* had a chip out of one side; so had the crossbar of the lower-case *t*. The lower-case *e*, the most used letter on any typewriter, was blurred with wear, its upper loop encrusted with dirt so that it tended to be only a dark blob with a hook beneath it.

'Could take days to find a typewriter like that,' ventured Makins. 'Unless it's tucked away somewhere in Blezard's offices.'

'Come on, George,' said Roper tartly. 'You can do better than that. Who do we know for sure has got a typewriter—and one that *really* gets hammered?'

Makins's eyes took on a sudden bright gleam.

'Bloody Westlake. Who lived next door.'

'Right,' said Roper.

PRICE RAPPED DOWN twice on the grinning brass goblin. On Roper's other side stood WDC Anderson with a zippered document-case under her arm. The sky was overcast, the drizzle ceaseless, tempting Roper to draw the conclusion that the world would end like this; no bang, no whimper, only the steady splash and drip of falling rainwater.

A bolt was taken off the cottage door, and there was Hollister, his jaw dropping, as Price was later to relate, somewhere down by his carpet slippers.

'Afternoon, Mr Hollister,' said Roper. 'Sorry to trouble you again, sir, but we'd like a word with Mr Westlake.

Very briefly, sir.... If he's not too busy.' Which he was, because Roper could hear the typewriter rattling away from the depths of the hall.

'Why, yes, I suppose so,' said Hollister reluctantly, but with what Roper considered a masterly exercise in the recovery of his aplomb. 'All of you?'

'Yes, sir, please,' said Roper, his smile still fixed meticulously in place. 'If you don't mind.'

'Yes.... Right,' said Hollister. Facial expression good, script bad. He'd *definitely* been caught on the hop. He opened the door wider, and left them to enter and wipe their shoes on the mat while he went down the hall to fetch Westlake.

Westlake was wearing a pink shirt today, and a scarlet choker almost hidden under his several chins. And he was more out of breath than he had been yesterday; asthma, probably. But, whatever it was, it seemed certain that he could never have overcome a healthy woman such as Mrs Blezard had been; neither could he have picked up her corpse, let alone carried it for any distance.

He patted his chest to signify his condition further. 'Sorry.... Out of puff today.... Afternoon to you. Enter. Please.' A hand flapped like a seal's flipper to usher them into the front room. 'Do go in.'

They arranged themselves in the capacious chairs, Westlake in the one he had used on Wednesday afternoon, WDC Anderson in the one of which Hollister had sat on the arm. Hollister was about to lower himself on to the settee next to Price, but didn't quite reach it before Westlake reached across and touched his arm.

'Puffer first, Rollie,' wheezed Westlake. 'Must have puffer.'

Hollister hastened off to another room.

'Asthma,' gasped Westlake. 'Very bad. Be all right when I've had a squirt. Sorry.'

Hollister returned as quickly as he had gone and held out a pharmaceutical spray to Westlake, who was now gulping for air like a goldfish. With fluttering fingers, Westlake seized it and pumped a couple of doses into his open mouth. Roper watched the colour slowly return to his face.

'We *can* call back, Mr Westlake.'

Westlake's hand flapped again to decline the offer. 'No.... Really.... All right in a jiffy.... Worse to see than it is to have.'

The moment passed. The spray was handed back to Hollister, who capped it and put it on the shelf above the fireplace before settling down again on the settee next to Price.

Westlake had begun to breathe easily again.

Hollister was lighting a cigarette. In the dreary grey daylight, he looked quite old this afternoon. He was wearing another bagged-out cardigan, a glimpse of grey sock showing at the worn toe of one of his slippers. He was definitely the poor relation here, the hired man.

'Now, how can we help you, Superintendent?' asked Westlake, still with a wheeze in his voice but clearly now recovered enough to call the meeting to order. 'Have you offered them tea, Rollie?'

'No, sir, thank you,' broke in Roper, before Hollister had a chance to reply. 'Don't want to keep you too long. A couple of minutes and we'll be gone again.' He left a pause hanging. 'I was wondering if WDC Anderson here could tap out a few words on your typewriter, sir.'

Westlake was puzzled. Hollister had briefly frozen.

'Why, yes,' said Westlake, 'I don't see why not. We've certainly nothing to hide, have we, Rollie?... But

I'd be interested to know why.... I'm sure my typewriter is an entirely innocent party. Mm?' He beamed, and leaned sideways and reached out to squeeze Hollister's wrist. 'Show the young lady the way, Rollie, there's a good fellow. And take the sheet I'm using out of the typewriter for her, will you? And put a new sheet in.'

'We've brought our own paper, sir,' said Roper. Beside him, Anderson had unzipped her document-case and was taking out a brand-new packet of Basildon Bond blue envelopes.

'Aren't you people supposed to have a warrant or something?' asked Hollister irritably as he rose, perhaps because he now knew better than anyone else in the room what the outcome of this visit might be.

'I can get one, sir,' Roper replied amiably, smiling up at him. 'But Mr Westlake seems agreeable enough. And it's a lot of bother, sir. Paperwork. Visit to the magistrate. Phone calls. I'm sure Mr Westlake understands.'

'Quite,' agreed Westlake. 'Don't make such a fuss, Rollie. Go on. Chop-chop. There's a good fellow.'

Hollister definitely didn't like the 'chop-chop', although Westlake had uttered it guilelessly enough.

'This way,' he said, and Anderson passed her case across to Roper and followed Hollister along to the study.

'It's all *very* mysterious, Superintendent,' confided Westlake, hugely delighted at being so close to the centre of a possible drama. 'Will I be able to use whatever it is for a plot, d'you think?'

'Do you write mysteries, Mr Westlake?'

'I write about the biggest mystery of all,' replied Westlake gravely. 'Love.'

'Then, I'm sure you'll find a way, sir,' said Roper, with equal gravity. From the next room came the soft ratcheting of a typewriter being fed with paper.

'Is it an electric typewriter, sir?' asked Roper.

'Yes, indeed,' said Westlake. 'One of the first. An old and very dear friend, that typewriter.'

'Do you ever have it serviced?'

'No,' said Westlake, horrified. 'Never! Bad luck. I'm very superstitious.'

In the next room, Anderson's fingers were dashing out Mrs Blezard's name and address. The ratchet sounded again. Then Anderson was coming back with a tight-faced Hollister behind her. She handed the newly typed envelope down to Roper, and he took from the document-case a magnifying glass and the photographic enlargement of the original envelope that Butcher's constable had intercepted from Mrs Blezard's postman. He compared the two under the glass. In the final analysis, it would need an expert witness, but at this stage Roper was expert enough.

'Please sit down, Mr Hollister,' he said.

Hollister resumed his place beside Price, rose again briefly to stub out his cigarette, then sat down again with his hands tightly clasped together between his knees.

'Did Mrs Blezard ever use your typewriter, Mr Westlake?'

'No,' said Westlake unequivocally. 'Never.'

'How about you, Mr Hollister?'

Hollister didn't reply. Westlake's expression was suddenly one of concern. 'Well, answer the man, Rollie. It's a simple enough question.'

But still Hollister made no reply. Then, with a sudden and unexpected vehemence, he addressed himself spitefully to Westlake. 'You don't understand, do you, you bloody old fool? She was my daughter.'

FIFTEEN

HOLLISTER DRAGGED a handkerchief across his nose. In the study next door, Price was interviewing Westlake, the rumble of their voices rising and falling. Anderson had her notebook opened on the arm of her chair.

'I'm sorry,' said Hollister, balling the crumpled handkerchief between his hands. 'The last few days have been very hard. I couldn't let anything show, you see.'

'Why not, sir? She was your daughter, after all.'

'Oh, it's a lot more complicated than that,' sighed Hollister. 'A hell of a lot more.'

Roper could have told him that it usually was.

'Were you blackmailing her, Mr Hollister?'

'No,' replied Hollister passionately. 'Of course I bloody wasn't!'

'The envelope we intercepted had something like a blackmail note inside it.'

'I only ever typed envelopes for her. No letters.'

Roper took due note of Hollister's use of the plural. 'Type many of them, did you, Mr Hollister?'

'Yes,' said Hollister. 'Quite a few.'

'What's "quite a few", Mr Hollister? Ten? Twenty? A hundred?'

Hollister shook his head as he tried to cast his mind back. 'I honestly don't know,' he said. 'I typed more for her lately. A couple a month, at least.'

'Since when, sir?'

'Oh,' mumbled Hollister, hanging his head and staring

down at the handkerchief he was still toying with. 'Last Easter. About then.'

'So about six months, sir?'

'Yes,' said Hollister. 'Sounds about right.'

'I'd rather hear it from you, Mr Hollister.'

'Yes, then,' snapped Hollister. 'Six months. I typed those envelopes for *six months. That* better?'

Roper ignored the outburst. 'And you never saw what she put in these envelopes?'

'No,' said Hollister. 'Never.'

'But you had some idea of what the contents might be?'

'No,' said Hollister. 'I keep telling you. I only ever typed the bloody envelopes.'

'You know, Mr Hollister,' said Roper patiently, 'I'm going to ask my DC to stop noting your answers for a minute or two—and ask you that question again. Only this time I suggest you take your time answering it. *And* tell me the truth, sir. And if I think you're *still* lying I'm going to caution you formally and ask you to accompany us to the police station. Now, sir, did you or did you not have any idea what Mrs Blezard put inside those envelopes?'

For a few moments more, Hollister did battle with himself, turning the ball of handkerchief over and over between his hands. Whatever conflict was going on inside him was clearly a painful one.

'Yes,' burst softly from him at last. 'Yes. I knew.... But they owed us.... *Everybody* owed us.'

'Us?' said Roper. 'That's you and your daughter us, is it, Mr Hollister? Or some other us.'

Hollister looked scornfully at him. '*Our* us,' he said, as if Roper should already have understood that. 'Hannah...and me. She was my *daughter,* for God's sake.'

'And who exactly owed you, sir?' asked Roper.

'They all did,' said Hollister bitterly. 'That bastard next door. He owes.' He jerked his head in the general direction of the study.

Roper presumed he meant Westlake, which went some way to reinforcing the conclusion he had drawn yesterday: that Hollister only lived with Westlake under some kind of sufferance. And yet, somehow, that conclusion did not seem to operate the other way around.

'What does Mr Westlake owe you, sir? In the particular.'

'Everything,' said Hollister rancorously. 'From the breakfast he gets in bed each morning, that bloody coffin of a car I have to polish, to the sleeping pills I count out for him each night. The man's a buffoon. Even his writing's rubbish.'

'But he keeps you, sir,' Roper reminded him. 'Or isn't that so?'

'Pocket money,' sneered Hollister. 'Thirty years ago, I could have kept him. And a damned sight better than in this crabby little place, too.'

'I see, sir,' said Roper. 'But tell me, Mr Hollister, your daughter had a smart house next door. Why didn't you move in with her?'

'I was going to,' said Hollister. 'It was just a matter of time. A few more months. We were going to set up house together.'

'Next door?'

Hollister shook his head. 'God, no,' he retorted fiercely. 'We both of us couldn't get far enough away from this damned place.'

Roper at last saw the light or, rather, at least a distant glimmer of it. Mrs Blezard did not have a house to sell; her bank account here in King's Minster was down to eighty pounds; she had borrowed a few hundred off Marshall as recently as Monday lunch-time, and a few months back a few thousand, without security, from Arthur Chaucer—that 'bridging loan' as she had called it. And Hollister, unless he had more tucked away somewhere, looked as if he had only a few pennies to rub together. Ergo....

'So where were you going to set up this house, sir?'

'Spain,' said Hollister. 'It's all arranged. Or it was.'

'And this house in Spain is paid for, is it, Mr Hollister?'

'It's taken us years,' said Hollister. 'Every penny we could lay our hands on.'

The light that Roper had earlier glimpsed grew brighter. A house in Spain was one thing; living in Spain, perhaps in idleness, was quite another, especially for two. It would require money in some quantity, and perhaps more than Mrs Blezard's monthly salary-chit from the factory. Hannah Blezard would never have considered living in paupery. So Mr Bohun senior had been right. A lot more money must have poured from Mrs Blezard's handbag than had ever, at least legitimately, been tipped into it, and certainly more than she had ever received from Blezard's Electronics.

Roper returned to the matter of the blue envelope, and its curious contents. 'You never saw what went into these envelopes, you say?'

Hollister shook his head.

'But she told you the general idea, didn't she, Mr Hollister?'

Hollister nodded. 'Yes,' he sighed. 'She told me.'

'So now tell me, sir, please.'

THE DEEPER Roper trod into the morass of human motivation, the more he despaired of the species, and there

surely wasn't a body of written law in the entire world
that was large enough to encompass the infinite com-
plexity of man's skulduggery. Mrs Blezard had indulged
in remote-control blackmail, or at best been guilty of ob-
taining money by deception.

'Who did she show these letters to, sir?'

'I don't know,' said Hollister. His dark eyes rose and
met Roper's doubting ones. 'I *swear* I don't know. She
always said that it was best I didn't. In case it went
wrong. She didn't want me party to it.'

'One of her men friends, perhaps, sir?'

'Had to be,' said Hollister. Roper measured him, and
decided he was now telling the truth. As Clark had been
last night, Hollister was rapidly reaching the end of his
tether as his emotions, perhaps repressed for the last few
days, were at last catching up with him.

'Who were these men friends, sir. Any idea?'

'There were several,' said Hollister. He paused to blow
his nose again. 'Several.... That little pipsqueak Chaucer.
Hannah had *him* around her little finger.... And a chap
called Marshall, from the factory. And that boy I told
you about the other day, although I think she was gen-
uinely fond of him for a while. Ridiculous, of course, a
lad like that, but Hannah was terrified of hitting forty.
Having a boy that age falling for her.... Well, you can
imagine.'

'And you think she showed a particular man friend
these letters, told him she was being blackmailed about
something or other, and the gentleman in question paid
up for her. That it?'

Hollister nodded. 'Yes,' he said. 'I think so.'

'Out of the goodness of his heart, eh, Mr Hollister?'

Hollister glanced up inimically, looking for irony, but

finding none. 'You never saw her alive, Superintendent,' he said. 'She was full of fire and life, charming. She deserved better than she got with that bastard Blezard.... He left her bloody nearly destitute, do you know that?'

Hardly destitute, thought Roper, but he didn't pursue it. And if he had wanted a character reference for the late Mr Blezard he would rather have plumped for Mrs Crispin's.

'We know that Mrs Blezard had a new will drafted last year, Mr Hollister. Do you know where it might be? Only we haven't been able to find it, sir.'

'Yes,' said Hollister, to Roper's surprise. 'I have it...all her private papers...upstairs in a deed-box.'

'Gave them to you for safe keeping, did she, sir?'

'No,' said Hollister. 'Not exactly.'

'So how do you come to have them, Mr Hollister?' asked Roper. 'Exactly.'

'I picked them up on Monday night,' said Hollister. 'And her handbag. I couldn't just leave them there, you see. Something had happened to her. I knew it.'

Like a discarded kettle of yesterday's soup, the deeper Roper stirred into all this business the murkier it became. 'I see sir,' he said, with commendable self-control. 'You *knew* something had happened to her. Are you psychic, Mr Hollister?'

'No,' said Hollister. 'She rang me every night at ten-thirty. Without fail. Even when she was away somewhere. We'd become very close.'

Roper leaned back in the capacious leather settee, his thinking momentarily blurred by the constantly shifting scene that Hollister was putting to him, and feeling doubt as palpably as a cold draught on a winter morning. He recalled the look of hurt and shock on Florian Westlake's face when Hollister had flung at him the accusation that

Westlake was a bloody old fool. A few moments after
Price had gone into the study to talk with Westlake, he
had returned for Westlake's asthma spray. Whatever anger had lurked in Hollister for God knew how many
years, Westlake hadn't known of it. Until today. For three
years, Westlake and Hollister had lived next door to Hollister's daughter. And Westlake hadn't known about that,
either. Nor would he have known about the nightly telephone calls that Hannah Blezard made to Hollister, since
he went to bed at nine-thirty every night with a fistful of
sleeping pills inside him. All of which begged so many
questions that Roper was hard put as to which one to ask
first.

'I think, Mr Hollister,' he said patiently, 'that I'd like
you to start again, sir. From the beginning.'

LIKE MOST PERSONAL remembrances, Hollister's recall of
them was a jumbled disorder of years and incidents, leap-
ing backwards and forwards in time as the memory of
one happening sparked to life the memory of another.
Roper listened, prompting only occasionally. Anderson
had stopped taking notes; since most of the anachronistic
jumble was irrelevant to the matter in hand, there was
little point. It was easier to listen now and unravel afterwards.

Hollister's life seemed to have been a mess from the
very beginning. Separated parents. A commission in the
Army in the closing days of the war had seen him helping
to create order from the chaos of a displaced persons'
camp in southern Austria. In the mean time there had
been a marriage. It had failed. And, like most ex-soldiers,
military training had given the young Lieutenant Hollister
no equipment to face the equally harsh realities of peace.
He had sold shoes, electric-light fittings; at one point, his

lowest, he had been employed as a chauffeur. He had not so much gone into acting as drifted into it. As an extra in crowd scenes, as a waiter with a line or two, bit parts. Then, in the first year of the fifties, his name began to appear, even if low down, on the bills. Another marriage, his second and last, in 1951, to an aspiring actress. It had finished within eighteen months; he had arrived back from the studios one night to find an empty wardrobe and a letter on the bed. A few months afterwards, another letter arrived, this one from a Reno lawyer informing him that he was divorced, that his wife was remarrying and would make no further claim upon him. The slide into drink soon followed, and with that decline came a similar deterioration in the parts that were offered him. By the late fifties, there was one year when his sole spell of acting was in a television soap-commercial—as a re-moval man. His final fall from grace came in his ap-pearance at the South London Magistrates' Court in the middle of the sixties. He had struck a policeman who was in the process of taking him in on a drunk and dis-orderly charge. He was fined ten pounds, which he did not have; the alternative was seven days' imprisonment.

His rescuer was Florian Westlake, in the court as a spectator that morning and by way of doing some re-search into the lesser purlieus of British justice. He had recognised Hollister as the small-time screen actor he had once been, paid the fine and bought Hollister a meal, a new suit and a haircut.

FOR SIXTEEN YEARS, Hollister had lived with Westlake in the latter's flat overlooking the river at Chelsea. Then as Westlake's asthma had progressively worsened, and his doctor advised a cleaner air than London provided, he and Hollister had moved down here to Dorset, to this cottage, where the two of them had lived ever since, Westlake writing his romances and Hollister dealing with the more mundane chores of gardening, shopping and seeing that the bills got paid on time.

And then, like a plot from one of Westlake's books, or one of Hollister's B-pictures, Hollister became friendly with the young widow next door; only to discover within a few days that she was his daughter, born in Los Angeles and brought back to England by her mother within the year, when that lady's second marriage had failed, and her proposed Hollywood career similarly. She had been told by her mother that her father was dead, and he on his part had not known of her existence.

'But you kept all this from Mr Westlake, Mr Hollister,' Roper broke in. 'I don't understand that.'

'No,' said Hollister bitterly. 'You wouldn't. But, then, *you* haven't been owned lock, stock and barrel by someone else for twenty years, have you? Fetching and carrying, dosing him up with aspirins every time his nose runs, taking him up his breakfast in bed—on his special plate, with his special bloody cup and saucer—washing the plastic flowers in his bloody window-boxes, polishing that bloody stupid door-knocker....'

Roper heard out the list of Hollister's grievances in silence, until he finally came to the point and belatedly answered Roper's question.

'She was the only private thing I had, the one part of my life that Westlake didn't know about. She was mine, Superintendent. *Mine.* For the first time in my life I was able to make plans. And bloody Florian didn't know about them. Can you imagine that?'

Roper presumed the question was rhetorical. In any event he didn't answer it. 'Tell me about Monday night,

Mr Hollister. What time was it when you went across to Mrs Blezard's house?'

Brought up short amidst his reminiscences and bitter accusations, it took a few moments for Hollister to bring his mind back to order and recall the events of Monday night. The handkerchief by now was twisted from corner to corner like a rope.

'Monday,' he said, distantly, frowning. 'Yes.... I was out at the dustbin.... I heard the sound of her garage door.... Did I tell you that? Ten o'clock.... I remember the time because the news had just started on the box.... I didn't think much of it at the time. I simply thought it was Hannah coming home.... I'd thought she'd been out when she didn't ring back about my message on her answering machine.... Well, that was always the first thing she did as soon as she got indoors—run through any messages on the machine. I waited until ten-thirty, the time she always rang across. Ten-thirty, on the dot. Always. But on Monday she didn't. So I rang her again, and *still* got the machine.' Which accounted for the first two blank passages that Roper recalled hearing on that tape. 'Which I thought was odd, because all her downstairs lights were on. Anyway, about a quarter to eleven, after ringing again, I decided to go across there. I had this feeling...here.' Hollister tapped his forehead. The handkerchief slowly unwound. 'Vibes. Bad ones. I *knew* something had happened. I'm not sure what the time was then.'

'How did you get in?' asked Roper.

'She'd given me a key,' said Hollister. 'Keys, in fact. A Chubb and a Yale. But I only had to use the Yale; the Chubb was already unlocked, which it only ever was when she was in.'

'What size shoes do you wear, Mr Hollister?' asked Roper.

'Eights,' said Hollister. Which was another set of foot-prints accounted for.

'Go on, sir,' said Roper. 'You went into the house....'

'I stood in the hall and called out,' said Hollister. 'She didn't answer. I thought she might be having a shower and hadn't heard me. So I went upstairs. There was no one in the bathroom, nor in the bedrooms. I went back downstairs. Saw the hi-fi was switched on. And the elec-tric fire. And that wasn't right, either. I went out to the pool.... Its door was open.'

'Open, Mr Hollister?' interrupted Roper. 'Or just un-locked?'

'No,' said Hollister. 'Open. Wedged open with half a brick.'

'Did you leave it like that?'

Hollister shook his head. 'No. I shut it. It wasn't all that warm outside, and the house was losing all its heat. I looked around the garden for her, thought she might have had an accident out there. I couldn't see her.... I went back inside...and I began to notice things.'

'Like what, sir?' asked Roper.

'Two cups on the coffee-table. And two whisky-tumblers. One still had a finger of Scotch in it.'

'You saw *two* tumblers, Mr Hollister?' Roper broke in again. 'You sure?'

'Yes,' said Hollister. 'Quite sure.'

Roper tried Hollister out on Kim's game, and Hollister was remarkably good at it. He remembered everything that had been on the glass-topped coffee-table: the news-papers—the *Financial Times* on top; the unused glass ashtray; two coffee-cups—beige ones with dark brown rims; two cork coasters; and the two cut-crystal whisky-tumblers that Roper had *not* seen. And if there had indeed been two tumblers on the table when Hollister had visited the house around eleven o'clock on Monday night, then Roper was forced to draw two more conclusions: that young Clark had been telling the truth when he had spoken of Mrs Blezard expecting another visitor that night; and that that visitor had murdered her, taken her body out to sea, and only then remembered that he had left his fingerprints on a glass and had to return to the house to wash them off and put the two glasses away. The two cups and saucers would not have mattered; he hadn't touched those.

And from those two conclusions Roper drew yet another: that Mrs Blezard's car had been left in Witling Lane, a quarter of a mile from the house, because her murderer, possibly on his way back from his night's work, may have seen the shadow of Hollister....

'How long were you in the house, Mr Hollister?'

'Oh,' mumbled Hollister, frowning, 'it must have been midnight at least.... I sat there waiting.'

'Did you go near the windows?'

'Yes, I expect so,' said Hollister. 'Several times. Looking out for her—you know? I was worried.'

'She was thirty-five, Mr Hollister,' Roper reminded him.

Hollister flared. 'She was my *daughter,* for Christ's sake. And the *pattern* was all wrong. She hadn't phoned. The pool door was opened. Someone had been—and she never went out and left dirty cups and saucers and glasses lying about. She was like me. Tidy. It struck me as being all wrong. I can't tell you how, exactly, but I knew it was *all wrong.* She would never have gone out and left the house open like that. And without a handbag.'

'Did you touch anything, Mr Hollister? Wash up the glasses, perhaps?'

'No,' said Hollister. 'I was too on edge. I don't think I touched anything except the pool door and the curtains. And I turned off the electric fire.'

Hollister had not used Mrs Blezard's front gate on Monday night, but come through a gap in the hedge that bordered the two gardens.

'Did you look in her garage?' asked Roper.

'Yes,' said Hollister. 'Soon after I went over there.'

'And was Mrs Blezard's car in it?'

'No,' said Hollister. 'Definitely.'

HOLLISTER HAD BEEN upstairs to fetch the deed-box that he had taken into his charge on Monday night, together with the handbag that his daughter had obviously been using that day. And a photograph-album.

Roper opened the handbag first. Grey leather, brass fittings, good quality like everything else of Mrs Blezard's. The contents were unspectacular. A wallet with a couple of ten-pound notes in it, two credit cards, three postage stamps and her driving licence. A wad of paper handkerchiefs, a purse with a few pounds' worth of coins in it, and her set of door keys. Eye make-up, a lipstick, a powder-compact. But no car keys.

Hollister swore that he had not opened the handbag, but only picked it up from the settee as an afterthought on his way from the house.

'If I'd seen those door keys, I'd have been more worried still.'

'If you were that worried, Mr Hollister,' said Roper, 'why didn't you ring the police?'

'Because I had nothing to go on, did I?' said Hollister. 'And you seemed very unconcerned when we called here on Wednesday afternoon,' said Roper. 'And all the time we were talking you had your daughter's private papers and her handbag tucked away upstairs. You also knew by that time that your daughter had been drowned. And you still kept quiet about going across to her house on Monday night. Very strange reaction, that, Mr Hollister, for a father.'

Hollister didn't answer at once. His hands were back to fiddling with the handkerchief. 'You're wrong,' he said at length. 'I was half out of my bloody mind.'

'But there was a lot you should have told us. And didn't.'

'Yes,' said Hollister, 'I know. But there was a lot at stake, and I'd had a couple of hours to pull myself together—and I swear I didn't know then that she'd been murdered. I knew that she'd left me everything, you see, and that it hadn't all been come by honestly. I thought I could play everything down...perhaps wait a couple of years...when everyone had forgotten what had happened....' Hollister's voice tailed away, perhaps because even he was forced to realise the naïvety of what he was saying. Roper gave him the benefit of the doubt. There were crimes of omission and crimes of intent, and heaven alone knew what had passed through Hollister's mind after he had heard the announcement on Radio Solent of his daughter's body being fished out of the river.

Roper turned over a few pages of the photograph-album. And soon saw why Hollister had removed it from Mrs Blezard's on Monday night. Many of the photographs were of Hollister, several of them of Hollister and Mrs Blezard together; the beach in the background looked like a slice of Spain.

Roper took up the deed-box and balanced it on his knees while he opened it. It was jammed with papers.

Her will, nominating Roland Jervis Hollister as her beneficiary; marriage certificate, passport, a cash-book, the
deeds to her Spanish villa and all the legal documents
and records that its purchase had entailed. And a thick
swatch of share certificates, in plastic envelopes, purchased through a Spanish bank and a Spanish broker, all
of them in the name of H. G. Hollister, her maiden name.
Roper didn't know the current value of the peseta, but
the values of the shares looked as if they ran into several
millions of them.

'We know that your daughter borrowed ten thousand
pounds from someone a couple of months back, Mr Hollister,' said Roper. 'Would you know what she wanted
that for?'

'Yes,' said Hollister. He really did look very old, very
tired. 'She needed it to pay the Spanish builders. They'd
finished the job a couple of months ahead of time and
wanted cash. On the nail. It was part of the agreement,
but it caught us out. We expected them to finish late.
And Hannah was temporarily out of cash after buying all
those shares. She'd ploughed in everything she'd got. The
dividends and her money from Blezard's were going to
keep us, you see. And it was a bad time to sell shares.'

'So she borrowed?'

'Yes,' said Hollister. 'I don't know who from, but she
borrowed.'

There was still plainly much about his daughter that
Roland Hollister had yet to learn. And Arthur Chaucer
could say goodbye to his ten thousand pounds, that was
equally certain; unless the lads from the Fraud Squad
could work a miracle for him.

ROPER HAD RISEN and was buttoning his raincoat. Anderson was zipping her document-case. Hollister was still

sitting hunched on the settee, on the arm beside him the receipt that Roper had just given to him for the handbag, the album and the deed-box.

The floorboards creaked in the passage. Florian Westlake, Price behind his right shoulder, stood in the doorway and looked disconsolately over the back of the settee at the huddled figure of Roland Hollister.

'I thought you were my friend, Rollie,' he wheezed. 'I really did.'

Hollister slowly stood up, picking up the receipt from the arm of the settee as he straightened. He looked at Westlake coldly and levelly for several seconds.

'It was an act, Flo,' he said. 'I hate the bloody sight of you. I'm sorry.'

SIXTEEN

ROPER, PRICE and Makins sat around Roper's desk, the contents of Mrs Blezard's deed-box spread in front of them. It was four o'clock of that same afternoon, the sky still an endless sombre grey, the rain incessant.

The investigation had moved. Not far, but it had moved. Whoever had been Mrs Blezard's other visitor on Monday night had called after Stephen Clark had left and before Roland Hollister had arrived. And gone back to the house again after Hollister had finally quit it. To wash those forgotten whisky-tumblers.

Roper had hoped to find a name or two in Mrs Blezard's cash-book; but there were no names, only dates and sums of money she had obtained on those dates, five hundred here, five hundred there, occasionally a thousand. The dates went back three years, a month or two after her husband had dropped dead in his factory. His death certificate, tucked at the bottom of the deed-box, gave the cause as an aneurysm of the aorta. Hollister's name had been written into Mrs Blezard's will by hand, in dense black ink that had soaked deeply into the heavy paper. The two witnesses to her signature had been Ernest George Hawkins—Westlake—and Ailsa Crispin, her two neighbours. Beyond that, the contents of the deed-box revealed nothing that Roper did not already know. It was disappointing.

At five o'clock, alone, he dropped in at the mortuary. The autopsy on Norman Oates was finished. Wilson, still in his green overalls, was sitting at the desk checking over his notes while the attendant was hosing down the stainless-steel table in the centre of the room.

'Coffee?' asked Wilson, as Roper sat down opposite him.

'Not in here, thanks,' said Roper.

'The most hygienic place in town,' said Wilson, smiling wickedly.

'Rather buy you a beer later,' said Roper, 'in a dirty old boozer.'

He waited while Wilson finished scanning his notes, crossing out a word here and there and substituting another. Water gurgled down a nearby drain set in the tiles.

Wilson capped his pen at last, sat back, took off his spectacles and drew a thumb and forefinger together across his eyelids.

'Right,' he said, leaning forward again and hooking his spectacles back on. 'One male body, believed to be that of Norman Leonard Oates, late of thirty-one, Rope Walk, this parish. Caucasian. Underweight, undernourished, probably smoked forty a day, and his last meal was a couple of pints of stout—possibly Guinness. Died of stab wounds. Six in number. All of them in the stomach and abdomen.' Delivered, as Wilson had earlier prognosticated, underarm.

'What sort of knife?'

'Long one,' said Wilson. 'Carving-knife. Something of that sort. With a blade about an inch wide, thin, triangular in section. You're definitely looking for a man. A woman couldn't possibly have done it. Wounds too deep.'

'What sort of man?'

'About six feet, give or take a couple of inches. And left-handed.'

'How do you know that he was left-handed?'

'The direction of the wounds,' said Wilson. 'From the

assailant's point of view, they all sloped up to the right. Sure sign he was cack-handed.'

It wasn't much, but it was better than nothing. The killer now had a sex and belonged to that minority of the population that was left-handed.

'How about nail-scrapings?'

'Nothing significant,' said Wilson. 'Most of the dirt seemed to be engine oil. And he'd recently clipped his nails. Sorry.'

'Pity,' said Roper. 'How about those bruises around his ribs?'

Wilson thought that those were not connected with the stabbing or, at least, were not contemporary with it. Bruises like those would have taken several hours to develop to that state.

'How many hours, Mr Wilson? Roughly?'

Wilson pursed his lips. 'Ten. Twelve. Perhaps even longer.'

Clark, thought Roper, although he didn't say so. Clark had visited Oates early on Wednesday morning, and Oates had died on Wednesday night. Roughly twelve hours in between. DS Clark still wasn't out of the woods.

'He lost a lot of blood,' said Roper.

'At a guess, about twenty-five per cent,' said Wilson. 'The lowest stomach wound would have been a gusher.'

'And gushed all over his killer.'

'He'd have been smothered,' said Wilson. 'Whatever he was wearing, he would have had to burn it. Right down to his socks, I should think.

AND THEN IT WAS nine o'clock. Roper had taken an early dinner in the Duke of Wellington, where Price and Makins and WDC Anderson now were. Rodgers had gone home for the night. The town was quiet, apart from the occasional car splashing through a puddle in the High Street.

With a smoking cheroot by his cheek Roper was sketching out a family-tree of two murders, perhaps with two progenitors, perhaps with only one, but unlike family-trees these two had to be laid out from the bottom upwards. Mrs Blezard at the bottom left of the page, Norman Oates at the bottom right. The space above Oates's name was noticeably blank.

Mrs Blezard had died around ten o'clock on Monday night. She had had three visitors, two she had seen and one she had not: Stephen Clark; the murderer listed at the top left hand of the page as 'X'; and her father. Roland Hollister had gone across to Mrs Blezard's house at quarter to eleven, having heard the creak of her garage door some forty-five minutes before that. Stephen Clark had left Mrs Blezard's house at nine-thirty. So everything had happened in that blank hour and a quarter.... Except the murderer's return to wash those two glasses. At some time between nine-thirty and ten forty-five on Monday night, Mrs Blezard's murderer had been...and gone, probably in her car, and taken her body with him to dump it out at sea somewhere to the north of the river mouth. To achieve that, he had crossed the river on foot by means of the bridge, having left the body in the car or perhaps wedged between those alder trunks, which was likelier, and borrowed Chaucer's cabin cruiser. He had got rid of the body, returned the boat to its moorings, then retraced his steps across the river to where he had left the car.

And at some time in between he had remembered those two glasses. Must have brought him up with a start, that. He would have had to go back to the house. That night. Probably in a cold muck sweat. Perhaps he had intended putting the car back in its garage, but had seen Hollister moving about in the house, and had had to sweat it out until he was sure that Hollister had gone. But if that was so, then X, whoever he was, must have been back in the vicinity of the house by midnight.

Could he have done that?

Yes. Easily. He could even have stopped off for a beer—as Chaucer had, a few minutes before eleven o'clock—and thereby established an alibi of sorts; and then gone back to the house to wash and hide away those whisky-tumblers. Chaucer had had a motive. Mrs Blezard had still owed him ten thousand pounds, perhaps not a great deal of money to a man who owned a chain of baker's shops around the county, but certainly a large enough sum to make even a moderately wealthy man rankle. And perhaps that had not been all she had had out of him. Had he been one of her remotely controlled blackmail victims, even a substantial subscriber? He might have been lying when he had told Roper that his relationship with Mrs Blezard had finished. He would have known his own boat. He might have hot-wired it *after* he had done his dirty work to provide the police with a diversion.

Or could it have been Hollister? Plenty of men had murdered their own daughters for one reason or another, and Hollister had had a particularly good one. And the opportunity. To all intents and purposes, Florian West-lake, a.k.a. Ernest George Hawkins, was rendered unconscious every night by ten o'clock. He would have heard none of Hollister's comings and goings. A villa in Spain and the promise of more money than Hollister had ever seen in one piece in all his life. Not that he would have got away with it, even if he had sat on the contents of that deed-box for twenty years. But had there been a moment of aberration, on Monday night, when Hollister had thought that he might?

And was the flashy Mr Marshall, MA(Oxon) et cetera, another likely suspect? Were his frequent visits to Mrs Blezard's house all that he had said they were? According to Marshall, he had rung Mrs Blezard or, rather, her answering machine at twenty to midnight on Monday. What a shrewd move that would have been, *if* he had killed her. What Marshall lacked, however, was motive. He had lent Mrs Blezard a few hundred pounds that lunch-time; he would hardly have been likely to go to her house only a few hours later to get it back.

Or was there another man in Mrs Blezard's life, someone Roper didn't yet know about? Another lover, or ex-lover, or victim? Had Stephen Clark told the absolute truth? Had anyone?

And there was still the business of the late Norman Oates, even when the Blezard investigation was wrapped up. Stephen Clark had been Mrs Blezard's boyish admirer, Oates had taken photographs of Clark's sister playing netball, DS Clark had given Oates a good hiding. And Mrs Blezard's address and telephone number had been in Oates's tatty red notebook, and a fragment of Oates's red shirt had been found snagged in the paintwork of Mrs Blezard's conservatory windows. Plenty of connections there, but no logical way of stringing them all together. So perhaps it was pointless to try to link them. Perhaps they were simply a series of discrete events—apart, that is, from Oates taking pictures of DS Clark's daughter and Clark later visiting him with a view to meting out some justice of his own.

The knife that had killed Oates was still to be found. It could have come from anywhere, and gone anywhere. Possibly the river, possibly stuck into a field somewhere and heeled in, where it might remain undiscovered for a dozen years. Wilson had suggested a common or garden carving-knife, wielded by a left-handed man, six feet tall or thereabouts, and powerful with it, who must have left Oates's terraced cottage spattered with blood.

ROPER TOSSED DOWN his ballpoint. He had written nothing in the last ten minutes. He lit another cheroot. Voices in the corridor were Price and Makins coming back from their break along at the Wellington. It was still only half-past nine. For most of the human race the weekend had begun several hours ago; for Roper and Price and Makins it looked like being another working one.

For half an hour they bandied names, possible scenarios, possible motives, but all of it ploughing back over the same old ground. They looked at all the photographs again. Makins proposed that he climbed into his car, drove across to the disused sewage works and went through the motions of stealing Chaucer's boat, in the dark and against a stopwatch.

'What's the point?' asked Roper.

Makins shrugged. When it came to the point, he didn't know. It was something to do. They had reached an impasse. At ten-thirty, Makins signed off, doubtless to pursue his wooing of WDC Anderson into the small hours, and Price and Roper adjourned to the private bar of the Wellington, which, in contrast to the saloon, was empty and with a couple of vacant stools at the counter. Price ordered a fruit juice, Roper a half of bitter. It was winding-down time. With the narrow view into the saloon came the hubbub of boozy conversations, the bleeps and splutters of the Space Invaders machine, and the smell of wet raincoats.

'Cheers,' said Price.

'Good luck,' said Roper. He sipped the froth from his bitter. For the first time in a week, with any luck, he would be home and in bed before midnight, and a few weeks hence he would slip into retirement and hopefully never have to look at another dead body. It might even be that he would have to hand this case over to Price because the murderers—in the last hour he had begun to think of murderers in the plural—were still to be found. The idea didn't please him. He was a tidy man, and the possibility of driving home from duty for the last time with a couple of unsolved murders left behind for someone else to pick up seemed a ramshackle way of finishing a career.

'You haven't thought of staying on?'

'No,' said Roper. 'Not a lot.' He had been offered the vacant Chief Super's job, but piloting a desk for another five years definitely lacked appeal; and, besides, he had no intention of turning Sheila into a copper's wife, with all its ramifications, the way Mrs Clark was a copper's wife. A woman deserved better than that. And, anyway, there was another world out there where you only heard about murders at second hand.

His cheroot-packet was empty. He pushed the brass bell-push let into the counter for service, handed over three pound coins, received in exchange ten cheroots and a ten pence piece.

'When I first started buying these bloody things,' he grumbled, as he stripped off the Cellophane wrapper, 'I used to get change out of half a crown.'

He struck his lighter. Perhaps, if he had not, if he had chosen to light his cheroot a moment earlier, or a moment later, had not glanced over the pale flame at that most particular second, the cases of Mrs Blezard and Norman

Oates might have been consigned for ever into the County archives, never to see daylight again.

He gave Price a nudge as he snapped his lighter shut. 'Saloon bar, Dave. By the pumps. Navy blue raincoat.'

Price craned his neck to get a better view.

'Who is he?'

'Looks like Arthur Chaucer,' said Roper. A young lad near the pumps turned away with a brace of pint jugs. The figure behind stepped forward to take his place. It *was* Chaucer, ostentatiously brandishing a twenty-pound note to catch the barmaid's eye.

Price, who hadn't seen Chaucer before, was no more impressed with him than Roper had been. 'Looks ordinary enough.'

'So did Crippen,' said Roper over his glass. The bell rang for last orders. Somebody near Chaucer vacated a stool. He quickly annexed it. He ordered a Scotch—it looked like a double—picked up his change, mouthed 'Cheers' to whoever had served him, sipped from his tumbler, reached for a water-jug.

'He's left-handed,' said Price.

And so he was. Roper should have recalled that when he and Makins had spoken with Chaucer yesterday Chaucer had been wearing his wristwatch on his right wrist, but Roper had forgotten that. Not that Chaucer's being left-handed signified anything; several million others also were.

He was talking to somebody who was out of sight behind the counter, a quick exchange with a joke in it. Then he was momentarily obscured in the press for last orders.

Roper sipped at his beer and drew on his cheroot. A potman came through the door between the private and the saloon to pick up empty glasses. Out in the street, car doors were beginning to slam, and the lights were being turned off a few at a time in the saloon bar. A group of devotees around the Space Invaders machine were still at it.

Price put down his empty glass and slid it to the back of the counter. Roper's joined it, but his fingers stayed crabbed over its rim and Price heard him mutter: 'Well, I'll be buggered. Must be Hallowe'en.'

'What's up?' said Price, his gaze following Roper's into the emptying saloon bar.

A wet Ben Marshall, in a rush, an umbrella hooked over his arm, was exchanging a fistful of coins for a packet of cigarettes. From the drenched state of his coat, it was obvious that he had just come in from the street. As he was turning to hurry away again, Chaucer caught sight of him and reached out for Marshall's sleeve, said something. Marshall shook his head. Chaucer flashed his wristwatch. Then Marshall nodded a reluctant agreement, and stood by while Chaucer tried to catch someone's eye on the business side of the counter before the closing-bell rang. Which it did, as two more whiskies were put on the counter in front of him and he collected his change.

'Cheers,' mouthed Chaucer.

And Marshall lifted his glass. And Roper, watching, was drawn to pondering what odds a bookmaker might offer against the chance of walking into a country pub late on a Friday night and finding two left-handed men in dark blue raincoats taking a drink together. Because Marshall was also wearing his wristwatch on his right wrist, and drinking left-handed, as Chaucer was; and Roper had also suddenly recalled something that Rodgers had told him yesterday morning—about Mr Marshall.

Price was still none the wiser, because he had not seen Marshall before, either. 'Who's the other one?'

'Marshall,' said Roper. 'The bloke who identified Mrs Blezard's body for us.'

'Smart,' observed Price. 'Expensive raincoat.'

'And bloody wet,' observed Roper.

'It's raining,' said Price.

'Ay,' agreed Roper. 'But *why* is he wet?'

'Because he's walked here in the rain,' said Price reasonably.

'Ay,' agreed Roper again. 'But why did he do that? On a night like this. When he's got a car.'

'Maybe he felt like a breath of fresh air.'

'You reckon?' said Roper. 'Fancy betting your pension on it?'

MARSHALL WAS JUST shaking out his umbrella before stepping into Chaucer's new red Peugeot when Roper's hand dropped on his damp shoulder and held him fast.

'What the hell...?' exploded Marshall angrily, straightening and turning quickly and bunching a fist that Roper caught by the wrist with his other hand a moment before it could do any damage. Then, belatedly, Marshall realised who he was threatening, and the fist uncurled and dropped back by his side. Behind him, Price was telling Chaucer to drive off and slamming shut the Peugeot's passenger-door. Marshall watched its tail-lights fade. 'Christ,' he raged. 'What bloody right did you have to do that? I've got a bloody two-mile walk now.'

'Car in for service, is it, Mr Marshall?' asked Roper.

In the light of the street-lamps Marshall's face stiffened perceptibly.

'Not that it's any of your business,' he said. 'But, yes, it is.'

'And how about your other raincoat? That gone in for a service, too, Mr Marshall?'

A muscle twitched high up on Marshall's cheek. Car doors were still thudding shut along the street, voices rose and fell as drinking companions bade each other goodnight.

'I don't have another raincoat,' said Marshall. 'Now, if you don't mind, I'd prefer not to stand here in the rain answering stupid questions.'

'I won't keep you, Mr Marshall,' said Roper, 'but just one more stupid question. I'd like to know what garage your car's in, sir. Just for the record.'

With Roper in front of him and Price behind him, there was nowhere for Marshall to go, and Marshall looked as if he'd give his eye-teeth to be somewhere else. Roper waited, rain running down his face. Like Marshall, he wanted to go home. It was late, he was tired and, even though what had started as a hunch looked like paying off, the sight of a man slowly crumpling before his eyes gave him little gratification.

'Well, Mr Marshall?'

Marshall took a long tired breath. His gaze dropped to the wet pavement, rose again, met Roper's. He was done for, licked. He expelled the breath he had taken in.

'It's in *my* garage,' he said. 'And it's a long story, Superintendent.'

Roper drew aside. 'If you'll just step this way, Mr Marshall. I've got all the time in the world, sir.'

SEVENTEEN

MARSHALL, his fingertips still stained with fingerprint ink, lit another cigarette with shaking hands. His shoes had been taken away. They were size eight, and thus completed the set.

'You still don't want a solicitor present, Mr Marshall?' asked Roper, across the narrow table in the interview room.

Marshall shook his head. 'No,' he said. 'No point, is there?'

Roper reached out and switched on the tape-recorder again. 'In your own time, Mr Marshall.'

Marshall drew deeply on his cigarette. Across the room Rodgers, roused from his bed at midnight, sat at another table with a ballpoint poised over a pad.

'It was an accident,' said Marshall. 'I swear to God it was an accident.'

'But you did push her into the pool?'

'Not deliberately. I swear I didn't even mean to push her. I was only trying to fend her off.'

'So you were quarrelling?'

'Yes,' he said. He took another greedy drag of the cigarette. 'We were quarrelling. She'd had another one of those letters. It was a demand for five thousand, the biggest one ever. I told her I couldn't manage it. Not with the auditors coming next week. There was no way I could lose that kind of cash in a few days, even on the computer. And she said, if we didn't pay up, the blackmailer would blow us wide open. And I told her I didn't care any more. He could go to hell for his money.'

Or Arthur Chaucer could, thought Roper. Because, he recalled, the urgently required five thousand was exactly the sum Mrs Blezard had promised to repay Mr Chaucer on Wednesday.

'When did these blackmailing demands start, Mr Marshall?'

'About Easter-time,' said Marshall. 'Soon after we'd both agreed that we couldn't cook the books any more.'

'You *both* agreed that you'd have to stop?'

'Yes,' said Marshall.

Roper took his hat off to the late Mrs Blezard. A con-artist if ever there was one. Having agreed to call it a day, she had obviously then started writing the blackmail letters to keep Marshall at it.

'It's called embezzlement, Mr Marshall,' Roper reminded him. 'How long had the two of you been embezzling?'

'Oh…almost five years. Soon after we met.'

'How much?'

Marshall knew to the penny. 'Two hundred and eighteen thousand—including the blackmail money.'

'And the company didn't miss it?'

'The annual turnover's seven million plus,' said Marshall. 'Amongst that lot, a quarter of a million spread over four or five years is peanuts.'

'And the accountants never noticed, and the Customs and Excise…and the Inland Revenue?'

'No one,' said Marshall.

'And where did all this cash go, Mr Marshall?'

'I gave it to Hannah—Mrs Blezard. Most of it went into the bank, some of it to buy a villa in the Algarve.'

'The Algarve, Mr Marshall?' queried Roper. 'But that's Portugal, surely? You sure this villa wasn't in Spain?'

'No,' said Marshall, frowning, brought up short for a moment. 'What's Spain got to do with it?'

Roper didn't answer. The deed that Roper had seen referred to a house and its surrounding land in Spain. So if Ben Marshall was telling the truth—and from the state he was in Roper was sure that he was—then he had been conned out of all that money he had worked so hard to embezzle. If Mrs Blezard had been going anywhere, it was to Spain…with her father.

'Whose idea was this embezzling, Mr Marshall, in the beginning?'

'Hers,' said Marshall. 'Not much in the early stages, but when Blezard died and left her virtually nothing, then it really took off. She told me if I helped her to get back what she was owed we'd go fifty-fifty. And when we'd got enough together we'd slip away somewhere and nobody would be any the wiser. She'd carry on getting her director's salary, the rest of the board would be glad to have her out of the way, and I'd resign gracefully.'

'And both live happily ever after?' said Roper.

'Yes,' said Marshall. 'That was the general idea.'

Roper returned to the question of the letters.

'Any idea where they came from, Mr Marshall—who wrote them?'

'I thought at first that it had to be someone in the accounts section at the works,' said Marshall. 'He or she seemed to know exactly how much money had been taken. But I found excuses to get rid of them all over the months. And the letters still kept coming.'

'And it was always Mrs Blezard who paid the black-mailer off, was it?'

'Yes,' said Marshall.

'Did it ever occur to either of you to wait about on the off-chance of seeing who it was?'

'We did that twice—or, rather, Hannah did. But he must have spotted her because he didn't make the pick-up; and both times he upped the demand. The second time, she had to sell one of her pieces of china to make up the difference.'

'When was that, Mr Marshall?'

'Back in the summer,' said Marshall. 'About July.'

Which was probably the antique piece that had so up-set the senior Mr Bohun when he had been negotiating Mrs Blezard's insurance. When it came to pulling the wool over Marshall's eyes, Mrs B. had certainly known her business.

'It never occurred to you that Mrs Blezard wrote those blackmail letters herself, Mr Marshall?'

'Of course it didn't,' scoffed Marshall. 'Why should she?'

It seemed that Marshall, for all his degrees and quali-fications in the world of financial matters, was a raving innocent when it came to handling life in the round.

'How long have you known Mr Chaucer, Mr Mar-shall?'

'Not long,' said Marshall. 'About a year.'

Roper could have pointed out to Marshall that three years back he and Chaucer, on the face of it, had been Mrs Blezard's lovers contemporaneously; but he didn't.

'Mrs Blezard borrowed ten thousand pounds in cash off Mr Chaucer recently, Mr Marshall. Any idea why she'd have to do that?'

Marshall's eyebrows shot up. 'Ten thousand? From Chaucer?'

'You didn't know?'

'No,' said Marshall, his eyebrows still arched and his forehead puckered. 'I've no idea.'

Which was probably the truth. It was going to take several weeks for the Fraud Squad to sort out Mrs Blezard's financial machinations—if they ever did.

'Let's go back to Monday night, Mr Marshall,' said Roper. 'From the moment you arrived at Mrs Blezard's house.'

Marshall had received a telephoned summons at the factory on Monday afternoon. Mrs Blezard had received another blackmail letter that morning.

'I told her then that I couldn't manage it. Not with the auditors coming. There wasn't time. It was impossible.'

Which would account, Roper guessed, for the frightener-letter that Mrs Blezard had concocted later that afternoon, and given Stephen Clark to post for her that night.

'She said at least we ought to talk about it. I told her I'd be along at nine-thirty. Which I did. It was all very amenable at first. We had a drink. There were a couple of cups on the coffee-table. She told me her neighbour had been in—Mrs Crispin. I asked her if she was sure it wasn't that bloody boy again.'

'What bloody boy was that, Mr Marshall?' Roper broke in.

'Some lad,' said Marshall. 'He did a spot of gardening for her back in the summer. And I think he took too much of a fancy to her.'

'Go on, Mr Marshall. You had a drink together....'

'We talked about the blackmailer. Tried to work out

who the hell he could be. Then she started to insist that we'd have to pay up. The letter said within forty-eight hours. I told her we couldn't. So far as I was concerned, it was the end of the line. Then we heard a noise in the garden. I went out there with a torch and had a good look around, decided it had only been a fox. She was waiting for me in the conservatory doorway. And started nagging me again about the blackmail letter. I told her to forget it.' Marshall stubbed out his cigarette and shakily lit another. He blew out a horizontal column of smoke. 'She grabbed my jacket—we were on our way back into the house…from the pool. I stopped. She shook me, told me I was a bloody fool, we'd both do ten years, we'd lose everything we'd worked for…. I was angry. I grabbed her wrists and pushed her away…. Not hard—I swear I didn't push her hard. She sort of twisted—as if one of her ankles had gone—and stepped sideways, into the pool—only she caught her face on the corner of the tiles—the edge, you know? I heard it.' Marshall closed his eyes and drew his shoulders tightly together and thrilled with horror at the memory of it.

MARSHALL SIPPED FROM a cup of water. The last few minutes had not been easy for him.

'She went under,' he continued in the same flat voice, 'and floated up again. But too far away for me to reach. And it was the deep end—I don't swim, you see. Never learned. Never wanted to. I panicked. Looked all round for a broom or something to hook her out with. And by the time I found one…she was dead. I tried to revive her, but I wasn't sure how to do it. I knew I couldn't leave her there—someone might have seen my car in the lane and put two and two together. So I thought I'd take her out into the country and put her in a ditch. I used *her* car—the keys were in her handbag. Seemed more sensible than using mine. Then, once I'd got her on the back seat, it suddenly occurred to me that I'd have to look for a ditch with water in it—and we'd had no rain in weeks. So I drove along to the old wool-jetty, but there was a couple snogging in one of the parked cars and it was as bright as day up there. And I had to do something quickly. Then I remembered the boats moored by Hawkesley's yard—wondered if I could start one up and take the body out to sea.'

Marshall took another sip of water and dragged the back of his hand across his mouth.

'I drove across to the old sewage works and hid the car in the trees. Then walked back across the cathedral grounds and came back to town over the bridge. I found a boat with the control panel on the outside. A white one.... Do you know what "hot-wiring" is, Superintendent?'

'I do, Mr Marshall,' said Roper. 'Indeed I do, sir.'

It had been eleven o'clock by then. Marshall had taken the boat across to the other bank, put Mrs Blezard's body aboard it....

'Did you wedge the body in the fork of a tree-trunk, Mr Marshall?' broke in Roper again. 'Just for the record, sir.'

'Yes,' said Marshall, 'I think I did.'

But Marshall, as Roper had suspected, was no mariner. He knew nothing of sandbars and currents, nor indeed whether the tide was on the ebb or the flow at the time he had dropped Mrs Blezard's corpse over the stern of the boat.

He had not gone far out for fear of not being able to

navigate himself back again in the dark. Of the distance he wasn't sure, but he thought the trip out had taken him a little over five minutes, and similarly the journey back.

'When did you remember the whisky-tumblers, Mr Marshall?'

'The moment I climbed into the car to drive it back,' said Marshall, showing no surprise that Roper knew about the two used whisky-tumblers he had left behind in Witling Lane. He had driven there post-haste, terrified that someone else might have been there in the mean time. And, of course, someone had, and that someone was still there....

'I saw someone looking out of the downstairs front window—a silhouette. It looked like a man. I'd got as far as the gate. So I climbed back into the Sovereign...didn't even shut the door...drove on about a quarter of a mile, and walked back to my own car and moved it further along the lane out of sight, and prayed to God whoever he was hadn't seen it.'

Which he probably hadn't, thought Roper. The front hedge would have obscured it, and Hollister had come and gone from Mrs Blezard's across the back garden that night.

'He stayed until midnight,' Marshall went on. 'But even then I wasn't sure if he'd gone or not. I went back in through the conservatory—I'd wedged the door open with a brick when I carried her out. The brick had gone, so I knew he'd had a good snoop-about. But the glasses were still on the coffee-table. I washed them, and put them back in the cabinet in the dining-room.' Mrs Blezard's car keys had been pushed into a roadside hedge near where Marshall had left his BMW.

It had not been until three o'clock, lying awake, unable

to sleep, that Marshall had had the notion to record his voice on Mrs Blezard's answering machine. Which he had done at once. Not at twenty to twelve but at five past three the next morning.

'So you lied about that, too, Mr Marshall?'

'Yes,' sighed Marshall, 'I lied.'

'When did Mrs Blezard have that machine installed? Do you know?'

'I forget exactly,' said Marshall. 'About July time.'

'Do you know why? To do with the business, was it?'

'No,' said Marshall. 'Nothing to do with the firm. She'd been getting a lot of dirty phone calls. With the machine, she only ever got them when it was switched off.'

Oates, thought Roper. That heavy breather on the tape had been Norman Oates. Had to be.

IT WAS HALF-PAST ONE of Saturday morning. The chain-smoking Marshall was down to the last half-dozen of the cigarettes he had bought last night in the Wellington. He took a sip of the coffee newly fetched for him.

'I thought I could cope,' he said. 'I thought, even after I'd met you at the mortuary, that I'd covered all my tracks.'

But within an hour of returning to his office on Wednesday afternoon Marshall had received another chastening telephone call. From Norman Oates, although he had not known who the man was at the time. Oates had been the fox in the garden on Monday night. Oates had seen everything. Oates had photographs of Marshall hooking Mrs Blezard out of her pool with the end of a broom, taken through her conservatory window. A thousand pounds in used notes, left by eight o'clock that night

Sellotaped under the directory-shelf of the public tele-
phone-kiosk by the town gate, would be rewarded tomorrow by the photographic negatives that Oates had
taken of the incident in question. Sellotaped under the
directories in the same telephone-booth. Some time after
nine o'clock.

'And did you pay, Mr Marshall?'

'Yes,' said Marshall. 'The next day was pay-day at the
factory. It was all in the safe, mostly in used notes. I took
out a thousand and did what the man said. But I waited
in my car—from where I could see into the booth. At
about half-past eight, a white van stopped outside it. A
man got out. I couldn't see all of him. He went into the
booth—and was back out again in a couple of seconds,
so I knew he hadn't made a call. I followed the van. He
drove it up an alley at the back of Rope Walk. I got out
of my own car just in time to see him going into one of
the back gates. I followed him, saw his kitchen light go
on.... And I knew that the money had to be back in the
firm's safe before the next morning, or all hell'd be let
loose.'

Marshall's gaze came up for the first time in several
minutes and met Roper's squarely.

'I knew I was going to have to kill him. There was no
other way. I had to have those photographs and I had to
get the money back. I wasn't even sure how I was going
to do it—bare hands perhaps.... I was bloody desperate.'

Marshall had squeezed himself through the gap in the
featherboards of Oates's back gate. Chaucer never could
have.

'I watched him through the window. He was getting
stuff out of the refrigerator to make himself some sandwiches. Then I saw this carving-knife on the draining-

board by the sink, and I thought if I could just get hold of that....'

Marshall's voice tailed away. He took another mouthful of coffee.

'I saw him put the money on the table. Gloating over it, the little bastard was. I jumped him. I was in there. I had the knife. I don't even think he knew what was happening for a moment. And I didn't, either. I'd lost my head by then—just knew it *had* to be done.'

Only, afterwards, Marshall had not been able to find the negatives or, if he had, had not been able to recognise them.

'So I burned everything I could find.' But what Marshall had not realised was that modern technology had seen to it that photographic negatives did not catch fire easily. So he had used wads of Oates's old prints for kindling. For almost two hours, the front bedroom curtains closed and Oates's dead body down in the scullery, Marshall had frantically tended his fire, until he had burned every last negative he had been able to find. And then not been *really* sure that he had burned the vital ones. The knife had gone down the drain in the back alley.

'So when I rang you the other night for an engineer, Mr Marshall, you'd only just got home after killing Oates?'

Marshall nodded. 'Yes,' he said. 'I thought you were on to me. Scared the hell out of me.'

A knuckle rapped twice on the door of the interview room. It was Price, followed by one of the technicians from Forensic. Roper switched off the tape-recorder.

'How was it?' he asked.

'Bloodstains on the driver's seat,' said Price. 'Looks

and smells as if he tried to take them out with carbon-tet. and bleach.'

'So you haven't been using your car for the last couple of days, Mr Marshall?'

'No,' said Marshall, shaking his head.

'And your white raincoat? The one you were wearing at the mortuary?'

'I burned it,' said Marshall. 'The factory incinerator. And my suit.'

'Bully,' said Roper, reaching out again to switch on the recorder. 'Now we'll put that on record for posterity, Mr Marshall. In your own time, sir....'

IT WAS HALF-PAST TWO. Marshall was exhausted. The tapes Roper had used were presently being transcribed on a typewriter upstairs to make the statement that Marshall would sign in the morning before he was arraigned.

Marshall lit the last of his cigarettes before he was taken down to the basement.

'And all because I went into a pub with a new raincoat and an umbrella,' he said ruefully.

'No, Mr Marshall,' said Roper, 'not entirely. One of your directors was singing your praises to one of my sergeants. He told us you hadn't taken a day off for a long time. And I reckoned you'd got that Bondi Beach tan of yours *very* lately. And it suddenly occurred to me that the likeliest place to get a healthy tan like that around here was under a sun-lamp—like the one Mrs Blezard had in that conservatory. And I guessed you'd known that lady a damned sight better than you'd let on.'

'Smart, aren't you?' said Marshall with weary irony.

'Sometimes, Mr Marshall,' agreed Roper. 'Not always, but certainly sometimes.'

IN THE FLOODLIT YARD, Roper buckled himself into the Sierra.

In eight weeks he would be a civilian again for the first time in thirty-four years. But, as Phil Butcher had said in the Wellington the other day, a lot could happen between now and then....

The dashboard clock read three-fifteen. Above the floodlights, the sky was the colour of a copper's raincoat. And it was still raining.

No Birds Sing

Jo Bannister

A CASTLEMERE MYSTERY

Castlemere—the kind of hard-luck place that provides a constant challenge to its crack team of detectives. And this time their skills are put to the test in very personal ways.

A string of violent crime—train robberies, a dog-fighting ring and a rapist stalking the area—forces both Inspector Liz Graham and Sergeant Cal Donovan to go undercover. The rapist is attacking blond, fortyish, successful women—and Liz fits the profile. Acting as a decoy, she's unprepared for the shattering repercussions in the department, her marriage and herself. As Donovan joins the vicious ranks of the pit bull circles, both cases take shocking and deadly turns....

Available August 1998
at your favorite retail outlet.

Take 2 books and a surprise gift FREE!

SPECIAL LIMITED-TIME OFFER

Mail to: The Mystery Library™
3010 Walden Ave.
P.O. Box 1867
Buffalo, N.Y. 14240-1867

YES! Please send me **2 free books** from the Mystery Library™ and my free surprise gift. Then send me 3 mystery books, first time in paperback, every month. Bill me only $4.19 per book plus 25¢ delivery and applicable sales tax, if any*. There is no minimum number of books I must purchase. I can always return a shipment at your expense and cancel my subscription. Even if I never buy another book from the Mystery Library™, **the 2 free books and surprise gift are mine to keep forever.**

415 WEN CJQN

Name	(PLEASE PRINT)	
Address		Apt. No.
City	State	Zip

* Terms and prices subject to change without notice. N.Y. residents add
  applicable sales tax. This offer is limited to one order per household and not
  valid to present subscribers.
© 1990 Worldwide Library.

MYS98

DEATH OF A HEALING WOMAN

ALLANA MARTIN

A TEXANA JONES MYSTERY

Texas border country. A place of desolate beauty, ancient mystery, modern danger—and home to Texana Jones, owner of the local trading post. Still reeling from the murder of two close friends, Texana discovers the murdered body of reclusive Rhea Fair, a healing woman whose death is too easily dismissed as another casualty in the violent world of drug smuggling.

Texana won't accept this, and delves into the mystery. The key, she believes, is a missing woman in a rental car, who had come to see Rhea. Sifting through clues as fine as grains of desert sand, Texana uncovers the explosive link between Rhea, her murdered friends and the killer....

Available August 1998
at your favorite retail outlet.

 WORLDWIDE LIBRARY®

FREE BOOK OFFER!

Dear Reader,

Thank you for reading this Worldwide Mystery™ title! Please take a few moments to tell us about your reading preferences. When you have finished answering the survey, please mail it to the appropriate address listed below and we'll send you a free mystery novel as a token of our appreciation! Thank you for sharing your opinions!

1. How would you rate this particular mystery book?

  1.1 ❑ Excellent   .4 ❑ Fair

   .2 ❑ Good   .5 ❑ Poor

   .3 ❑ Satisfactory

2. What prompted you to buy this particular book?

_____

_____(2, 7)

3. What are the most important elements of a mystery fiction book to you?

_____

_____(8, 13)

4. Which of the following types of mystery fiction do you enjoy reading? (check all that apply)

14 ❑ American Cozy (e.g. Joan Hess)

15 ❑ British Cozy (e.g. Jill Paton Walsh)

16 ❑ Noire (e.g. James Ellroy, Loren D. Estleman)

17 ❑ Hard-boiled (male or female private eye) (e.g. Robert Parker)

18 ❑ American Police Procedural (e.g. Ed McBain)

19 ❑ British Police Procedural (e.g. Ian Rankin, P. D. James)

5. Which of the following other types of paperback books have you read in the past 12 months? (check all that apply)

20 ❑ Espionage/Spy (e.g. Tom Clancy, Robert Ludlum)

21 ❑ Mainstream Contemporary Fiction (e.g. Patricia Cornwell)

22 ❑ Occult/Horror (e.g. Stephen King, Anne Rice)

23 ❑ Popular Women's Fiction (e.g. Danielle Steel, Nora Roberts)

24 ❑ Fantasy (e.g. Terry Brooks)

25 ❑ Science Fiction (e.g. Isaac Asimov)

26 ❑ Series Romance Fiction (e.g. Harlequin Romance®)

27 ❑ Action Adventure paperbacks (e.g. Mack Bolan)

28 ❑ Paperback Biographies

29 ❑ Paperback Humor

30 ❑ Self-help paperbacks

6. How do you usually obtain your mystery paperbacks?
   (check all that apply)
   31 ❑ National chain bookstore (e.g. Waldenbooks, Borders)
   32 ❑ Supermarket
   33 ❑ General or discount merchandise store (e.g. Kmart, Target)
   34 ❑ Specialty mystery bookstore
   35 ❑ Borrow or trade with family members or friends
   36 ❑ By mail
   37 ❑ Secondhand bookstore
   38 ❑ Library
   39 ❑ Other _____(40, 45)

7. How many mystery novels have you read in the past
   6 months?
   Paperback _____ (46, 47)   Hardcover _____ (48, 49)

8. Please indicate your gender:
   50.1 ❑ female   .2 ❑ male

9. Into which of the following age groups do you fall?
   51.1 ❑ Under 18 years   .4 ❑ 35 to 49 years
   .2 ❑ 18 to 24 years   .5 ❑ 50 to 64 years
   .3 ❑ 25 to 34 years   .6 ❑ 65 years or older

*Thank you very much for your cooperation! To receive your free
mystery novel, please print your name and address clearly and
return the survey to the appropriate address listed below.*

Name: _____

Address: _____City: _____

State/Province: _____ Zip/Postal Code: _____

In U.S.: Worldwide Mystery Survey, 3010 Walden Avenue,
P.O. Box 9057, Buffalo, NY 14269-9057
In Canada: Worldwide Mystery Survey, P.O. Box 622,
Fort Erie, Ontario L2A 5X3

098 KGU CJP2

WWWR98F2